franklet

demons for social networking

soical networking demons for social networking for social demons for networking social for social social for networking demons social networking for demons for demons for soical networking demons for

a novel

Social Networking for Demons

a novel.

By **franklet**.

Friends 18 mutual

dedicated to precious demons everywhere....

....you know who you are....

....and Tori for lending me the fairies' ears.

"trouble needs a home girls.   will you give her one?" -*Tori Amos* - *"Trouble's Lament"*

This is a work of fiction. Any resemblance to actual events is a trick of the light.

Chapter 1 – Wish I May

[assistant blocks the camera and leans in to put makeup on a young woman, thin-faced and large-lipped, in her mid-twenties. The assistant's large, jean-covered ass looms large, leaving only the left eye of the young woman visible. It is a deep, almost purple-black blue. The edge of the young woman's face shows her puffy lips curving upwards into a smile as the assistant moves off camera.]

"ACTION."

"Like I said, I'm not sure...it could have gone any other way. Cassie was so full of life and Thad, well Thad loved her more than anything. But Cassie, she was like a sister to me, you know? She was everything a woman can be to another."
[young woman smiles mysteriously, tucks a lock of garishly pink-colored hair behind her ear.]
"My sister, my best friend, like I said. She was everything. All that. And Thad, she and Cassie they were so in love, star-crossed or some shit. Wait, can I say that?"
[she looks off camera, nods and looks back]
"I remember the night before it happened, they had come in from drinking at this bar on Bourbon, the Lucky. I think it's closed down since, I don't know. But they were pretty sauced up, you know? And all OVER each other, it was almost

7

gross. I was sitting on the couch, watching TV. I didn't have my own place see, I was staying with Cassie then. And they hovered in the doorway, maybe they didn't see me? I don't know, but they just kept kissing and he was pressing himself up against her, and like grinding, you know? Not that it was sick or anything, it was maybe innocent? I don't know. I mean they had been having sex for a long time, and Thad was really hot and Cassie was willing, so I mean, there's nothing wrong with that. They had been together for a few years, and like I said, they were meant for each other."

[she coughs, pushes her loose hair behind her other ear.]

"Sorry. I wanted to say something? Like should I go? Or sneak off or something? Give them some privacy? But I didn't, I didn't have anywhere TO go, it was a one bedroom? I just stopped watching and burrowed into the couch. That's when I saw it."

[she stops, swallows visibly and smirks.]

[off camera a man says, "And what did you see, May?"]

[she laughs nervously, tucks her hair back against her head, though it hasn't moved.]

"I don't know? It was like a shadow or something, just past them; outside the hallway. Maybe...I imagined it? I told the police and they said I probably did. You know, like after the fact. People do that, right? So, I just turned to watch more TV and I was thinking, 'Isn't Cassie lucky? Thad is so hot and they're so in love, star-crossed, you know?' But I said that already?"

[she forces a smile, with obvious effort.]

"When I looked back, Cassie was gone. Like she hadn't ever been there. It was crazy. The police said I probably fell asleep or something. Except, I remember watching the TV and hearing the sounds, the sucking and kissing sounds, you know? Not like gross sounds, you know, not really, I mean Cassie was overweight, but not gross sounds, right? But she was gone and I got cold all of a sudden, but Thad was still there, only he was staring at me."

[she shivers slightly, then another mysterious smile.]

"I didn't know? The police, they said, it's normal to forget that kind of stuff, after something terrible, I don't know. But Thad came over and he started staring at me. I didn't know what to say, and that shadow, it was there, like hovering over him and around him, maybe coming from him? They said I probably just imagined that, you know, because of what happened next. But I really think I saw it."

[she puts her hand off-screen and grabs a bottle of water, takes a sip.]

"And he told me, he said, 'May?' and I said, 'Yeah, Thad?' And then he was like, 'I feel like going to the Omni Royal and climbing up to the roof.' I was confused, so I said, 'Cassie going with?' And he sort of cocked his head to the side, like he was hearing a voice or something, you know? And he said, 'No. She's cooking. We had a fight.'"

[she stares, flatly, into in the camera as though she had just made a funny joke, an inside joke.]

"But you know, I didn't think anything of it. But I guess I had fallen asleep, you know? How else could he have gotten her there? They were JUST there in the doorway, like all over each other. How had they gotten somewhere else? I hadn't heard a fight either? And Cassie's place, like I said, it was one bedroom, I could see the kitchen from the couch."

[she tucks both sides of her pink hair behind her ears, sits up straighter against the seat and looks directly, forcefully into the camera.]

"It's not my fault, you know? It was late and I was tired and Thad was always there, how could I have known? I had JUST SEEN THEM. But the police are sure I fell asleep. They said he cut her up and cooked her body parts on his stove. They never did find the weapon he used to kill her. They said it was a knife, but with serrations like they had never seen. Super sharp. What happened to it?"

[she cocks her head to the side, very, very slightly. The camera goes out of focus for a quick moment, then back to normal and her head is straight, her dark eyes on the camera, her puffy lips smiling.]

"But the weirdest thing, I mean I had no idea at the time, and I said earlier and I meant it, like Cassie was MY SISTER or BEST FRIEND or some shit, she was the best person I had ever known, I don't care what people say about her. It wasn't me, you know? I didn't start it, like at all. HE kissed ME. And he BIT my lip. When I told the police about it, they asked if we had been having an affair or something, and I told them, 'No.' Because we hadn't. Thad was hot, but I would never do that to Cassie. Still, they looked at my lip the next day and compared the bite mark, but it was too faint by then. He drew blood and wiped it off and said he was sorry. Then he left. I think he jumped off the Omni Royal like two hours later? I don't know the exact time or anything. That's like morbid, trying to piece all of that together. The police said I must have fallen asleep again, or that maybe I imagined he came back, you know, after the fact."

[she looks skeptically into the camera, and shrugs.]

"All I know is that they were in love you know? You could just tell. It's all so sad, but Cassie's in a better place now or something, right?"

[the camera zooms out and shows May sitting on wooden-backed chair, wearing a blouse and a skirt, incongruously staid balanced against her pink hair and snide, smuggy expression. Then the picture winks out.]

...

"Have you ever been to this place?" Jeremy asked May, yelling over the sound of the bland techno music coming from the large speakers down towards the stage. It was dark and cloudy with smoke, both cigarette and cigar and it smelled vaguely of sweat. Lurid pink lights were in sconces on the walls but they did not give enough light to tell what color the walls might be, encased in shadow as they were. Most of the tables were empty, except for three close to the stage, which had three separate groups of men filling their space. One was a trio of heavy-set black men, all wearing jerseys and sporting bald heads. They were cat-calling the woman on the stage, waving pink-light-tinted bills at her. The other two groups were both pairs of white men, each comprised of one larger, fatter man and one thinner, slighter man. Though they looked nothing alike otherwise.

"Yeah. My friend works here." May said and pulled Jeremy in close to her, wrapped her slight arms around his thick waist. He was not terribly fat, but rather muscular with copious amounts of padding around the trunk and chest. His face was broad and young looking, for his age, but his hair was a vivid orange, not a natural looking color and in the pink light it made him seem cartoonish.

"Is that her?" Jeremy asked, pointing at the

woman on the stage.

May shook her head. "No. She's getting off soon. I was thinking maybe we could take her out with us..."

Jeremy looks deep into May's eyes, which in the pink light had the strangest overtone, like pink paint scraped over purple wood. She smelled of smoke, independent of the smoke of the place and her hair, a blue as vivid as his orange hair, stank of sweat and some other odor, perhaps stale wine, which he could not quite place. But she was thin, had a wide mouth with puffy lips which felt softer than they looked. He liked kissing her, though she seemed to like it more, sometimes pushing herself against him with as much force as her small, thin body could manage and purring like an angry cat. But he almost felt like she was unaware she did this.

He wondered about what she had just suggested. After all, she had picked him up a few days ago, it wasn't like they were dating, he told himself. And the look in her eyes, the smell on her, she was definitely THAT kind of girl. A whore. A slut. The kind who had friends who were strippers that like to fuck strange men with their girlfriends at the same time. He was into it, especially if the other girl was as thin as May. The thin girls, the ones with the small breasts and narrow hips, the ones that if you looked at them at right angle at the right time you could imagine they were younger, innocent. Not that he was INTO that, not really, all that stuff was just random stray thoughts, nothing that he plotted on. Those other girls, they HAD told him they were older, hadn't they? He shook his head, trying to get rid of thoughts about that. It was useless anyway, and he didn't want to seem nervous or scared in front of May.

"Sure. What's her name?" Jeremy asked, putting on his smarmiest smile, the kind he used on old women when he wanted to do something chivalrous or kind and seem like he cared.

May shifted against his body, the bony protuberances of her hips poking his meaty thighs. She was half a foot shorter than him but that did not deter her from pushing herself up on her tip-toes and kissing him again. Then she stuck her tongue in his mouth, and he tasted the now familiar sour taste of her. It wasn't precisely unpleasant, considering some of the other women he had had, but it was strange. Like she had just been eating meat or something.

"Jazzy." May said, with a smirk. The corners of her mouth, wide and puffy as it was, were the only things that moved. Jeremy found the expression beguiling, and had she not smelled like she hadn't bathed in two days, charming. As it was – he got hard anyway.

"What kind of name is that?" he asked, as the woman on the stage left and another, darker, came out.

"Her real name is Jazmine," May said, "Jazzy is just a nickname, her entertainer's name."

"Entertainer's name?" Jeremy scoffed. "That's rich,"

May eyed him, her head cocked slightly to the side. He was not entirely sure, but it suddenly seemed as though the air above May's head warped a bit and a leaking shadow from the pink-tinted walls circled around her before blending back into the other long shadows cast by the low lights. Jeremy blinked several times to dispel this feeling, that that shadow had somehow been real and alive.

"There she is!" May exclaimed and tugged at his sleeve, her grimy hand leaving a slight smudge on the fabric of the t-shirt, but Jeremy hardly noticed or cared about that. His eyes followed hers towards the stage and the vision there.

She was everything May was not, lush where May was thin and womanly where May was boyish. Jazzy's hair was longer too, and multicolored, though the pinkish lights made it hard to tell exactly what colors, not to mention the clouds of smoke that began to swirl around the stage. All she was wearing was a thin-stringed pair of panties, not quite a g-string, but close. Her firm, rounded breasts hung suspended above her diaphragm like a pair of creamy skinned alien eyeballs, perfectly round and devilishly pink areolas glistening with moisture. Her nipples were hard. Jeremy watched

Jazzy twirl around a pole, crawl around on all fours and playfully nip at her breasts with her teeth, transfixed, unable to look away. His cock was pressing hard against his jeans.

May's hand, when he grabbed it, felt more like a claw than a hand, as if it ended in sharp appendages, rather than normal human fingernails. Jeremy gasped and tried to move away, but May was suddenly in front of him, covering the whole of his vision, her eyes holding his and her hair swaying as she slowly shook her head. Her grip on his shit did not let up, but it was not painful. He realized she was attempting to stroke him over his jeans. But she was definitely not smiling, in fact there was a distinct aura of displeasure wafting off of her that when combined with the raw lustiness of her semi-clawed hand made Jeremy's head ache, his temples throbbing as though he had just done a too-heavy workout and his blood was pumping far too hard. The sound of May's voice, growling, made its way to his ears and her hand began to move faster.

"She's hot right?" May said, in an off-hand, distracted manner, moving her head, but not her body, so that Jeremy could again see Jazzy. But Jazzy's number was over and she was exiting the stage.

"Yeah..." Jeremy muttered, his mouth dry. His erection was beginning to ache, not pleasantly, but not painfully, yet, against his pants. He shifted and May stopped. She smirked up at him and tossed her hair in that way women sometimes did, the way that meant something, though Jeremy never quite knew exactly what.

May turned away from him and her head cocked to the side again, and once again a shadow was around her, hovering, menacingly and it throbbed in time with the blood pulsing in Jeremy's body, with the music, with the phantom feeling of May's bent hand that he somehow still felt grasping him too roughly. "Let's go get her."

Something was different in May's voice, it was the same voice, but only for a moment, one horrifyingly violent stretch of time during which Jeremy's whole body slipped out of his control and he fell against the wall, nearly falling to the floor, unable to speak. A presence was descending over him, pressing down, like that weird dream he had had when he was a kid, where he was lying in his bed, asleep, but feeling awake. And his body was pressed against itself, surrounded by the feeling of true evil, a knowledge that some presence was holding him down, in preparation for some terrible act. He had not thought of this dream in twenty years, but he did so then and he knew, it was the same presence.

May's hand wove through his own and pulled him forward through the smoky pinkness of the strip club, past bouncers who merely nodded at her, and didn't see Jeremy at all, their eyes passing over and through him as if he were made entirely of pink smoke. Down a long, very dark hallway they walked, May's voice saying something, but nothing Jeremy could make out. Yet his mind filled with images, of an expanse of flesh and a pair of firm, delicious breasts, hovering beneath a headless neck. His groin burned and pushed forward, his erection growing harder, madder. May's whisperings increased in frequency and then they reached a door. The door opened, of its own accord it seemed at first, the haze of Jeremy's thoughts not noticing the scantily clad, sweaty brown woman on the other side of it, sizing May up and like the bouncers, not seeing him at all. He laughed to himself - "What am I, invisible?" after he saw the brown-skinned woman.

There she was, hovering against a wall of mirrors, and bright bulbs, her face smooth and young, the streaks of maroon clearly visible in her hair now, Jazmine. Her body was covered, though not by much, a thin shirt stretched taut and skin tight that traveled from just above her nipples to just below her navel's top. Beneath that was a pair of low-rise jeans, ragged at the top and tapering into a skinny cut near the ankles. Jeremy's mouth was no longer dry, he was salivating. May's voice, though her mouth was not moving, still seemed to be in his ear, he could hear it, though he could not hear the words.

After that they passed out of the club, as a

threesome, Jazmine having spoken softly, alluringly to Jeremy, feeling his biceps and pressing herself against him, so that her hips, soft and round, pressed against his insane erection. Though May had the shape of the others, the sluts who had gotten him in trouble back home, something about the unfettered, unconditional womanness of Jazmine was intoxicating in a way he had never before experienced.

Jazmine several times would lean over and whisper into May's ear and May's eyes would catch Jeremy's, darkly sparkling with an intention that he could feel in his crotch all the way up to his sternum. She WANTED IT. THEY wanted IT. And he was going to give it to them both, those sluts. The entire cab ride from the last club they went to passed in a blur of motion, Jeremy's mind far away, floating over the Gulf at night, stars distantly leering.

When the cab stopped they were outside a semi-rundown duplex amidst a street full of them, Jeremy could not tell one from the other. As he got out of the cab he swayed, had he not been certain it had not happened he would think he was high. He felt high, not drunk and not blitzed or anything, but airy, light-headed with a giddiness he associated with the specific combination of drugs and orgasm and a crying woman beneath him.

They went inside and when the door closed behind him shadows detached themselves from the walls and danced around May, they had faces, screaming faces, soundlessly screaming faces, impatient with fury and hopeful in their rage. This no longer seemed frightening to him, the presence he had felt earlier was flitting about, and he was open to it now, because of May.

Then she was there, her tongue pushing gently into his ear. It was erotic and mean at the same time, she just kept pushing, as thought the taste of his inner ear was couture to her and she could not find enough of it. But she was whispering as she did so and grinding herself against him from the side, her legs wrapped loosely around his left side, pumping like a man or a rabid dog.

"What's happening?" Jeremy said as the room titled and the lights went out. But May did not respond, she just shifted around him pulling her clothes off as she did so and another set of hands were pulling at his, from behind. He closed his eyes and enjoyed the feeling, of their hands caressing him, down his back, nails scratching slightly, up his thigh, across his taint and then over his chest, flicking his nipples. When he opened his eyes though, it was just May, there was no sign of Jazmine. He sniffed, remembering that she had smelled vaguely of orangey perfume, but the only thing he could smell was the musky smokiness of May.

"Where's Jazmine?" Jeremy asked as May

knelt before him and took him in her mouth. Her eyes, dark already, were in the unlit room two apertures into nothing, empty and sucking. Her mouth, a round hole of blackness kept swallowing his whole cock, then releasing it, not bothered at all by the girth. It was a thick dick, roughly the size of a composting cucumber. Few women had made such an easy time of it. In fact, Jeremy had liked that, the sound they made when it choked them, the way their head pushed back against his hand just before the tears rolled out of their eyes. But there was none of that with May, her wide mouth, puffy lips kept swallowing him all and opening wider, the lips flattening against his stomach, balls, as if she wanted more, as though her mouth was a bottomless, abysmal nether.

Then he could not think straight as an orgasm rocked through his body while his whole shit was inside her mouth, he grabbed the back of her head anyway, a useless gesture and rammed himself forward, determined to catch the feeling. The only sound he heard from her was a slurping purr. When he pulled out and made eye contact she said.

"She's over there."

And so she was, lying down on a sofa, her legs spread awkwardly, her head leaned back against the armrest and her hefty but firm breasts floating forward in defiance of gravity, was Jazmine. There was no light in the room, except for a candle someone had lit and it cast shadows over every part of Jazmine. The shadows were shaped like hands and they caressed Jazmine, suggestively, sending sensations to Jeremy of her body, the softness of it. The slick sheen of sweat between her thighs and the hefty, unmoving weight of her breasts as he cupped them.

He did not remember entering her, only he had. May standing behind him, arms wrapped around him, telling him that she loved him and, by she, he knew May meant Jazmine, not May herself.

"Star-crossed lovers, that's what you are, look at her. Jeremy. Look how much she loves you!" May's gentle voice chided.

And he did, slowly, as if more space than was possible separated them, Jeremy leaned forward, thrusting into Jazmine as hard as he could, so hard that her pelvis was slamming painfully against his, but she made no noise. "Do you love her?" May asked.

"Do you?" she asked again, insistent. Her voice had deepened, broadened and taken on a quality that was the sound equivalent of a shadow, dark. Ephemeral.

"I DO." Jeremy said as he rammed himself into her, harder and harder. She surrounded his whole body, not just his cock, like his whole body was thrusting into hers and coming out, his whole self a sex organ and she a hole, wet and receptive, like May's mouth.

Then he climaxed inside her. Her body went limp beneath him and her head rolled to the side and then fell off to the floor, the same expression, of shock and terror, that he had seen while he fucked her frozen upon her face. May's hand wrapped around the outside of his and only then did he realize that something was IN in his hand, something hard and unyielding. Looking down at it, he could see it was a thick, heavy meat cleaver, dripping in blood. Before he could react or move – May was moving his arm, arcing it backwards and then slammed it down with far more force than her thin body should have been able to produce. As though she had harnessed his strength as well. The meat cleaver came down just below Jazmine's shoulder, neatly severing the arm against the armrest, causing it to flop, slick and heavy, to the floor.

After that Jeremy's eyes rolled upward, the room traveling from his feet towards his head until the ceiling collided with him and something pushing him from below slammed into him, knocking him into unconsciousness.

When he woke up, a lamp was twinkling on an end table in the room, the sofa covered in a thick woolen blanket; soft, susurrating music – vaguely Goth playing in the other room. He pushed himself up from the floor, noticing the sticky, tacky feeling of his hands as they made contact with the floor. Before he could scream, May was there, her wide mouth smiling, her head cocked to the side. She was moving towards him, dancing erotically as she did so, an obvious imitation of how Jazmine had moved on stage.

"Do you feel like going outside?" May asked, "Maybe seeing the top of the Omni Royal – at night?"

"We should run..." May said, a breeze rustling her dirty, bluish hair. Atop the Omni Royal Hotel with a crown of stars diamonding her head and the slight nimbus of emptiness where a shadow had been, Jeremy stared at May, dumbfounded. He was unable to piece together just then who she was, or how they had met, or become entwined. Flashes of memory came to him, like stills on a television set, the implication of motion there, if not the actuality. May was all dark smiles, eager even, her whole body bouncing on her tip-toes with an energy that might have been manic or something perhaps darker. But Jeremy, squinting, could not see the shadow around her. It had to be there, he told himself. He HAD seen it. Hadn't he?

Slowly, languid in her rooftopness, May came over to him and wrapped her thin, boyish arms around his thick trunk, her cold hands brushing against his fat-covered muscle. She leaned her head against his chest and he could again smell the sourness of her, the reek of her hair and unwashed body. At the very least she had washed the blood off her face. He grimaced as other memories, these more frightening and full of joy at the same time, assaulted his mind.

Jazmine.

What HAD he done?

All the stuff in South Carolina with the girls, he had at one point argued they should be considered women, after all they had fucking pubes, didn't they? Knew how to suck dick, right? They weren't virgins or anything close, he was SURE of that, if nothing else didn't THAT make them women? He knew the law said otherwise, but what was law against human nature, he'd often thought. After all, wasn't it illegal to drink alcohol once? But those things he'd done with those girls had been natural, an urge of the body, exorcised once, twice, three times. Done. The charges had been thankfully mild, he'd served his slice of time and fled as soon as he could. He never did that registering shit. He was an American, who were THEY to tell HIM where he could live for the rest of his life because of some teenage whores?

But Jazmine, she was a whole different thing. The shadow was responsible, he knew it. He could FEEL it. So as he held May he looked down at her, searching for it again. When he could not see it, he pushed her away and out, his strength far exceeding hers. She grunted and looked up at him, her too-dark eyes almost pleading, her wide, puffy mouth pouting. "What IS it, honey?" May said.

That was new.

Not the pouting or pleading, but the term of endearment. He stared at her, squinting again, looking for that shadow, looking for the menace that had floored about her earlier, looking for reasons why they had done what they had done. What he could now remember, if only in brief snatches.

Jazmine's shocked expression as the meat cleaver sliced in her throat. The gurgle as her blood had poured down her neck. The vague sucking sounds as May kissed him while he paused between chops. He had done it, of that he was sure. But it wasn't his fault, somewhere that shadow was lurking and May was the source of it.

He pushed her further away, past the tips of his fingers, the sound of her feet crunched on the gravel of the rooftop. She really looked hurt now.

"What ARE you?" he asked, in a quiet whisper, one that was carried by a sudden gust of wind towards May. She snapped away as if he had yelled at her.

"Yours." she purred. "We're LOVERS. Star-crossed or some shit." Anger laced her tone as the last words slipped out of her wide mouth. "You said so...and we..."

May swallowed back whatever she had been about to say. She looked away, then tucked her hair behind her ears. Jeremy searched her whole person with his eyes for that shadow, but it was gone. He sunk into himself, denial setting in. His hands were clean. It was all her.

"Yeah. We should run..." Jeremy said, but what he was thinking was: "You're some kind of demon and I'm going to kill you before they take me away."

May looked at him, concern washing across her features. He cocked his head to the side and smiled at her, his knowledge of her future pleasing him. He never saw the shadow arcing around his head.

Chapter 2 – Driving Mr. Daddy

"Can you slow down?" Karla asked, sheepish, not bothering to turn her head and look at her father. Instead she focused on the cars passing slowly by, like vehicular sludge. Ahead there was a bottleneck, where three lanes of Interstate merged to become two. Part of the familiar route on the way to school every morning during rush hour traffic in Greenville, South Carolina. Her father DID turn to look at Karla, though he did not slow down. Instead he sped up and snarled, not at her, but at the man he had seen do what someone did every morning at this point. It was never the same person of course, that would be absurd, but it happened every time nonetheless.

A man driving a gold Lexus darted out and tried to speed past the bottleneck, using the soon to be ended third lane to jump ahead of the people like Karl, who though he was still moving faster than the lane to the right, was moving slower than the third lane, to his left. Karl swore after his snarl and sped up, intent on insuring that driver did NOT make it back into the line of cars ahead, at least not before he did. He knew that Karla would be grabbing at the oh-shit handle and tensing in her seat, refusing to look forward out of fear of an accident. He tried not to be angry at her for this. Why couldn't she trust him to have her safety in

28

mind?

At the last minute Karl saw the car ahead brake and allow the gold Lexus to slide in front of it. He screamed and hit his own brakes, his right arm flying across the seat to brace Karla, though she wore a seat belt and was too old for such a gesture. She had in fact, the week before during a remarkably similar incident explained quite matter-of-factly to him that his arm would not keep her from flying out of the windshield in an impact or her head from slamming into that windshield or the dashboard below it. Karl had tolerated the lecture in silence. Then he turned the radio up and hoped Garth would keep her silent. But that was the week before.

Karla mumbled a held back shriek at the suddenness of his braking, at the squeal of his brakes and the fishtailing of the back of the pickup. Both her hands gripped the oh-shit handle. Karl wanted to sigh.

He could remember her, when she was younger, just large enough to see over the dashboard and so slight the strength of his one arm was a guaranteed protection, a desired bulwark against the suddenness of tragedy that could descend upon her. Karl thought he knew something about that kind of suddenness - that brand of tragedy. He was forced to admit, if only to himself - he didn't really know Karla anymore. When had that happened? How had it happened?

And whose fault was it? Her fucking cunt of a mother's? Had that whore somehow transmitted from prison some aspect of her whoreness to the teenager? Karl would like to think this was the case. It was easier to imagine than knowing somehow he had simply stopped knowing her because she had become a young woman; with desires and hopes which no longer centered around pleasing him.

Swallowing his anger, he mustered an olive branch.

"Sorry, hon." Karl murmured.

Karla sniffed but did not say anything else. Inside, Karl was seething. That fucking asshole in the Lexus was already zooming ahead, laughing at him no doubt, enjoying that he had gotten over. Worse, that Karl knew he had gotten over. Always the worst part for Karl, knowing someone else knew.

Once they were past the bottleneck Karla's hands dropped from the oh-shit handle and she moved in her seat, putting hands in her lap, folded together, an image that to Karl's mind spoke of primness. The gesture made him want to laugh and sneer. It took an effort not to do so, to recall this was his daughter, not some barroom slut he had wrangled for the night. She WAS prim, wasn't she? He glanced sidelong at her.

He knew the answer. But he refused to give it, even to himself. She had slept with that piece of shit child molesting pervert. Karl could think of him no other way, despite the man's ridiculous claims that Karla was not a virgin when he was with her. That Karla was part of some pact at her school to get pregnant, that all the girls had been a part of it, the man was just the tool they'd picked for the job. He KNEW those girls. Knew their fathers and mothers and in some cases grandparents. Hell, he had gone to school with some of them as far back as the first grade . Karl had supervised numerous sleep-overs with some of those girls at his house. What the pervert had said was just not true. Karla had denied it, of course she had, but still. What IF she wasn't telling the truth? What if she had been sleeping around before she did it with that man? Karl cursed Karla's mother, but in silence, in his mind.

The cunt.

"Are you excited?" Karl asked, changing the subject. Hoping to see Karla smile, to see that effervescent little girl appear. It still came. At times. If not directed at him anymore. He saw it from afar, when watching her with her friends, a distinctly unpleasant thing for Karl. At times it made him feel like an outsider, an invader, because he had to spy on Karla to see such moments. Why couldn't she just be the happy girl she had been? Karla sniffed, turned and looked out the window again. Karl wanted to swear again, why did she have to be so. Fucking. Difficult?

31

Couldn't she see he was trying?

"Yeah." she said finally just as they began to speed up, the bottleneck clearing out.

Of course she was! Why wouldn't she be? It was her last day of high school. The last time he would be driving her to school. He was going to surprise her after graduation, with a car no less. He had already picked it out, it was a used, mint-green Camry but in good condition. She'd had her license for nearly a year, but driving had been something Karl was too scared to let her do much of. Giving her a car was his way of trying to move past that, of acknowledging she was the young woman he was now secretly afraid of. It was also his way to keep tabs on her, he had paid to have the tracker installed himself. He could follow her if he wanted and see where she'd go. But he had told himself that would be unnecessary. She wasn't going to do anything like that bad stuff. Not again. He glanced down at her hands, still primly held in her lap and saw them twitch, as if she knew he was thinking about the bad stuff again. He glanced down at her hands, still primly held in her lap and saw them twitch, as if she knew he was thinking about it again.

"Are you girls going to do something special?" Karl asked. It was Friday night after all and they usually spent the night together at one the girl's houses. He both hoped and didn't that it would be his and Karla's. He knew if it was he would resort to spying on the girls, trying to catch moments of Karla's girlhood still intact. And other moments, things he shouldn't want to see, but fuck, he was still a man, despite that fucking cunt whore trying to emasculate him even from prison. How the hell did she keep getting motions into courts from behind bars? Weren't they supposed to prevent that kind of thing? He wished, not for the last time, that Cindy had not been able to learn of what Karla had been through with that pervert, but apparently they had access to local papers. It had also been all over the Tri-County Area news. You would think those crazy criminal bitches would be worried about other things that who got arrested and for what, but Karl's friend Todd said otherwise. He would know since he'd worked at the prison for a decade and commented more than once how much those cunts liked that kind of shit. They thrived watching the local news for any signs of people they knew getting arrested and hooted and catcalled at the television when they did.

"There's a Class of '98 party tonight." Karla said, softly. He knew that tone. She wanted to go, but was afraid to ask. A graduation party? That didn't sound TOO bad, Karl had to admit to himself, but he scowled anyway, on principle.

"Where?" he asked, his tone assuming the rough quality he thought of as DAD in capital letters.

"At the American Legion. It's a dance thing,

like supervised. With chaperones and teachers and stuff." Karla said, her recrimination leaking through her obvious annoyance with him. Karl brushed this aside.

"What time?" Karl asked, making no effort to moderate his tone.

Karla scoffed and looked out the window. Her hair, in a loose bun-thing held together by a scrunchy, was the exact shade of reddish brown of Cindy's. The neck beneath, slightly concave and thin, bony almost, was redolent of his ex-wife as well. In fact, from behind with that scoff and posture and the ice between them she might as well have been Cindy for all the difference it made. Only when she turned back did he see his button nose and high cheekbones on her, mixed with Cindy's mother's lips and chin. She was a very pretty girl, his Karla, there was no denying that, he only wished she could remain just that, a very pretty girl. Why did she have to become a woman with all the inherent bitchiness that entailed? Her green eyes lit up as they caught his in the brief moment he looked over from the road and stared at her.

"8." she said huffily.

"OK." Karl said, sighing. He drew inside himself and focused on the road. They'd be at the school soon, ten minutes at most. He didn't want to spend the entire time fighting. Though, with Karla, she would remain angry at him long enough for him to calm down and get angry all over again. It was a lose-lose and he knew it. He smiled, chortled and drummed on the steering wheel. They were cruising near sixty now.

"Well, it sounds like fun."

"That's it?"

"What else is there?" he said, wishing and not, that he had more to say. He was proud to hold back his sigh and mutter.

"You're not going to demand to go? Or tell me I can't? Or ask me about..."

Karl made a noise in his throat. A warning. Karla's mouth snapped shut with a loud clack that must have hurt as much as it was hard to hear.

"Fine." Karla said, her mouth clenched shut. "Thanks."

"You're welcome." he grumbled.

"What are you going to do?" Karla asked and wonder of wonders she sounded as if she were sincerely interested. Her voice even wavered a bit, could she actually be sorry for being a younger version of her bitchy mother for the past minutes?

"The usual I suppose. Pizza and a beer and some WarCraft."

Karla laughed. A sound that was as unusual as it was thoroughly welcome. It was pure and though she was laughing AT him he basked in it. For a shining moment his little girl was there, encased in crystal and frozen forever as that diminutive of expectation and hope and unconditional Dad-worship. He felt like a hero again. He drummed lightly again on the steering wheel and actually sang a few bars of Journey.

"You are such a dork, Dad." Karla said. And just like that they were OK again.

"Well, someone has to be, besides one day you'll see it's the dorks that are worth knowing!" Karl protested, but his voice sounded false in his own ears. He just wanted her to like dorks instead of the bad seeds. He himself had played varsity football, had smoked and dealt weed, had banged cheerleaders raw dog, including Karla's mother Cindy. He had cut school, burned things, got in fights and stole cigarettes, even vandalized shit and once ate mushrooms. No, he had never been a dork, even if by Karla's standards he now was. When HAD Journey become a signifier for dorkitude? Plenty of women thought otherwise, judging by the number of times single moms threw themselves at him.

Thinking of this soured his buoyancy and he stopped drumming on the wheel, leaned forward much like an older man, feeling every bit of his forty-two years. They rode the rest of the way in silence.

When he dropped Karla off and they said good-bye it was as if they had found a cloud and settled it over themselves inexplicably, shadowing everything they did with the potential for a storm. It made him wary and made her frown and scratch lightly at her exposed forearm, a habit that had always confused Karl. Where had she learned it? Karl almost said something, he almost told her that no matter what, he LOVED her, was PROUD of her and ALWAYS would be. She was GRADUATING for Chris-sakes! But he didn't.

And she slammed the door shut, half jogging towards that group of large-breasted girls she ran with. The pack of them somehow all looked and dressed differently and yet achingly similar. Bunched up hair, tight jeans or shorts, tennis shoes and arms crossed over chests or under, chins upthrust and expressions giddy or pissy. He had not thought of them as a pack until after that stuff with the pervert, but now it was natural and impossible to think of them in any other way. He sat for a moment staring, wondering which of them would become Cindys or Marcys or Janets.

Marcy and Janet, both, had called him within the past week. Their ex husbands, like his own wife were gone. One was supposedly in prison, like Cindy. But unlike Cindy who had simply written bad checks to cover her Riverboat casino debts, Janet's ex had been a meth dealer. Karl didn't understand the whole meth thing. He had gone to a meeting at the school about it, a too-long lecture on the signs to watch for and shit. He hadn't paid much attention, it was before the pervert, and Karla didn't do drugs. But Karl suspected some of those little cunts she ran with did. And ideas were infectious among teenage girls.

Only months ago he would have been appalled at his own thoughts, those girls had grown up with his Karla. He KNEW them. And yet it felt right, terribly right, to think of them as cunts. What ELSE could they be? With their tight clothes and gum and overly made up faces caked with color. Their little boyfriends who were too old and too young at the same time. Their drinking games and.....

Karl shook his head. He HAD to stop that line of thought before he got well and truly pissed. He noticed then that Karla was staring back at him, her expression a mixture of annoyance and baby-rage. He could practically hear her thoughts and those of her pack.

"What's he DOING?"

"Why is he STARING at us?"

"Gah, Karla, your Dad is such a freak!"

Slamming his hand down on the gear shift, Karl peeled out. Faster than he intended causing him to nearly clip a long-limbed, wisp of a skinny teenaged boy walking across the street. Karl leaned his head out of the window, his face blustery and red.

Before he could say sorry the kid had actually shouted at HIM! "Hey WATCH it fart-knocker!"

Karl could only gape as the kid sauntered off and joined a pack of boys, tall, thin, gangly and full of the same cocky confidence Karl had once exuded. The beam of a high school athlete at his peak and prime. The boy was ugly despite that, his face mottled with pimples and his nose slightly off-center, but that hardly seemed to matter to the pack of girls. Karl's hand shook as he fought down the urge to get out and teach the shit a lesson. Hell, that boy was as tall as he was if not taller, didn't that make the skinny shit a man? As much as Karla's dalliance made her a woman? Well no man was going to talk to Karl that way, not and just skidaddle off. What the FUCK?

But the sound of a car horn going off crazily some distance behind Karl pulled him back and with a muffled curse Karl threw the pickup into gear and drove off.

Chapter 3 – Breaking the Tides of Darkness

There are always newer versions.

Wes thought this, to himself, though alone he said it aloud. There was no one else around to hear. His life was one of cocooning, at least that's how his mother referred to it, his sisters and his former friends. They had all banded together once, back in like 1998 – in an attempt to get him to change. To stop. To grow, they had said. Or was it to grow up? He couldn't really remember. Who could? That was over ten years ago.

His room hadn't changed much since. The desk he sat at was still crowded with stacks of paper, none of it useful, all of it disregarded until that rare moment when it became too much, some sunny Saturday when the idea of nice smelling candles and a breeze through the window was more compelling than the mindful direction of animated forces. The piles were different and they were the same. A pattern, his mother had said. Something about a pattern of the same waste. He really had tuned her out after the first few minutes, his mind doing as it usually did during one of her lectures, falling into strategies for mock battles in his favorite real time strategy computer game.

WarCraft II: Tides of Darkness.

Something about the directing of hordes of small grunting creatures, of detailed little knights or

booming dreadnaughts – this had been an
enormous pleasure to him, one that did not abate
when he could no longer physically make himself
stare further at the screen. Not even when he had
defeated every level, then defeated hundred upon
hundreds of designer levels downloaded from the
Internet. All of that was before he had discovered
the cheat codes. Once he had those, the game
turned into something else, an experiment in
massive warfare. Just how many howling two-
headed Ogres could he send against a specific
target and destroy it and with what losses? What
about using only Dwarven miners or Troll Axe-
throwers instead? The cost was astronomical until
he found the equilibrium for each unit. But he
played every level this way, thousand of hours,
whole years of his life, examining the possibilities
of unlimited gold, populating the game's fake world
with so many creatures the demand on his
graphics card repeatedly overheated his whole
system. The processor couldn't handle it. He'd
had to get a new one, eventually another and
another. At that point he'd purchase the newer
version, WarCraft III, only to find it disappointing in
comparison, it offered none of the joy the previous
version had, with its convoluted story lines and
shorn battle specifics. There were no hordes in
WarCraft III to send, just small units of ten, maybe
twenty at most. Visually it had been nice but even
that had gotten boring within days. He hadn't

played it again once he had beaten the entire campaign. That made him chuckle balefully. When compared against his tens of thousands of campaigns in WarCraft II.... well. It was just funny.

He had even experimented with networked play – playing campaigns in WarCraft II against people online. Before the intervention though. The one staged by his mother and sisters and former friends. He would meet people from message boards, others who created their own maps for campaigns, like Wes did.   People who planned their battles as meticulously as he did. They'd trade IP addresses and then fight. Wes always won, but one guy, his name was Keith or Kevin or Curt or something, from South Carolina, the guy had actually come within ONE unit of defeating Wes, Wes's closest call ever. Something had terrified Wes about that, the idea of losing was much more than he wanted to handle, he could see past it, if he squinted: to a vast open vista of nothing, whence the game ceased to be of interest to him and life lost its point.

He knew one day he would find a new game, it was inevitable, he just couldn't picture that day in any tangible form. There were always newer versions of things and everything got old. But Wes was not ready to give up WarCraft II.

When he was cleaning up on those rare sunny Saturdays he would occasionally get reflective, as rare on those rare days as the days themselves, and think about the how and why of his WarCraft obsession. He was not a moron, he knew it for what it was, he hadn't needed the intervention to be told.

Fully ten years after that silly event Wes had stood in front of the large mirrors in his bedroom that made up the doors to his closet. His apartment was small, the bedroom only fifteen or so feet square, but an entire wall of that room was devoted to closet space and each of the six folding doors bore a full-length mirror. His head did not come near the top of the six foot door frame. He was five foot nothing, five-two in good thick boots. To call him scrawny would have been a passable compliment. His shoulders were actually less than an inch wider than his hips. He'd measured. His arms were sticks, his legs only mildly thicker sticks. There was a visible depressive concavity in the center of his chest where two flat lacks sloped towards visible rib bones. His muscles were more theoretical than actual. But none of that had stopped him from trying to enlist.

In fact, it was because of that he'd wanted it so bad in the first place. All those commercials, with strapping dudes in camo, square faces and strong looking hands gripping huge guns.... Wes had pictured himself growing into one of them, being forged and molded like one of the weapons in a fantasy novel, his favorite genre. He had been a healthy eighteen year old, mostly, despite his size and brittle skinniness. Nor did he wear glasses or have asthma, the standard markers of a weakling, like Calvin Courtes, his neighbor who had become a Navy SEAL. Calvin had never even come close to beating Wes at WarCraft, though they had played ten or fifteen times. Wes could still remember his ex-friend's hands at the intervention, held upward, palms out facing Wes, his square-jawed face beneath his glasses imploring Wes to "grow up" or whatever. That asshole.

But they had told him no. They'd said he was too small. That he didn't meet physical requirements. He'd been told he could appeal and he'd gotten the forms, but then he'd just put them on his desk, the starter papers for his future piles of useless papers.

Ten years and Wes was just as small – the only part of him that had grown was his stomach, outward and down a small amount.

Wes had done some reflection right after the Army had said no, back in 1996. About war mostly. Military glory. He had eventually decided it was all crap anyway. They told you what to do and you did it, not the other way around, not like WarCraft II. And you never saw the whole battle in the real Army, you never got the satisfaction of seeing your horde demolish the enemy. Not really. And all THAT had been before the second Iraq War. His rare reflections had gotten darker after that. Glory? In war? Who did they think they were fucking kidding? Not Wes Miller.

What was glory anyway, other than killing someone else's kids because some politicians told you to do it? How was that glorious? Didn't they ever THINK about that? And they rejected HIM. Assholes!

But WarCraft II .... what could be more glorious than discovering the exact right moves with the exact right units to achieve a victory that was bloodless outside the realm of the binary? That was a true example of a fine soldier, to Wes, no a fine GENERAL. He had no allusions, his place was in command, he would never be able to swing a sword like the grunts or punch like the big boys, no he had to use that thing they didn't, that tool of the truly glorious: his fucking mind.

Then after the Second Gulf War turned out to be all lies, Wes felt vindicated in a way that he desperately wanted to share with someone else. That urge had not been present in so long he didn't know what to do with it, how to act on it. His mother still called him, his sisters still came by infrequently, but they never stayed and he never visited any of them. Work was work, delivering pizzas kept him in his own car most of the time, listening to Rush and Limp Bizkit and plotting how he could level an Elven fortress with only hatchet wielding Peons. Could it even be done on the higher levels, with only Peons? Without cheat codes? That question had driven Wes for days of thought before he had attempted it, then weeks of trying before he succeeded. But he HAD. Now THAT was glorious!

And there need be no regret, no moment where you look back and say, damn, I killed all those people...because I was told to, and I did it for a lie. No guilt complex when you came back to the States and sucked on the government teat with some post-faggot stress disorder that turned you into the liability instead of the asset. It would make Wes laugh, to remember all those flag waving assholes, like his sisters and their husbands, the kind of people who had bumper stickers that praised the troops then voted against politicians that actually decided to take care of them once they'd returned to the States. How was that for glorious? Let 'em kill, let 'em rage and tell your little kids how proud you were of them until they came back, then they were just some crazy assface with a funny beard and a tic and you had to shield little Johnny from him. That made Wes laugh, if somewhat bitterly.

He didn't have to answer those kinds of dilemma in the game. All these kinds of thoughts swirled around in his mind and compacted against one another until the thoughts became something else, something inexpressible, just a feeling of rightness to his thought patterns and assumptions, a feeling he could not convey or transfer to another person, even if he wanted to or had someone he could try. It was like cupping fog and trying to give it away.

That hadn't stopped him from trying, when the second Intervention came. Eleven years after the first. They just showed up. His mother. His FATHER for fuck's sake and he hadn't seen THAT bastard in years and years. Where had they dug HIM up? Alongside his effing sisters and those brutes they had married, even two of the older kids, Mike and Janice, at least he THOUGHT those were their names. They were twins, and still teens, but obviously taller, larger, and thicker than he was. It made him want to snarl when he saw the group of them outside his door that sunny Saturday in May. How the FUCK could those KIDS be so much bigger than him? They had the same damned GENES. He was their UNCLE, he was supposed to be BIGGER.

He hadn't suspect what was coming though as he swung the door open to see his father and mother, standing next to each other, but obviously not sharing the space. The gap between them was empty of anything like love or joy or friendship even. That they LOATHED each other was obvious to anyone, even Wes, who zeroed in on this fact above all others as the group stood before his door.

It made him think of his childhood, of how his father had seemed like someone both to love and to pity and his mother someone who simply accepted that she was less because Wes' father told her she was. That had made Wes angry, stomping mad, until he found that he had agreed with the old man. Then the shithead had left, leaving Wes' mom with four kids, a shit-ton of bills and an extremely confused eight-year-old boy. How was it that the man had to leave then but could be here now? This was the question that Wes could not get out of his head, how was it possible they could share this space between them in front of Wes' door on an fucking May 14th, like a Saturday of nothingness in 2010 and yet his father couldn't be there when they had REALLY needed him.

Slowly, Wes began to notice the grave looks on their faces, his parents. At first he assumed someone had died and they had come to tell him, but then his mind again registered the presence of his sisters and brothers-in-law and niece and nephew and some ass-clown wearing a sweater vest in May! Those looks SAID someone was dead, but who? Memaw? Perry? Wes hadn't thought those names in months. Maybe years. A sudden, deep and ineffable longing for the leathery touch of his mother's mother's hands washed over him and he smiled. A wistful, bittersweet smile. This seemed to affect his parents strangely, they moved away from each other and let the sweater monkey sidle up between them, his hand extended.

"Wesley?" the man said, "I'm Dr. Shannagan..."

"So?" Wes said. "Mom? Dad? Rielle? What the fuck is going on? Is Memaw OK?"

Wes' mom shook her head sadly and turned away. What did that mean?

The man in the sweater vest held up a comforting hand, obviously comforting, towards Wes' mom, but also obviously asking for her silence. She sniffled in response.

"Wesley, your family has asked me to come here today to talk with you. Will you let us in?"

It only just then occurred to Wes that he had swelled up his chest and blocked the doorway with his arms pressed against both sides of the lintel. He looked at both arms, then back at the strange man.

"Um, yeah. Sure." Wes said. It was only after his hands dropped to his side and he turned his back on them that his firing neurons, which had been still rather wrapped up in his latest stratagem for WarCraft II, started to put pieces together.

Wes only made it three steps before he turned on them, his face twisted into a snarl. "Is this another INTER-FUCKING-VENTION?"

Dr. Shannagan paled slightly and pursed his thin lips. He was a very pale man, tall and svelte, wearing rimless glasses above an angular face of smooth skin below a balding pate. A small goatee of light brownish hair, lighter than what remained on his head rounded the doctor's face out. His whole demeanor, to Wes, screamed FAG, but he didn't say that. Still, Shannagan's face registered Wes' up and down look and nodded, as if this was expected.

"Perhaps we should all sit down."

This was a problem.

Wes' living room had a futon, but nowhere else to sit. He couldn't help it, he laughed. These idiots hadn't thought of THAT! But then he saw his sisters open folding chairs they had been holding that he hadn't noticed. This alone was enough to stoke fury inside Wes, his face went scarlet, his blood boiling.

"I'm not doing this shit again, I have stuff to do, I have work in like three hours, OK? I'm FINE. Everything's FINE! Why are you all looking at me like I'm a drug addict or something?"

Dr. Shannagan, to his credit, did not shake his head in derision, though most everyone else in the room did, even Mike and Janice, teenagers though they were. Those kids were too much like their father, Wes thought angrily. Rielle never should have married that fat jerk.

After everyone was seated Wes found himself painfully pushed against the ebon wood armrest of the futon his mother had bought for him years before when she'd discovered him sitting on the floor in front of the television. His sisters shifted, almost in unison in their folding chairs, Mike and Janice sat on the floor, like younger better-looking versions of Wes.

"Wesley..." Dr. Shannagan started, but Wes wasn't about to give up the high ground. He had learned that in WarCraft II. If you let the enemy strike first you usually lost, unless you WANTED them to strike first, unless you NEEDED them to strike first. That was definitely not the case here.

"Whatever." Wes said, holding up his hand mockingly at the man, who actually closed his mouth and cocked his head to the side considering for a moment before he nodded at Wes. Wes hardly saw this, he had already launched his attack.

"Listen, I go to work. I pay my bills, I don't drink or get high or fu...effing anything illegal! I don't steal or anything! I don't understand why you PEOPLE think this is OK! I'm a fuc...effing ADULT! I'm ALLOWED to live my life however I want!"

"And it's you people who need help! With your bumper stickers and your troops and pride for the military! As IF they aren't the most evil bastards ever killing people for lies! For OIL and shit and then coming home and getting drunk all the time and claiming post-traumatic stress McOrder and costing everyone millions! And for what? Some piece of desert we just gave up? Like the fact they went over there and had a tough time of it, wore through a few pairs of socks and sweated to the Oldies or got their assholes stuffed with sand – THIS makes them better than ME? Worthy of support? What the HELL! They got PAID to be soldiers! It's a JOB. Like any other. I could die behind the grill at Chipotle and no one would care, but if it were a Chipotle in IRAQ then what? THEY CHOSE THAT LIFE! Why does THAT make them heroes? Because they made a bad decision? And they call THAT glory, playing heavy metal music while you use a huge gun to kill unarmed beard jockeys who just want to live their lives and marry another virgin!"

Wesley spat the last words out with great stress on each. He hoped to drive his point home. That he was rambling was not something he was really aware of, or that his thoughts were incomplete and sounded like the ravings of the madman they all secretly apparently thought he was. But during the rant Dr. Shannagan merely nodded sagely, patiently as though the entire spill of word vomit made absolute sense, was perfectly legitimate, even enlightening or refreshing. Wes tried to ignore him, but the looks on the faces of his family members, their derision and shock and pity was too much, it left him talking almost exclusively AT Dr. Shannagan. His mother reached out and tried to grab at his hand and he batted her away.

"Well." Dr. Shannagan said after Wes paused to breathe, to gauge their reactions, to show them he was in control.

"It seems you've given all this a great deal of thought, Wesley." Dr. Shannagan said, his tone infuriatingly neutral, calm. "But we're here today because your family is concerned for you and thought it best to have a professional around, so you wouldn't feel isolated. I'm on your side."

The lack of stress on the word "your" felt telling to Wes and he glared.

Then he laughed. He pictured his little bitmapped Ogres and Grunts and Peons punching, hacking and slicing into the good Dr. How many would it take to conquer him? Wes even pondered, for a half minute or so, just outright challenging Dr. Shannagan to a battle, to a WarCraft II showdown, winner take all. He wanted to say, LOOK, Doctor, THIS is what I do and I do it better than anyone else. Better than you, better than anyone else can. And it makes me HAPPY? And you want me to stop? The ones who get paid to be killers and then expect to be heroes for it, expect people to bow down, to kowtow and look up to them, as if life handed them a raw deal and they somehow obliged to make the best of it. Like some handicapped sprinter or armless curler, some idiot savant. For fucks sake why couldn't they SEE?

Dr. Shannagan's face went troubled as Wes laughed.

"Would you mind telling us all what you think is funny?" Dr. Shannagan asked, calmly.

"You. This. I can't believe you all wasted this time and money on this. How much are they paying you to be here? Huh? I'm NOT fucked up, OK? I just know what I want, what makes me happy, what I like to do! How many of YOU can say that? Huh? Rielle? How's the PAINTING going? Oh WAIT! I forgot! You haven't done that since high school, since you got what? PREGNANT. And Trish? What about the dancing? Weren't you going to join some fancy New York City company? After all the money THEY spent on ballet lessons? Huh? Do you even GET to dance anymore? How stupid is dancing anyway? Yet I don't see a doctor here trying to convince YOU it isn't worth doing. And while I'm at it, why don't we ask Mike and Janice to give up their dreams, whatever it is THEY love, might as well drop the idea NOW before you kids love it too much, before Gramps the Disappearing Act comes back and decides he knows better." Wes fixed a stare full of years of anger at his father. The man's mouth stretched into a thin, angry line and he shook his head as if Wes had just spit on him or farted in public, at church. But Wes' mother, she choked out a sob and buried her hands in her face, obviously exasperated. This set her ex husband off, something Wes truly hated.

"See what you're doing to her?" Peter roared. "She just wants to KNOW you Wes! That's why we're here to find out why you've shut us all out and how we can get you back!" His dad looked to Dr. Shannagan then, as if seeking approval for what he had just said, for the veracity of his outburst. The old man had even thrown his hands up as he spoke.

Instead of giving obvious approval to Peter's words Dr. Shannagan held up a hand asking for patience. Peter nodded gruffly.

"Wes?" Dr. Shannagan said, his tone so even and ingratiating it raked across Wes' mind like an air-conditioning intake whining.

"Yeah?" Wes said combatively, turning to face Dr. Shannagan and Dr. Shannagan only. He wondered then just how he could end this farce, how he could get them all out of his house so he could be angry without doing anything really stupid. How could he explain to them? It made sense in his mind but he was beginning to see how it might not make sense if he tried to express it in words. He just wanted to play his damned game! He didn't have some lofty goal, he hadn't bought into that dream. There was no misty future out there for him full of swirling hopes and fuzzily smiling faces, a star-crossed love or beautiful work of art or mostly robotic best friend who wanted to be human. This was IT! Why was he OK with it but not them?

"How does it make you feel to see your family here, and to hear what they have to say?" Dr. Shannagan said.

Wes scoffed aloud before he could hold it back. They hadn't actually said ANYTHING! Other than that he was wrong, what he loved was wrong and he had to change. To make THEM happy. Unable to keep his emotions in check the anger seethed through him, making him bite his cheek.

He asked for NOTHING!

He paid his BILLS!

He even occasionally washed his own dishes!

HE LOVED HIS LIFE!

These thoughts rumbled through him on a loop, getting louder and more insistent each time, as though each one was itself a solid argument against everything he knew his family thought. Vainly, Wes tried to push them away, to start up another voice that countered them, that said, "Hey! You LOVE these people!" But that voice was like wind in a hurricane. Whisper in a throng of hooligans. It did nothing but confirm to him his own beliefs. He KNEW what right and wrong was. He was smart enough to know THAT much. So he snapped.

FUCK YOU.

The words came out softly at first.

Then louder.

Finally he was just shouting it at them, at Dr. Shannagan, at his parents, at Rielle's shocked face, at her awful brute of a husband's blowed cheek angry face. The piece of SHIT! Distantly,

Wes thought, this guy even LOOKS like one of the Ogres from WarCraft II!

He wasn't really aware of his father and brothers-in-law restraining him. Or what he said to them, or that he snapped at them, his teeth trying to bite at their wrists and elbows. It was distant, like watching a slow motion stop-animation from before cinema existed, with him the central character.

A farce, a comedy, not intended to be scary and seen as real, only an impressive feat of recording.

Chapter 4 – An Underwater Thing

"I knew you couldn't do it." Jerry Oxnard said, his teenager's Southern drawl dripping with acid.

Billy Drury flinched and then snarled, angry at himself for flinching and angrier at Jerry for calling him out. Billy's hands fidgeted at his side, aching for something. His body was dripping with pool water and the calm sound of other teens splashing was a constant background noise. Three long pools were spread out around them, two behind, one ahead, each full of lines of swimming kids practicing for inclusion on the school's swim team.

Jerry Oxnard's thin face, pointed at the chin and chiseled around the cheekbones, sneered. Muscles in his perfectly sculpted neck stood out as Billy stared, transfixed. His eyes malingered onward to Jerry's startlingly precise A-frame body, the broad but sinewy shoulders which tapered down to waist and hips of unreal narrowness with oddly thick pectorals and a washboard stomach above. Jerry wore a pair of navy blue spandex shorts and unable to resist Billy's eyes continued until they hovered frozen over the smallish bulge around Jerry's crotch. Stray thoughts invaded Billy's mind and he wondered if perhaps the Perfect Jerry Oxnard also happened to be blessed with a monster dick too. It would figure, Billy snorted in his own mind.

Jerry's eyes saw Billy's drift and he said

something cruel underneath his breath. Billy's fidgety hands balled into fists, his anger warmed up beneath evaporating drops of water. Though Jerry's body was perfect and his face cruelly beautiful he was also disgustingly smart and aware all of it. But Billy was taller and certain he was physically stronger, for whatever that was worth.

Billy's shoulders topped Jerry's and his head was high enough he could look down on the other boy easily, if not figuratively. Yet Billy's body was soft and curvaceous like a girl's, wide-hipped and flabby around the breasts. Jerry's taut muscles acted like lines on a map leading the eyes around his beauty whilst Billy's flesh flowed, lumpy and uneven, like unbaked dough. It was also scored in places with stretch marks from the growth spurts Billy had endured.

Not at all unaware of the deficits between them, Billy had never had the chance to put his strength to the test against Jerry. In his entire life Billy had always been soft. Sometimes quite fat even. But he had consoled himself at being stronger and taller than the other boys from a very young age. He was fifteen now and could easily get into R-rated movies. He couldn't grow much facial hair, but his chest sprouted awkward tufts around the nipples that added to his earnest desire to never be seen without a shirt. Other teens always seemed effortlessly aware that Billy was one of them though, even when adults failed to notice, and the teens treated him accordingly.

Tensed, Billy contemplated just attacking Jerry, getting it over once and for all and proving who was the better between them. The stronger. This made Billy take deep breaths and his boy-boobs heaved with the exertion, his stomach jiggled. He was not grossly fat, but he was fatter than any of the boys around. He was disturbed greatly by this.

Billy knew he should answer Jerry's charge with some quip of his own: a cocky, confident salvo. An insult or something, but he couldn't think of one. He was actually smarter than Jerry, test scores had proven it, as in Billy's opinion had classroom discussions. Not that he had ever seen Jerry's test scores, but Billy had a habit of eavesdropping on conversations and going unnoticed doing it thereby learning reams of detail about people, particularly Jerry.   It was a close thing however and those who had not seen both Jerry's SATs and Billy's could be mistaken for thinking the prettier, more confident Jerry the smarter of the pair. Billy exuded the slowness often attributed to large people: he LOOKED stupid and unwieldy.

Except in the water.

Worse, Billy knew this, he knew how people viewed him and his own perceptions colored it even darker than it was. If he hadn't overhead Jerry's admitted test scores he would have himself assumed the other boy was the smarter as well as the better looking.

Jerry snorted another laugh at Billy's heaving chubbery.

"I can SO. " Billy stuttered. "I'm just not good at it."

Jerry's face slipped into a mask of scorn and disdain.

"Yeah, just like you said you could beat the World Record in butterfly, remember? Except you were talking about a 50 meter record and giving your 25 yard time. Remember that?"

Billy HAD said that. In a fit of pique after reading about Mark Spitz's World Records at an Olympics in the seventies and noticing his own recorded times were faster Billy convinced himself he was just that good. And after one of Jerry's frequent sessions of belittling him, Billy had fired back that he was better than the World Record and was terribly chagrined when Jerry called him out on it and turned out to be right. Others had heard the claim and Jerry's rebuttal and Jerry had whipped them up, leading the others in making jokes about whales, walruses and sea lions and other fat things that swam well. Billy thought he could still hear the incredulity that must have rocketed through Jerry's thoughts at the time: THIS fat ass thinks HE can break a World Record? As fucking if.

Just do it, Billy's mind urged. Just HIT him.

He had fantasized about it so many times.

Consequences be damned. Billy knew it would mean expulsion from the gifted school he and Jerry attended. Fighting was perhaps the only thing that could bring such an end about, but it was part of the school's zero tolerance policy towards violence. He also knew his mother would FLAY him alive. Not to mention what his father would say. And then he'd be stuck going to the normal public high school, where his sister went. The school where being smart was not an asset and where being the.... other thing was worse than being the fat kid on the swim team.

He gauged his anger again, and his eyes trailed across Jerry's now dry body. Not for the last time Billy despaired over his feelings. Of all the boys to want, why did it have to be Jerry? Billy wanted so badly to hate Jerry, to despise him above all things yet his rage always devolved into envy: of Jerry's looks, his charm, his clothes, popularity and athletic ability. As much as Billy hated Jerry though he both wanted to BE Jerry and be WITH Jerry. Every time he faced this truth it only served to remind Billy of what he was not.

Not WITH Jerry.

Not good enough to be Jerry.

Not even worth half of Jerry.

The last thought happened often, and Billy would dismiss it when he could. His intelligence rebelled, told him it was nonsense, but his body had some other hold deeper, higher, stronger than any logical thought. He intrinsically knew his worth was separate from his physical shape, was a function of his intellect and not derived from some arbitrary standard of beauty. Yet none of that knowledge made him believe what his intellect tried to convince him was true.

"Of course you're not good at it!" Jerry wailed, laughing. His voice cracked but he went on, undeterred. A group of other swimmers were avidly watching now, some hanging off the edge of the pool, others gathered around. "You can't even do a fucking flip-turn, Fatty. Much LESS break a record, except for obesity. EVERYONE here saw you try and fail. EPIC fail." The last words leaked out like a fart in a tub.

Each of those words felt like a nail from a gun pressed into Billy's chest. Each nail firing into the lungs and catching Billy's breath making the next that much harder to take. He sucked in air, but it wouldn't come. Sneering teenage faces, on thin svelte bodies floated in and out of his vision, disembodied and bereft of personality. He wanted to swat at them, like troublesome insects. He wanted to rail against them, to scream:

I can HURT you all! I am stronger and bigger than all of you! Only my superior intellect keeps me from it!

But he didn't. He just stood there, drying out and seething. He stopped imagining himself punching Jerry, stopped dreaming of kissing him, of holding him and being held against him. Of the hope somehow it could be, that it should be.

"Leave ...me alone, Jerry." Billy said, through clenched teeth barely getting the words out. "You're such a dick." His voice caught as he called Jerry a dick and the words became even more garbled.

"You want my dick?" Jerry said, laughing, and full of cruel gleam.

Billy had nothing left to say. Sadly, just saying the word "dick" around Jerry made Billy's body respond, giving paid to Jerry's mishearing of the remark. Billy had to force himself to work that much harder to contain it.

By then Coach had noticed the stoppage of practice and the gathering on the edge of the pool, had sauntered over, his tight t-shirt and short shorts not at all comical on his rigidly muscular frame. The man, Coach Senz looked Jerry and Billy up and down and frowned, at Billy.

"Drury. Back in the pool." Senz barked at Billy.

When Billy tried to walk over to the training pool, where swimmers did sprints of individual strokes, Coach Senz shook his head "no."

"No, Drury. The coaching pool."

Jerry's laughter was relatively silent, a chortle of a smile mostly. He knew better than to draw Senz's attention to him. His coterie of followers, that was what they obviously were now, did the same, all of them were watching as Billy turned, slump shouldered and went to the coaching pool. Billy did his best to drown them all out.

The word drown struck Billy then. It catapulted around his brain, bouncing from side to side like a pinball. Drown. Drown. Drown.

The coaching pool was where senior kids, those who had already had an earlier practice at fourth hour during the school day and two assistant coaches taught freshmen, mostly, how to execute flip-turns or proper stroke, how to breathe properly and very rarely even how to dive correctly. It had surprised Billy when he saw that and he had cringed inwardly at the sight of the very thin, scrawny boy being positioned on the edge of the pool as he was taught how to dive while everyone else pretended not to watch. He had wondered: who tries out for the swim team without knowing how to dive? Or how to do a proper backstroke or butterfly? And now here he was trundling over to that very pool, looking like some retarded adult who could not hack it with people his own age so hung around those much younger, using the steady compilation of experience and adult knowledge to press advantage over those who had yet to have either.

Billy spent the rest of the swim practice with a grimace on his face as an assistant coach braced his midsection and had him flip over and over in the water, constantly exhorting Billy to "breath

INTO the flip!" or "watch the BUBBLES, Drury!"
Each time Billy flipped under water the world would
roll and he'd lose a sense of himself as some
overwhelming emotion overtook him. He wanted to
say it wasn't fear, but Billy was afraid it was. How,
he would think just before the flip, am I going to do
this? What if I... but he never completed the what-
if, he just let the assistant coach roll him and the
world would turn upside down, the air bubbled out
of his nose and his senses went flat. By the end
he hadn't made any progress, he knew it, the
coach must have known it as well, but he didn't say
so. He offered some quiet platitude, but Billy knew
then it was his last practice. There was no way he
could endure another.

    The next day, after school, Billy was kicking
rocks down a dirt trail just behind his house, a trail
that ran next to a ditch. The ditch was supposedly
for draining, to stave off another flood like the
mythical one which had hit Baton Rouge in 1982, a
year so distant Billy could not readily conceive of it,
yet that ditch never got full. Not that Billy saw. His
head down, his feet trundling, he almost ran
headlong into Mike Devall, without warning.

    "Billy!" Mike squawked just as Billy's head
raised and he saw Mike standing there, filling his
vision, his hands held up protectively. Billy
scowled.

    Mike was one of those kids in the
neighborhood Billy had liked before he had

switched schools, back when his size had meant something and his intellect had been less of an issue. But Mike had ended up going to school with the idiots in the neighborhood as opposed to the gifted school Billy attended. Mike was not an idiot, though, and Billy knew this. Still, he held his scowl after noticing Mike.

Mike for his part was staring back at Billy, in an odd manner, as though he had maybe not seen him before, maybe he didn't know him, despite having just said his name. Billy replayed that in his mind and realized it had been a question.

"Billy?"

"Mike?" Billy sneered back with questioning, mocking arches of his eyebrows.

"What's up?" Mike asked, looking askance at him.

"Nothing." Billy said in the tone that said something was definitely up. Billy remembered they had once been closer friends, as children, but that was in a different, more magical world. Not THIS world, of new sex and flip-turns and teenage humiliation, papered-over envy and competition.

Billy wavered on the spot. Should he ask or just brush it aside and wander off? He had his own problems, not the least of which the prospect of facing Jerry Oxnard at school the next day, seeing the beautiful boy's sneering, laughing face and knowing it was backed with ammunition. All the heft of Billy's intellect would be useless then and he knew it, though not in those words. What was Mike going to add to THAT? Besides, what was Mike to him really? A memory? A ghost? A former pal from before when Billy wasn't Billy and Mike wasn't Mike.

Mike sighed. Billy kicked a rock in his general direction and noticed Mike for the first time. They were the same age, Billy remembered, and unlike everyone else their age, Mike was almost as tall as Billy's six foot four frame. But unlike Billy, who was chubby and soft; even through his baggy clothes, it was obvious Mike was lean and lithe, more like Jerry Oxnard than Billy. This fact made Billy's decision.

"What's wrong?" Billy asked.

"My family." Mike said sadly. "My uncle is cray and my parents are getting a divorce I think and my sister...." He swallowed whatever comment he was going to make and made direct eye contact with Billy. Meaningful contact. His eyes said, "You KNOW." But Billy didn't know, whether because his own problems mattered more or just willful ignorance or a smart kid's lack of common sense. He had not been friends with the neighborhood kids for years, he was no longer privy to their battles and tides, gossips and dramas.

For a moment Billy reflected, trying to remember Mike's sister. He vaguely recalled that she Mike's twin. Identical even, so much so that as very young kids when playing House Billy had once kissed Mike, thinking he was Janice. It was kind of funny, considering, that it was the first time Billy had ever considered what HE was, the first time he thought of himself as different from the other boys. Months before the Playboy incident. He blushed furiously, remembering the Playboy incident and that kiss. Mike had been there for the first, and the second, obviously.

"How's Janice?" Billy said, trying to deflect, to crush the memory.

"She's...mean." Mike said. Billy blinked in confusion, this was NOT the answer he had expected. Mean? It was just too young a word, or maybe too old. It didn't seem to fit with his idea of Mike, until Mike's mouth closed upon releasing the word and Billy nodded, as if in understanding. He understood, so he thought. It did fit. Jerry Oxnard was mean. Beautiful, like Janice, but mean.

"What did she do?" Billy asked. Mike moved closer to him, almost imperceptibly. Billy's back tensed and he looked away. Nervous.

"She found my porno." Mike said. Then he kicked another rock in Billy's direction. "Do you remember when we kissed?"

The question threw Billy for such an emotional loop, his body responding long before his brain, his erection sprung up, forcing his thoughts in the same direction. Furiously, he tried to control it, instead turned away, his face reddened. Slowly, he got control, of his thoughts, his body. Mike was not Jerry Oxnard. Mike's face had pimples, his nose was a shade too large and his mouth too thin and narrow. These features somehow worked on his twin sister Janice though. She was by all accounts the hottest girl in the neighborhood, Billy had heard from his eavesdropping habit. Mike, he also know, was not pretty, not cute, not the kind of boy girls like, though Billy wasn't sure how he knew this. He was also wrong.

When he didn't respond to Mike's question, Mike pushed forward. "My girl...." he paused, "..friends," the pause was long, the "s" hard and forced. "...think I'm weird, except Julie. I told her. But not my sister. I mean, she's going to tell my parents, I know it. Do you ever feel scared by it? That others are going to find out?"

Billy gaped at nothing refusing to look at Mike. He wanted to believe Mike was talking about what Billy wanted. It just seemed impossible. So unlikely that Billy had to be misinterpreting, somehow making up the connections in his mind and strengthening them, maybe as a reflex against Jerry Oxnard's presence in his mind.

"I..." Billy started to say but intellect flipped an override switch.

No. It said. *Don't.* It whispered.

It's not what you think and he'll laugh at you.

Much like the world underwater during forced

flip-turns, everything else felt out of focus and tumbled about. Out of reach and yet pressing, softly, all around. He was turning and still at the time and as confused, as unable to compel himself to do what he knew he could do. Should do.

"It's OK." Mike said after a moment's quiet. "Maybe it is just me."

This hung between them like air bubbles released beneath the surface during a flip-turn. Billy wanted to grab at them, but they were just air, empty and soon out of reach. Mike sighed.

"Well," Mike said, "It was nice seeing you again, Billy..."

Billy nodded. After Mike had gone away Billy kicked hard at more rocks and swore loudly.

Why was he such a loser? Why couldn't he just SAY what he thought? Why couldn't he just MAKE those flip-turns?

I am good enough...

Smart enough...

Billy snorted softly to himself and sighed a suffocatingly pressured filled noise then began to make his way home, kicking more rocks and twigs and trash the whole way. He saw other kids from the neighborhood, Jason and Preston Cauley, Darren Jones, Mike Devlin. But they just glared at him from afar, said nothing. Jason was larger than the last time Billy had seen him, filled out with thick muscles and yet still inches shorter than Billy. Billy's head cocked to the side as he stared.

They're no match for me and they know it.
But look at Jason's chest, it's so beautiful.

Billy tried to pay them less mind, to not see Preston's lengthened face and note how handsome it appeared. He had never thought that about Preston before.

At home Billy's parents spoke to him and his sister, but he paid them no mind, lost in his own trepidations and plots. His mind whirled, trying to find excuses to explain his inability to flip-turn. Something to justify the lack.

Maybe if I brought some of my ribbons from summer swim team to school...

Those were winning ribbons by and large but Billy could not think it would seem anything but desperate. Jerry's pretty face laughing at him, sneering at him, floated across the idea of desperation. Billy shuddered. He decided to do nothing instead.

Hours later Billy lay in his bed slowly tossing a Koosh ball into the air and narrating his catches. His narrations were varied, sometimes they were fantasies about unreal things, other times they were color commentary on his last-minute game saving catches that kept the Koosh from hitting the floor. He slowly went numb and the suffocating thing inside him dimmed and puffed away. All he wanted as he drifted off to sleep was to avoid the humiliation he knew was coming.

He didn't set his alarm clock. When his

mother came to wake him, Billy feigned illness and she grudgingly agreed to allow him to remain at home, unseen by a doctor. She called the school and let them know. Billy spent the day watching television and eating, he neither bathed nor brushed his teeth nor changed out of his pajamas. He tossed the Koosh ball for several hours.

By the time his mother came home he was bored senseless but strangely unable to do anything about it. His video games sat unused, the Koosh ball abandoned, the TV off and his books all closed. Homework had never even been contemplated. Thankfully he had not spent much time worrying about Jerry after he masturbated when the Price is Right went off. Mike he didn't think about at all.

"You seem better..." his mom said, annoyed. Billy nodded.   "I feel better."

It was now Friday night. His mind formulated a plan and he knew it required she believe him well enough to leave the house. The plan had been forming unseen in his mind for some time, as if crafted by some other agency, some independent thing.

"I feel a lot better actually."

"Wonderful! Maybe you can..."

"Do you think I can go hang out at Mimi's tonight?"

"But you're sick."

"Not anymore, really Mom. Please?"

She sighed. Perhaps not at all fooled, but eventually she nodded. Mimi lived several streets over and was well known to her, if not precisely liked.

Billy walked there early, long before the party he had heard about but had not planned on attending started. There was only one car in the drive, nothing to give tell to the party he had purposefully not told his mother about. He shoved his hands in his pockets as he approached Mimi's front door.

Mimi answered the knock and let Billy in, with only the slightest look of confusion at his super early arrival or mere presence. He didn't see her again until the place was teeming with other teenagers. Several older boys appeared with plastic sacks of alcohol. Tens of people Billy knew but didn't socialize with showed up, most of whom glanced at him without speaking. But Billy didn't care, he was waiting for Gretchen.

Eventually a group of nominal outcasts came in, Gretchen Wilkins among them. Billy steeled himself and let the independent mind within have control. He grabbed some liquor and guzzled it all down. With each gulp his comfort increased and his control slipped away. He got shit-faced quite quickly. Then he cornered Gretchen.

"Hey Gretch." Billy slurred and leaned into her. She was easily a foot shorter than Billy, her blond hair in a messy French braid and her brown eyes clouded from weed. Her floor-length skirt was floral patterned and smelled of cigarettes and patchouli. Billy swallowed a burp.

"Hi Billy." Gretchen murmured and looked him up and down. "Thought you were sick."

"I wanted to see you." Billy lied. The plan, now fully engorged inside him, was to get Gretchen to make out with him. Thereby changing the topic of conversation so that no one would care about whatever horrid things Jerry Oxnard had or would say. It wasn't much of a plan and Billy knew it.

The party kicked into full swing. More liquor, more teens, louder music, more hormonal air shifts. Billy made small talk with an obviously uncomfortable Gretchen, who kept leaning away from him every time he lurched at her. Far more people showed up than Billy had expected, more than he imagined had ever been to one of Mimi's bashes before. Groups Billy thought of it as insoluble were intermixed. Jocks and loaders, cheerleaders and fat girls, drunken band geeks and supercilious Latin club nerds hovered around college drop-ins playing beer pong.

"Stop it Billy!" Gretchen finally said and shoved him away. "I don't want to make out with you OK?" She didn't say it cruelly, just with obvious, open disinterest. And a large dose of confusion. But Billy was too drunk to care. He reached out and grabbed her breasts. Just at that moment Mimi appeared and hooted at them.

"I thought you were..." she started, then swayed and burped at the same time. Distracted, Billy was unable to stop Gretchen from shoving him away and fleeing.

"..Shick?" Mimi slurred. She seemed to have forgotten that she had seen him already.

"Nah," Billy muttered. "Didn't feel like going to school today."

Mimi laughed, swayed again and groped at a lanky, scruffy boy with a mohawk who had sidled up to her. Billy knew the guy's name was Morton but he also knew he had never been directly told this and therefore possibly was not supposed to know such. Even nearly drunk he maintained that facade.

Morton eyeballed Billy, questioningly and with a grumpy expression on his bearded face. "Who's HE?"

Billy smiled. Because he was supposed to, though it was difficult, like the world was rolling around him and full of water. Neither Mimi nor Morton registered anything of Billy's hesitance or mood.

"Everyone's here..." Morton said, leadingly. Mimi threw her arms out wide and repeated it.

"EVERYONE'S HERE!"

Billy turned to slink away unnoticed and he realized something with unusually clarity. Everyone was there and they had somehow, inexplicably all paired off. Even Gretchen who was making out with some extremely large bear-shaped guy Billy did not know. His stomach twisted and constricted painfully, but not because of Gretchen. Right next to Gretchen was Jerry Oxnard – his face sucking on Ava Timber's lips. Billy's desires sank from the place they lived within his brain down to the gut where they bloomed like a red tide into something gross and bloated. "Billy!" Mimi shouted, exuberance wafting off her. It didn't seem feigned. Perhaps she actually liked him, as a friend, he mused. They had had moments of confidence in the past.

She nudged at his shoulder with something hard and covered in paper. Billy let his gaze linger on Jerry for a long fantasy moment before he glanced down and saw that it was a bottle of some liquor in a paper sack.

"want shum MadDog?" Mimi slurred. He took a huge swig and gasped as it burned going down. It tasted awful. Like forty-year-old cough syrup in a half-asleep nightmare. But it soon loosened his limbs and eased the thing swelling in his stomach. He cocked his head to the side. Then he yelled.

"YEAH!"

"YEAH!" Mimi shouted back. Morton frowned. Several others repeated the shout, some without disengaging from their kissing. Billy wandered away from Mimi and Morton, unwilling to keep watching Jerry make out with Ava.

Hours passed in a haze as he wandered

around the house and yard, with teens slowly passing out in odd places like the bathtub or flower beds. Suddenly Billy found himself alone for the first time since the party began. People were around, but comatose. A largish sofa was inexplicably empty near the door of the room. Billy's sight went cloudy for a moment and he blinked furiously to clear his sight. When he could see again he had somehow moved to hover over the sofa and could not recall having done so.

A melancholy descended upon him then. A realization of his singularity, his uncomfortable aloneness within himself. His conversations with Jerry replayed in his various motions, both slow and fast-forward. He had relived, in drunken teenage estimation, the varied weird of those moments, the impact on his future and the seeming bleakness of it. He was prescient, he knew, in those moments, seeing something beyond himself, or perhaps very, very deep within himself. As though he had been granted guest rights to a coming part of his life where the aloneness he felt pushing on him from all around was not just some thing he couldn't control. Some action he could not do. Some flip-turn he could not make. But a real, vestigial part of him, an unseen limb of dubious function, a secret   self. An underwater thing.

Amidst these thoughts he stumbled into the sofa.

A snuffling grunt rose from it and Billy started

back. Lying, his perfect mouth open, his eyes lightly closed, one leg thrown down and hanging, limp towards the floor, was Jerry Oxnard. The pretty boy wore a Polo shirt and a pair of khaki shorts, both with small, wet stains on them. He smelled strongly of the same liquor that was flustering Billy's own mind. And he was dead asleep. Snoring.

Looking around, furtively, Billy searched for Gretchen. The last he had seen her she had been mouth to mouth with Jerry. But that was fuzzy in his memory, somehow incorrect. There were other people around, though they were all asleep as well. Billy stifled a belch. He did not think he knew any of the others. No Mimi. No Morton, or Mike or Charles or Ava or Mike or Janice or anyone he could readily name. Just drunken teens oblivious to his presence. And Jerry.

The party had descended into the quiet interregnum between bangs and people were all held down by whatever passion lived within them and required escape. Billy felt alone with Jerry, who was passed out on the front room sofa.

His hands itched. The feeling that had dropped to his stomach rose up, angrily, and raced outward to his hands, to nest in the tips of his fingers.

This he thought *I can do.*

The world consisted of only that room, that sofa, and Jerry. All of it danced around Billy, thanks to the liquor, spinning in a rather delightfully scary manner, not at all unlike being underwater during a flip-turn, and Jerry. Always Jerry. Billy eased himself to floor before the sofa, his tongue gently tipping his lips, head turning side to side, swaying as he looked for anyone who might be awake or watching. But there was no one.

Gingerly, he reached over and grabbed the small metal handle of the zipper on Jerry's khakis. Then he pulled the zipper down. Billy's heart fluttered so fast every part of him shook, except his hands, which remained exquisitely in control. They reached inside the opening of Jerry's shorts, Billy's fingertips, one of the few parts of him that could be called slender. He edged and sought and found Jerry's flaccid, small penis. Attention riveted, Billy pulled Jerry's penis free of its warm den and allowed it to sit, exposed in the breached opening of his soiled shorts. Billy's eyes could see nothing else then, his ears gone deaf to the world around, he could not have resisted the motion dragging him forward even had he wanted. The flip-turn had begun, executed flawlessly and the rest must be gravity or fluid dynamics or inertia or whatever ruled the motion of a human body above as below water. Billy's head dipped towards Jerry's crotch and took Jerry's penis inside his mouth, tasting the piss on the tip and not caring. He bobbed up and down upon it, unknowing if he was doing it right, uncaring. The sound of footsteps reached his ears and his body reacted instantly. Within a second he had pulled away and was standing up, red-faced, swaying and close to puking from the roiling inside him. But his eyes did not leave Jerry's glistening dick. It had not changed. Nor grown, it was the same, it just sat there, sad and small and wet. It was only the sound of drunken laughter that pulled Billy's eyes off it.

Mimi was there, with Gretchen and Morton and several others, all of them staring at Jerry's little prick and laughing. Distantly, Billy heard one of them say, "I think he peed on himself!"

Billy's heart fluttered, angry that they had not understood, had not grasped what had really happened. Couldn't they see it? Were they blind? But he laughed along with them, joined in the mockery of the sleeping beauty while inside the thing that had moved his hands, that roiled his stomach, that ruined his flip-turns sulked and settled in until it could surface again.

Chapter 5 – Cassie Before the Fall

"Do you ever wonder?" Cassie murmured,
as Phil's arms wound around her soft, chubby
shoulders. His presence was comforting, in the
manner of remembered autumns and beige anti-
septic quiet. At times she wondered if she was
settling, after all Phil *was* a nobody, but then she
would remember that she hadn't done much yet
herself either.

Yet.

Still at times, it felt like settling. Not right then
however. It was warm and enveloping.

"About what?" Phil said, his warmed-honey
voice caressing her as much as his nose, which
pressed gently against the side of her neck,
against her slowed carotid artery.

"Losing people." Cassie said, annoyed.

This is what I meant by settling! He can't
even follow a conversation. We HAD just been
talking about this, HADN'T we? Nothing had been
said in the interim, nothing more than arms being
wrapped around and nuzzling.

"Not really." Phil said. His thick, stubby
hands wandered down her sides and pulled gently
at the elastic of her panties which showed up just
outside her low-rise jeans. That a man could do
this to her never ceased to amaze. She was fat,
she knew it. Her bulk rolled over the edge of those
low-rise jeans, stretching those Victoria's Secret

panties into blue silk sausage casings. Yet Phil could caress her over that fat, there and elsewhere, his hands and erection giving no indication he found this to be problem. That knowledge, more than his hands themselves, sent those electric chills up her spine. Phil himself was thick. Squat. Muscular with a bulge around his trunk, nothing unusual for a man past thirty but not yet forty, who had worked construction for Tori knows how long.

"I do." Cassie said. She wanted to be able to talk about this, naturally, with someone who could feel what she did. Who could find it...meaningful. The other people in her creative writing classes seemed to get it, but they were all gay or other fat girls, or punks who thought being angry was *no bueno.* None of them were available to be more than what they were to her.

Yet these people read her most intimate thoughts, in the form of stories and poems. They criticized her. She could hardly explain how.... *close* this made her feel to them. When they GOT her, it was far more satisfying than just about anything she had ever felt. Because it lasted.

Phil sensed her mood and disentangled a bit, so he could make eye contact. Then in a sparkling moment, one that Cassie would remember until the day she died as being a pristine example of the kind of thing that should stick with a person, Phil said: "You want to talk about this more, don't you?"

Cassie bit her lower lip and nodded, pleased.

"Ok." Phil moved again, propped himself up on one elbow.

Cassie grinned and rolled over, her bulk shifting a bit and making her panties ride up uncomfortably. She was too used to that to care much. Besides, she had Phil's interest and his closeness.

Was this a good time to test him?

"I've never lost anybody. Like never. Not a relative, not a friend, no one I know has died, no one since my great-grandmother when I was seven. I didn't even know her though. She made me that quilt. All I remember of her was that smell, the acrid, smokey smell that was all over, it was the first time I realized that old people smell different, you know?" Cassie shuddered. She smiled, pleased at her words. "Still when she died I didn't feel anything, you know? My mom she cried, but only while we were in the service and my Grammaw, she cried too, but after the service was over she was laughing. At the wake." Cassie paused to add significance to this. Phil nodded. Maybe he understood. "After that – no one. This kid died when I was in the tenth grade, he was riding his bike down Perkins road and a car just like hit him. I knew him, sort of, he was in the Latin Club too. I had even talked to him a few times. But he wasn't, you know, something? Right? And a week after he died no one was talking about him anymore. And then that other kid, that Jerry Oxnard, the one who threw himself off that office tower in like Hong Kong or something? My best friend Lettie, she actually dated him and I had like ten classes with him! But when I found out he was dead? I felt nothing. I mean NOTHING." Cassie said.

Phil nodded, yet again. He had gone to the same high school, but had been ten years ahead. Maybe he was familiar with Jerry's story nonetheless. Yet his nod was infuriating. What did it mean?

"Ok?" Phil said.

Cassie sighed.

"So why don't I feel anything when people die? What happens when my mom dies? Or Grammaw? Or Lettie? Or Nora?" Phil's mouth thinned in distaste at the mention of her sister Nora. He hated her. The feeling was likely mutual, but Nora didn't really like anyone. It was clearer as the years passed just about everyone else not related to her felt the same way. Their own mother sometimes wouldn't say the girl's name in Cassie's hearing for months on end.

Phil started to say something, but Cassie bulled through.

"I mean, what if I'm not prepared for it? What if I turn into jello on the kitchen floor and lose my shit? What if I just start counting flecks in the linoleum and singing Tori Amos until my throat hurts and all I can do is lip synch?" She laughed. It was a running joke between them, how people lip synched when they thought no one was watching, how they got all passionate with it, pulled faces and acted dramatic. Phil did not laugh. "Or what if I just really DON'T feel anything? What if my mom keels over tomorrow and I can't cry? How do I go on from that? What will that say about me? Will I have to, like rethink everything about who I am? And for real, you know all I want is to be a writer, how can I write about death when I can't FEEL it?"

This last part actually made her voice waver and shake, much like jello being removed from the fridge. Her blue eyes met his green ones, searching. He KNEW how important writing was to her, how much she defined herself by the what ifs of it, the steerage level hopes of something grander with a balcony and white napkins.

Phil nodded, yet again. Fury rose in her, a need to say something, anything that would make him stop with the fucking nodding.

"Well," Phil said, slowly, as if he was searching her eyes like a dog seeking a treat, for the words she wanted him to use. "That's what will make you the best writer, right? Because you can FAKE it? Right?"

His smile said he was proud. Cassie drew away; without thinking about it, she just did. His smile warped into a frown. His hands grabbed at her sides, haphazardly, his calloused fingers found the softness just above her bunched panties and held. She did not struggle.

"I guess. But all the good ones, they KNOW. I read them sometimes, and it's like they know things I don't, they see things I can't. They can take something like their Mom dying and make it into something, you know, like imagine she's inside a urn and talking to them and they hear her voice or something. And..." Cassie's voice had grown so excited, carried steam as an idea began to roll out under the inkless press of her mind. "Other people can hear it too and they all act like it's normal, like in their world Mom doesn't die, she just goes into an urn for eternity like I Dream of Jeannie and you have to listen to her tell you to wash the dishes or wear less makeup if you rub it too hard." She smiled, pleased.

Phil just stared, unmoved for a long, dolorous moment. Then he, too, smiled and said, "You should write THAT, Cassie."

He always said that to her when she floated an idea. It was mind-boggling how stupid he could be.

Couldn't he see how DERIAVATIVE the idea was? She had to come up with something NEW, not some REHASH of what others had done.

It was JUST an example. A way of showing her superiority, her fleet-thought-footedness against his methodical plodding.

"Yeah." Cassie said. *I am settling.*

Phil pulled her closer, "But Cassie, I don't THINK it will be that way for you. How could it be? You feel for everyone? When Nora was sick last month and no one went to see her and Paulie was pulling double shifts, didn't you go to her? And don't you take care of Jeffrey, more than anyone in his family does? Not to mention your little cousins, I can't remember their names, the ones with the psycho super fat Mom? You're over there cooking and cleaning every other week when she looses her marbles and starts eating herself into a coma, AGAIN."

Cassie bristled. She had always wanted to write about her family and in one sentence Phil had beautifully described her Aunt Marissa. The woman DID seem to descend with biweekly regularity into near insanity which culminated with a binge-eating session. That left the corpulent woman in a torpor of sleep for three, maybe four, days. During those times her cousin Prisc would call, she was only thirteen, and oldest of of the five, asking if Cassie could come over and help them. Their father was a good guy, but he was oblivious and always away with out-of-state work. She supposed Phil had a point there, she DID give a great deal of herself for others, far beyond what anyone did for her and she never got mad at people for it. Not that she didn't think about it, she did, she would fume for hours over it. But she it was something she had to keep inside. Besides, she'd hoped it would make her a better writer.

"Maybe you're right." She said. Blandly.

"I just can't see you not caring, or not feeling anything if someone close to you dies. But I can't see you breaking down either. You're too strong for that."

He really believed what he was saying, it was almost enough to make her believe as well. Instead she altered the subject, just enough, to keep it about her idea without having to accept his praise.

"Still, I can't KNOW until someone dies and who looks FORWARD to that? I know I don't. But it's GOING to happen. It's just so WEIRD. That it hasn't happened? Most people have lost someone by the time they're my age, right? When did you lose someone the first time?"

Phil's eyes lost focus and he looked away from her, his hands tightened on her sides, but she thought maybe he wasn't aware of it. His hardened, calloused fingertips bit into the stretched flesh there, not sensually at all. She found she liked it.

"Do we have to talk about THAT?" Phil rejoindered. Cassie sighed.

No they didn't have to talk about it, she thought. But she wanted to. She wanted to examine the issue from multiple angles, to find the meat of it, to understand it enough that it imprinted itself on her, that she could then cast that imprint into a stamp, stamp her voice on it with her writing.

Again, Phil sensed something. "I guess so." he said.

Cassie annoyed, struggled away. This was not at all what she wanted. There was that idea again, that she was settling. That Phil was beneath her with his understanding and meek compassion. How could she explain it to him when she couldn't even get him to understand something as simple as her own lack of knowledge of death.

Phil grasped at her again, did not let her struggle completely away. His strength was annoying to her, it needled a spot she couldn't quite reach, a sore somewhere.

"Really, Mama Cass," Phil said, using his favorite nickname for her. "What does it matter? Can you be different? If you're going to feel something or nothing, then you're going to and that's that, right?"

She knew the word for this, felt her superiority that he would not.

Fatalism.

There was irony there too and she laughed, knowing she knew.

"I guess so." Cassie said, no longer burdened by the need to explain anything to him. Something was different now, something ineffable and airy between them. She could no more have caught it or seen it that she could remember being born.

"Listen, Mama," Phil said, pulling her close. His smell of sawdust and cheap cologne and body hair roaring into her nostrils did not cloud her thoughts with lust as it used to. She was done with that, but she could not stop him and she would not try. "Let's stop talking about death and do some living, what do you say?" She could feel his erection, thick and large, pressing against her. His hands were massaging her sides slowly and lugubriously rolling down her bunched up panties, oblivious to her fat rolls. She allowed him to engage, but did not return his kisses. They made love, fruitlessly for her but climatic for him. After he had passed out she got dressed, gathered her things and left quietly.

As she walked down the street towards her apartment, she and Phil lived in the same complex near the college, her panties riding up her butt, Cassie felt lightened, almost weightless. A new determination had found seed in her and grown, its growth imparting the very feeling of buoyancy that made her steps so light. She and Phil were done. She would no longer settle for anything less than love, less than a stellar, star-crossed love. Like she would not settle for being mediocre in her art. She laughed, tiled her to the side.

Because though Phil was very much alive, sleeping off their sex back in his apartment, to her he HAD died. And she knew the feeling, she understood it, could quantify it and felt her fingers itch at the need to go write about it. A furor overtook her light steps and she began half running for her place, to answer the need, to write, to express the swell within, the new understanding.

She had asked, she had wondered and the universe had answered. With a wind at her back she floated home, at times skipping like a child, at times smiling at nothing and everything, joyous at being alive.

Chapter 6 – Art Imitates Life

"You're beautiful... you deserve a beautiful life!" A man's heartsick voice said on the television set.

Lettie Stone snorted derisively before she changed the channel. Her sumptuous apartment in San Francisco was decorated in a palette of pleasing colors, bold reds and vivid blue – intended to evoke something modern, playful at the same time. She hadn't designed any of it, she'd paid an interior decorator, a friend, a fag, to do it. Despite living in San Francisco and being surrounded by gay men she was not very comfortable around them. They did have great taste, though she had to say, a thought she had often when reclining on her seven thousand dollar sofa, watching television.

She wondered, contemptuously, if some fag had written that line she had just heard blaring from the television. It wouldn't surprise her at all. They were obsessed with beauty, as they saw it, obsessed with sexualizing it, turning it into something to be *had* and *taken in*, fondled,objectified. The masculinizing of beauty was to Lettie an utter condemnation of fags in general.

She'd had a fag friend, back home. Before college, before grad school, before moving to San Francisco. She hadn't known he was gay at the

93

time, not at first, not until he came out during their senior year of high school - after her boyfriend had woken up from a drunken stupor at a party to find Billy's head bobbing up and down on Mark's cock. Lettie, undeterred, had asked the obvious question:

Was Mark's cock hard?

Their relationship had flounced after. For all she knew Mark had turned a fag, too. But Billy – that was an entirely different case. After that party, after the shame-faced next day at school when Billy proclaimed his gayness to them all (as IF they hadn't known already) he had rather quietly slipped away from everyone at the school, faded out as their high school days ended. Subsumed into some faggot cultural mire somewhere. She had heard about him a few times, seen him on Facebook, but they had not seen each other since graduation. She wasn't sure she wanted to.

She blamed Billy. She never would have gone on to date Jerry if Billy hadn't soured her on Mark. She never would have fallen for him, for his cocky brilliance, his too-thin yet flawless body, his effort-full love-making. Lettie hadn't been a virgin and Mark had been huge and attentive, but Jerry was radically different. Her orgasms had never been as good as they had with Jerry. Years had past and still she thought of him, remembered how insane it was to have him forcing her to climax with that sneering, cheerful smile on his angular face. Of all the men she had been through, Jerry had been the closest to ideal, or seemed it. Beautiful, but not girl pretty, masculine but not overbearing, cocky but not insulting. He had not been bothered at all by Lettie's talents and inevitable success. Among men it was such a rarity. Combined with the rest it made her hurt just below her stomach to remember him. She pushed the memory away.

Instead she focused on what that lame-ass actor had just said. The words cascaded down her mind into the deeper part - trenched off from rest, a place where it could soak and float back up as something else. Shifting against the chenille of the sofa's upholstery, Lettie sighed. Finally, the thought still unresolved, she turned the television off. Powered her stereo, choosing that Damien Rice song which had been her constant companion for the last week or so. She it sang it loudly.

Outside it was a balmy Saturday, like so many other in San Francisco. Some of the outside came in through the draper-ed windows, but not much, perhaps just enough. Though her work in the lab had garnered the patent for processing biofuels which led to her current life of monied indolence she did not miss the lab environment. Or the feeling of being singled out as the smartest woman around a group of pecking, undersexed males. Letting the thump of high-powered sub-woofer wash over her from the sound system, Lettie stood up. Stretched, yawned.

In her bathroom was a massive set of mirrors

fronting a pair of steel wash-sinks and an island tub large enough for four, sunken three feet into the floor. The details were typically faggy, ornate and crisp at the same time. She loved it every time she looked at it, reviled it in her memory when not looking at it or bathing in it.

Facing the mirrors, Lettie examined herself. Her frame was classic, a slightly under-exaggerated hourglass, with a still firm pair of breasts above a taut, unlined, naturally smooth stomach. Her satin bathrobe hung open and loose, framing the shape of her body but masculinizing it, robbing her of her edgy curves – straightening them. The tan bra she wore all but faded into her skin tone, as did the panties of the same color. For all she knew, standing right there could be a man with her face, her soft body. This made her frown.

She dropped the robe and it fell down, gathered around her feet haphazardly. Now the s-shape of her hips and breasts were obvious, and somehow the curve of her neck as well. As though her womanliness was a super-power and she had just changed into the necessary outfit to use it. Still frowning, Lettie ran her hands down her body, starting beneath her breasts and stopping just before the slight bulge of her pubic mound.

There was beauty, that was without question. Young still and in great shape despite her lazy living, her mind sharp and brilliant though having been used for little more than planning coyly sarcastic tweets over the past two years. She held her hands up, palms out toward the mirror, then slowly turned them around so the nails faced the the reflection. The shimmery gold polish glowed in the pleasant recessed lighting of the bathroom, atop her slender, unlined hands. Not a burn mark to be seen, highly unusual for anyone who spent as much time in a lab as Lettie had. And her nails, not fake, were long and unbroken, miniature claws each with approximately the right curvature to invoke pleasure but not pain when raked across a man's back.

After her bath, Lettie wandered through her walk-in closet, naked, slowly drying but steadily as she gently thumbed her clothes. She passed into the shoe room, an entirely pink square of confection, the walls plastered with shelves topped by pair after pair of shoes. Louboutins, Manolos, Jimmy Choos, blah, blah. She hadn't even bought most of them herself. Her personal shopper (yet *another* fag!) had. Still most of them were gorgeous, nearly works of art, at times making her afraid to actually wear them. That did not stop her from doing it, though.

Once she was dressed, in a simple black outfit, a mini with a tight bodice and a small, tulle ruffle around the hem – she picked a pair of deep gray Manolos, nearly black themselves. By the time she wandered out of the house the balmy Saturday afternoon had quietly faded into evening and her black dress gleamed pearlescent under the sodium lights as they popped on. Her shoes clacked against concrete for the seven steps it took until she reached her waiting car, the door opened and closed by a man whose name she did not know. He was new.

The car drove her to an event she had not really wanted to attend. But she knew she would. As she walked in several people said hello to her, none of whom she thought she knew. One, a robust woman in silk too tight for her size, gave Lettie a smile that offered more. Lettie smiled back and walked faster, her heels clacking against the marble floor. The room around her was elegant, tasteful and huge. A museum opening.

A man stopped and offered a tray to her with champagne flutes. She took one and sipped at it. The man was disgustingly attractive and her smile had no effect on him whatsoever. A bit disgruntled, Lettie moved deeper into the museum, merged into the welling crowd. There were various notables there, people she knew and did not know, and though she spoke, she found that she could hardly remember what she had said or what was said to her. At some point another waiter arrived with another flute and again her smile went unanswered.

Was every good looking man a FAG?

Lettie wondered. She downed the sparkling liquid and gave the empty flute to another handsome man with a tray, this time without a smile. She wasn't supposed to flirt with the help anyway.

Several hours passed, without anything of significance happening. Men smiled at her, their tuxes ranging from artful to garish to retro chic, everyone of them somehow resembling a plucked chicken. Not that they were not handsome, though most were far older than her, they just seemed somehow clipped. Several women flirted with her as well and she was forced to down a third flute to be rid of that frustration.

As the night dwindled into late evening she was drunk, but not disastrously so and ready to be taken home, even by one of the clipped men. Having been a beautiful girl before she was ever a beautiful woman she knew how to advertise her desire. Several men bit, but even despite her sloshiness, she sent the first three away with convoluted conversation stoppers about covalent bonds and wandering electrons. It was as if she were speaking a foreign language, the men's eyes would glaze over and their hands would twitch, then their feet would fidget until they had somewhere else to be. She was ready to give up after the fourth instance when a short, sallow-skinned, slit-eyed wisp approached her. His head was just above her breasts, his hair carefully spiked, his eyes a lustrous, shining black. Smouldering. His cheekbones were almost too high on his square face. He was quite handsome, in an exotic manner.

"I'm Pi." he murmured. Be he pronounced it "Pe-yo." Being a bit drunk, but not too drunk, she giggled but did not laugh. He seemed to be expecting this and smiled a crooked smile of perfectly straight teeth at her.

"You're the most beautiful woman I've seen..." Pi said but his voice trailed off, as though he were going to qualify the comment, maybe by saying "tonight," or "in San Francisco," or "this year." But he did not. His accent was strange as well, the inflection of English was almost British, but just slightly not. Lettie waited to hear how he would qualify her beauty and when he did not she turned to walk away. He was quite good looking but she had not earned half a billion dollars by being imprecise and she already knew she was beautiful. Only when his hand grabbed her arm and held tight did she remember. She *had* been looking for a hook-up. His grip was extremely strong.

She turned back around, ready to throw her drink, or what remained of it in his face when he just pulled her close, as though she weighed nothing and planted a very firm, very immobilizing kiss upon her. He had not stood on his tip-toes to achieve this, but had bent Lettie forward, leaving her dangerously unbalanced in her high heels, unable to easily pull away.

When the kiss was over, Pi's hands held tight to her forearms and gave her the balance necessary to ease upright. His grin as she stared down at him, dumbfounded, was all impishness.

Drunker suddenly than she thought, Letting swayed and said, "*How* beautiful am I?"

At least he isn't a fag.

The kiss had said that much. His size was a problem, though his body looked trim and athletic in his classic tux. And he was very well groomed, though not excessively so, his eyebrows were slightly uneven. She was going to let him take her home, but the rest was yet to be determined. It was not enough to simply want her, to notice her beauty, she was brilliant, as brilliant as she was beautiful. She deserved more. She required it, even for something in passing.

Especially from him.

He smirked at her and just shrugged. "Enough" He said, cryptically. She gaped, but he was pulling at her arm and walking, pulling hard enough if she fought back she would have to make a scene or fall down. Instead she let him lead her out of the museum to a bustling street capped by lights and a black sky. Small groups of other richly dressed people were departing the museum at the same moment, but Lettie paid them no mind. She felt like a stone in a torrent as he tugged at her, not towards any waiting car, but towards a line of ordinary cabs. Sighing, she allowed herself to be pulled.

He did not open the door for her. Instead he went around to the other side of the cab and spoke softly with the driver. Then he got in and waved for her to join him. Lettie was stunned. But she got in. As the cab drove down Market Street, creeping from light to light, Pi's hands rubbed against her knees and upper thighs. She refused to look at him. She watched the late night revelers whip by.

The cab eventually stopped at a warehouse like building in the Tenderloin. Pi got out and waited for her after he paid the driver, again not opening her door. Lettie got out. Her buzz waning but still strong enough to impair her. She let Pi lead her up into the building and past an undecorated raw space which might have once been a lobby. There was a defunct elevator shaft flanked by two that worked, the floors were smoothed planks and the ceiling was unpainted and blank. Three metal boxes had numbers affixed to them and were mounted on a wall near the doors. Pi whisked her into an elevator and pressed the button marked 3. There were only three buttons.

Once they reached the floor and the door opened she saw the entire space was one large, poorly furnished loft. Distantly, her analytic mind was calculating the value of the place, based on it size and the neighborhood. Several million at least. So Pi, whomever he was, was wealthy, if not nearly as wealthy as she was.

They had not spoken during the cab ride or elevator ride and did not speak as he walked her into a cordoned off area marked off by black sheets.

Not curtains. Sheets.

They moved gently in a breeze though Lettie felt nothing of it against her skin. Past the black curtains was a massive bed, an easel directly across from it and several low tables full of painting supplies.

Lettie sighed. Suddenly things began to make sense. An artist. A successful one, to judge by the space and location. The lack of furnishing now seemed not gross but perhaps unpretentious. She had never slept with a real painter before. Had she seen any of his works?

Pi, none to gently, placed her on the bed and began to systematically remove her clothing. He still did not speak. His face betrayed only an impatience. The kind of hurry one experienced in the middle of cooking while hungry. Lettie, half undressed, tittered with spikes of excitement at his touch as he removed each piece of clothing. Even when he jerked her bra over her arms and it caught in her hair. The tug made her warm, not angry.

When she was fully naked Pi shoved her backwards on the bed, using both his hands on her shoulders. She let herself fall, the motion swishing around her sumptuously, romantically. She was getting deeper into a moment, unlike anything she could recall having experienced before, even with Jerry, though her memories were fuzzy. Still, her left hand reached down and touched herself, gingerly, softly. She moaned, only slightly exaggerated, hoping it would draw Pi to the bed, into her.

Instead she heard the clack of wood on wood, the near silent squish of paint tubes and the delicate dunk of things being dropped into glasses of water. When she pushed herself up on her elbows and looked over at the easel, she was flabbergasted.

There was Pi, only he was naked, but barely. He was steadily squeezing himself into her clothing. It was all she could do to merely stare. She could not decide if this was a turn-on or a horrid, hateful turn-off. The indecision, the inability to know, rendered her helpless. So rare were the occasions when she did not know something, did not have the edge, was not more aware than those around her, even when she did not wish to be, it incapacitated her. All she could do was stare. Lettie's elbows sagged into the soft mattress, her mind dimly trying to decide if it was memory foam or not, as he pulled her tight dress over thin, if well-developed muscular man's legs and hips.

What she could see of his body struck her as

sexy, he was small but every bit of him was corded with muscle and seemingly hairless. Even his cock and balls had been so, and not at all small as she had secretly expected. Once he placed her shoes on his feet, the toes dangling slightly over the forward edge, she studied him up and down and realized the tightness, the unrelieved blackness of her clothes somehow fit him. It *was* sexy – in an exotic and frightening way. The alcohol in her system surged and she was woozy, enough she fell backwards on the extremely soft mattress, definitely memory foam, and rolled over on her side. Her bare ass and sandwiched vagina would be readily visible to Pi. She was moist and warm and ready.

Some time passed, in her state she was not sure how much, she did not think it was long. Lettie also did not think she had been touched. The sound of scritching could be heard, though all she could see was the black of sheets and a sliver of the floor.

With great effort she rolled herself over, feeling nauseated, but not enough to sick up. There Pi was, behind the easel, furiously painting, still wearing her clothes. He would look up at her for brief seconds and go back to hurried slashing strokes over the canvas. He bore a large erection beneath the tulle of her dress. Unwilling to wait any longer she began to pleasure herself.

As some point she ceased watching him.

She rolled on her back, her head opposite Pi and his easel, her hand thrusting in and out of her crotch to the timed scritches of Pi's brush. Her legs splayed wide so he could see it all if he wished. She knew little of portraiture, but dimly she wondered how he could paint her if she did not remain still. The thought was subsumed when a tide of orgasm started to crest within her.

At that precise moment a vision clarified itself out of the haze of her thoughts.

She was hovering over herself and the room. seeing her body in the throes of ecstasy. A creature of paints, swirling colors that were not quite her, yet were. Slashes, curves and roiling strokes – all of it added up to her, though it looked nothing like her as she saw herself. It was beautiful nonetheless.

Her attention shifted towards Pi and unlike what she saw of herself, as a painted representation, she could see Pi clearly. Or what had *been* him. The clothes were the same – hers – but the body was not. It had lengthened. Grown. Gotten slender in the shoulders and wider in the hips. His skin was lightening steadily. His high cheekbones were undulating under the facial muscles like sand in a withdrawing tide. Hair, by the quiet inch, was growing down from his artfully arranged spikes. Like a brush was sweeping color over primer the black hair changed until it was her shade of creamy, caramel brown. Her hand stiffened, her fingers still inside of her as her orgasm peaked. She could not stop it. Though she was now horrified and confused.

Her body thrust upwards as the strongest cum she had ever known wracked her frame. She vibrated across color spectrums and time warps and dreamscapes. She became something else in some other place and was pulled, screaming back.

When it was over she was panting, her arms fallen loosely over her body, too weak to even cradle herself as she wished. Her skin was slick with sweat and this was the first thing she noticed. Her breathing was hard and ragged. It slowed as the seconds ticked by. She huffed and found the energy to hug herself, to give comfort past the horror she could feel but could not remember.

Her vision clouded during the last of the orgasm, and only slowly washed out and came back into focus. The raw ceiling above, the hanging black sheets at the periphery of her sights. Slowly, timidly, she lifted herself on her elbows to stare at Pi, thinking she would share her vision with him. Gauge his reaction to her orgasm. A vague hope she could lure him into fucking her hovered around her thoughts. It was not insistent. She *was* satisfied.

Pi was gone. She realized she had felt something else besides the slickness of her skin as she had hugged herself moments before. Wrinkles. Gaping down at her sagging breasts and dimpled stomach she made squawking noises. Her hands came up and sought her face, feeling the age there. Lettie stroked across parts of herself at random, appalled and intrigued at the same time. Had Pi given her a roofie or mushrooms or something?

Her body ached in every joint and she could not have moved faster had she wanted to, whatever he had given her was *that* strong. Lettie got slowly to her feet. Padded over the raw floor to the easel, hobbling with aged steps. She stared open-mouthed at the painting.

What she saw made her stumble backwards and fall to the floor. The sound of something snapping at first made her think she had broken a paintbrush or something. Then a fiery pain lanced upward from her hip and leg. She knew it had been *her* hip which had snapped. A muffled croak of a scream escaped her withering lips, her tired, ragged vocal cords no longer capable of a full-throated shout.

Despite the pain she could not take her eyes off the painting. It was not of her. Vaguely she recalled having wondered about this, about portraiture and the need to be still, but hazily as if the memory had occurred years and years, decades, before. She moaned in pain. Moved a little closer to the painting, blinking to be sure she saw what she thought she saw.

The figure on the canvas, surrounded by

hanging black sheets and sitting half upright on a black-sheeted bed was a beautiful, high cheek-boned Asian man, in his mid-twenties, with artfully styled spikes of black hair and black eyes.

Not black. GREEN.

His form was painted, not realistically, but appeared so to Lettie. Like a photograph blurred at the edges, watered out and washed with unreal light. It hinted at motion, though it was still. The man's mouth was open in a silent scream. His eyes were wide open with terror, she was sure they could see her, they *KNEW* she was there, they pleaded with her for help.

Ignoring the pain as much as she could, memories of Pi coming to her, hazily as every other memory, but empowered by strong rage, Lettie got to her feet and scratched the painting's surface. Gouged the canvas with her long, broken, and yellowed nails. She screamed an impotently hoarse cackle.

When she had put ten long furrows across the canvas, shredding parts of the portrait of Pi, removing one of those pleading eyes, shredding parts of his perfect hair and perfect teeth. She fell back to the ground in misery as her hip radiated the most terrible feeling she had ever known.

From the floor she saw the sheets blow, in a gentle breeze she did not feel. She heard footsteps before she saw them, the loud clack of heels reminding her of something, something fine

and quite beautiful. But of what was lost to her.
She could no more recall it than she could have
stood in a body she no longer possessed. A face:
one she knew, or had known, or should know,
framed by luscious waves of caramel leaned down,
whispered into her ear.

    "You were so beautiful...."

    She knew the voice.

    It had been her own.

Chapter 7 – Share the Demon

Macklyn folded her hands over her lap, twisting her two wedding bands around her finger as she did so. Since Cassie was murdered Macklyn's life had been a seeming drudgery of unwanted motions, exercises and pale routines. It had been several years already and still she could close her eyes and hear her daughter's voice as though the girl was still near. As though the hope and urgency with which Cassie had said the word "Momma!" still resonated in the air of the open-space of Macklyn's living room. Her husband Stanford, not Cassie's father, was often gone later and later at work. His calls home came more and more infrequently.

Macklyn could remember so many details about her daughter, but at times she could not remember her face no matter how she squinted or dreamed. She would have to get out a photo album and stare, forlornly, at the photos until she was sure the image could not be burned any more permanently in her brain. When it faded she would descend yet again into a timeless funk which made everything on HGTV irrelevant. Enough to make her weep at the same time. She would question herself as a mother then.

"What kind of Momma am I?" she would ask Stanford after an episode of crying and unwilling forgetfulness. "That I can't even remember my own daughter's face?"

"Macklyn..." Stanford would say, his voice descending like Macklyn's emotions in just the space of time it took to mumble her name – from a calm high to a deep low. She knew he was coming to despise her, maybe he already did. Their marriage had not been the easiest or the best, but they had kept to it. Made it work. Slogged through her hearing loss and his heart problems, and his unmentionables. At times she seethed because Cassie had been the only one she could talk to about the unmentionables. Her own mother, Doreen, was far too much of an idle gossip. Macklyn was afraid if she told her about Stanford's thing not getting up Doreen would tell Macklyn's sisters and those cows would tell their redneck husbands and they would in turn belittle Stanford at Christmas. Macklyn knew there would be no coming back from THAT holiday.

"Macklyn," Stanford said to her after she cried that she was a terrible mother for not being able to remember her daughter's face. "She is in a BETTER place. You know that."

But Macklyn didn't.

She had known that, before. That's what happened when you died, she had believed it because she had to. Ever since Papaw Francis died and she could still feel the clammy hardness of his hands as he bounced her on his knee. Then he told her, loud as all get out: "Mackie you is the purtiest, bestest lil gran' daughter any old man could e'er want!"

Of course she had been the only granddaughter then. There had been no cousins, no siblings yet. They would come later in droves, after Papaw had died. They would only know him through his spotty smoke-filled wife and pictures. But Macklyn had gotten to know and love him as his special girl for nearly ten years.

It had been a hard thing, seeing death so early, and Macklyn had grown accustomed to it over her nearly sixty years. She did not fear it, except for her children and only in the abstract as she could imagine. She was not a deep thinker and she knew it. Still she could get weepy when talking about it. Especially to her only son, Cassie's brother Charles.

"Momma..." Charles would say with the faux patience of an intellectual speaking to a hick, a tone she knew he thought was well masked, but she knew him better than he could ever know. "What do you *think* happens after people die?"

She knew he was leading her into a specific conversation, one that he would dominate, because he was so much smarter, so much more than she ever was. One with an outcome he had already predetermined. That, however, did not dent her belief at all. And he was her only son, so she'd play along.

"Heaven, of course."

"So you think Papaw Francis," Charles would say, though his first name was Francis as well, named after the very man. They did not call him Francis. "..is up in Heaven?"

"Of course!" Macklyn would say, a bit of heat in her voice. She would try to hold it back, but it hurt her a bit to hear him doubt her beloved Papaw could be anyway else but looking down on her from above.

"And he's up there. Forever, right? Streets of gold, choirs of angels, etc. Etc?"

Macklyn would sigh. She was not interested in this conversation, but it would keep Charles talking to her and that was enough. "Yes, dear."

"What do you think he's doing, Momma?" Charles would ask snidely, his voice going softer than normal, leaning forward, eyebrows raised, to hear her response.

"He's watching over me and you and Cassie. Like a guardian angel!" Macklyn would exclaim.

"All the time?" Charles would ask.

"Yes."

"Even when you're taking a shit?"

Macklyn would suck in an exasperated breath at the mention of the word "shit" in that context. Her face would redden. The very IDEA of someone watching her go number two was so revolting as was her own SON talking about it. But he was always full of those kinds of ideas.

"What about when you're fucking, Momma?"

"Or gambling and smoking when you *know* you're not supposed to?"

"Or being mean to someone at work?"

The rapid fire of Charles' questions had thrown her off balance, then as always, it would mingle with her thoughts of Papaw and Mamaw and her first love. Also named Charles. Her friend Judy and others who had died as well, people she also missed terribly. The sure knowledge they were up *there*, waiting for Macklyn, watching out for her had always made the notion of death tolerable, something she could accept and soldier towards. Not cower in dread. But Charles' uncomfortable questions would go through her mind into painful doubt and aching, needy hope. It was not that Charles' intended purpose, shaking her faith, had succeeded, but instead it had reminded her she was still *here*. On Earth, while *they* were up *there* in Heaven, watching. And she missed them. The idea they would NOT be waiting for her, she would never again get to see Papaw Francis again, it hurt her more than she ever wanted to bear.

"But Momma," Charles would say, not unkindly – he was not a bad boy, despite the drugs and weird lifestyle, "Is that really what you WANT? The people you love forced to watch YOU all day, all the time? What about what THEY want to do? You can't even watch HGTV for more than two hours without getting restless, what if YOU died and had to watch me ass-fucking some guy I met in a bathhouse? Or Cassie sleeping all day while she was supposed to be writing? How would you choose between us? And what would you miss if you did choose? Imagine *that* stretched over *decades* Momma, and suddenly you're a different person and the person up over there watching – they can't know you anymore. Because you've changed so much, you're a STRANGER to them otherwise. With only the barest trace of the person they knew! Like a friend you haven't seen since elementary school."

This point, alone amongst all his rambling would strike Macklyn at her core, but she would already be crying gently thinking about her Papaw and could mask the doubt Charles had sown in her by claiming it was that. She would NOT let her son preach her out of her faith!

But Cassie dying. That had changed everything.

Her wedding rings, she had two – one with diamonds on it and one with none – were loose from the weight she had lost since the funeral. And the years since. She could turn them over and over so easily now. Sometimes they even slipped off and for days she would not even notice, until Stanford said something and she remembered she had a husband. Therefore she should have wedding rings.

As she turned them now, her hands folded in

her lap, she tried, unaided by a photo album to call up Cassie's face. Her daughter had not looked anything like her. She had not looked much like the man Macklyn had told everyone was her father either, Charles' dad Gerald. Macklyn knew Cassie was the product of her first love, Charles. And then Charles had *died* in that car accident before Cassie was born and Macklyn had been sure Cassie was her gift from Charles straight out of Heaven. Yet now she was dead and Macklyn, strain as she might, could not remember Cassie's face. She could remember details. Cassie had been overweight, like Charles, thought her brother Charles was not. And like her father Charles, Chuck as everyone had called him, Cassie had a rounder face, light brown hair, deep blue eyes and a beaky nose. But though Macklyn could recall each of these details individually, when she tried to put it together to make Cassie's face whole it was all blurry and indistinct, like she was seeing her daughter through fogged glass.

Stanford, who was still at work, would have yelled at her if he knew what she was doing. Told her to snap out of it. Get up and DO something, he'd say. Paint something, refinish something. He might even throw money at her to do it with, the tight-ass. She laughed bitterly at that thought. He was a tight-fisted son-of-a-bitch when it came to money. Or had been until Cassie died. Macklyn had the trump card now and Stanford never bothered to force her to play it, he simply gave her more and more.

"Momma?" Charles' voice came wafting from the kitchen. She had not heard the door open or the alarm beep to announce the door had opened. Had she mistakenly turned it off again?

"I'm *here,* son." Macklyn said, releasing her wedding rings and her attempts at recalling Cassie's face.

"What are you doing Momma?" Charles said, his feet echoing in the open space of the living room as he walked down the three wooden steps into the recessed area. "Why is it so *dark* in here?"

Macklyn blinked. Night had come and she had not noticed. She had been sitting in the dark. Without the dogs around this happened more and more often. But she had not been able to stand them after Cassie died, their neediness reflected her own and disgusted her. She had given them away within weeks of the funeral much to the shock of both Charles *and* Stanford.

"Sorry...." Macklyn said, sniffing a bit. She had been crying quietly too. She had not noticed *that* either. Charles bounded over to her and wrapped a single thin arm around her. He was like that, not a bad boy at all. Loving despite his need to be smarter than her, and everyone else. "Momma! You're crying again."

"Sorry!" Macklyn said and the tears came harder then. Wracking full body sobs. She couldn't talk to Charles about it, because it was his fault. Not that she couldn't see Cassie's face anymore, she could accept the blame for that, but that she *wouldn't* ever see Cassie again. Or Papaw or Judy or Mamaw or Chuck or any of them. And yet, though she knew it was his fault, she could never tell him this. What kind of mother would she be if she could? Being unable to remember Cassie's face was failure enough on that front.

But it *was* his fault and she knew that's why she was crying. Why she was sitting in the dark turning her wedding rings around her finger. Because she could not believe as she had before. Not really because of Charles, though his words had started it. Cassie's death had made it real in a way no other death had, or likely could have. The thought of Cassie in Heaven, miserable as she watched her Momma and her brother and her KILLER for Christ-sake, that *asshole* was *still* alive! The idea Cassie was up there watching all of them, all of that, and unable to do any of the things *she* loved, but stuck seeing them suffer or be happy, knowing how they missed her so terribly and were also happy regardless. This was more than Macklyn could conscience. It was wrong. And if that was wrong... then what else was wrong.

So she sat in the dark, hoping to recall her daughter's face, to know, that if she wasn't in Heaven, if her daughter really had just disappeared, at least in Macklyn's mind she would exist as long as her mother drew breath. But she could not remember her face!.

"Momma!" Charles said with urgency. "Where's Dad?" By Dad of course, he meant Stanford. Though Stanford was NOT his Dad. Why did she have to think of that right then, she fretted, only making her sob harder. "Momma? Are you OK?"

"Yes." Macklyn lied. But she wasn't OK. She felt terribly alone and faced with a wide world that had nothing after it, an emptiness so vast and scary she could not face it. A place that had eaten Cassie, and now held her memory hostage. Kept it away from Macklyn. Maybe forever. Charles pulled her tighter but his arms did little to comfort her. Though she did experience a small amount of pride she did not shrug him off as part of her very much wished to do.

"You can't keep on like this, Momma!" Charles said, so tenderly, with such abiding affection Macklyn's heaving sobs started all over again from the slight lull they had begun to achieve. "She's gone, Momma."

"Don't you think I know that?" Macklyn shouted, pushing Charles off of her. " No matter how stupid you think I am, I do know that! And I Know there's nothing waiting, that she's just gone, forever and there's nothing." Macklyn stuttered as she cried and screamed, wiping at her nose in the midst.

Charles froze and did not make any move to hug her again. He did go over and turn on one of the floor lamps. He sat down on the captain's chair across from the sofa Macklyn sat upon. His elbows hovering just above his knees, Charles buried his head in his hands and his shoulders hitched forward and backward like the fits of an engine which could not ignite. Macklyn had the urge to reach over and comfort him. But it was swallowed whole by her grief.

"I'm..." Charles began to say, his face still covered by his hands, but nothing else came out. Instead, after a long quiet moment of mutual sobbing she simply stood up and left him there. A sharp satisfying emotion trailed behind her, like a personal stink. She knew it was there but it was not something which affected her directly. She walked out of the house and into the backyard, stepping around the Gun-nite pool without looking down, crossing onto the lawn Stanford still kept meticulously clipped, though she had stopped pestering him to do so for well over two years. Her feet guided her to the shed in the back of the yard.

Once she had kept antiques and items she wished to refinish, to sell in her booth at the flea market, her "spending plenty" she called the money she made from such things. It had been a soothing thing at first: finding something distressed and fixing it up, finding just the right FEEL of color and application that made it gleam with old newness, or new oldness, or some other quality she lacked the erudition to elucidate. Charles could have done it, but though she had often used the money for his benefit and not hers, she had not shared the intimacy of the work with him or anyone else, not even Stanford or Cassie. It had been hers alone, a new baby to raise that would never leave, could never be so wrong it could not be redone. Would never do drugs or say it hated you or get murdered by the man whom you loved.

Macklyn had not been inside the shed since just after Cassie had been buried. She had given away most of what she had remaining, finished or not, to her sisters and Miss Jeannie, the old bat next door who kept a booth at the same flea market. Now, with night insects buzzing around and likely snakes in the long grass which lined the wooden slat fence just past the shed, she opened the shed's lock. Pressed the four digit code without paying much attention to what she was doing. The door swung open a fraction of an inch and let out a dusty breath of old wood, dried paint and the acrid, tangy whiff of paint stripper. She breathed in deeply and went inside.

She shut the door behind her and turn on the overhead light. There was still a large buffet against one wall, not sanded or painted, or stripped. One she had intended to give to Cassie and Thad when they got married. Three knickknacks sat atop it, unmoving and casting long shadows over the wooden top: all cast iron rabbits, which she had meant to paint and give to her own mother. Two chairs sat against another wall, ladder-backs, each painted a garish yellow she had meant to strip. They were old, old, old. With the right varnish would have fetched a hundred bucks each. The buffet was worth three times that, with all the carving on the lintels and doors and the heavy oak wood top. As she stared at these things, she wondered why she had come in here.

Macklyn walked over and pulled one of the garish yellow chairs away from the wall, sat down in it and stared at the buffet. In the glint of the light overhead she could see spiderwebs, mouse shit and a dead lizard. But not a single living thing.

For the tiniest moment Macklyn looked up at the thin aluminum rafters above and wondered if they could hold her weight. If she was brave enough to stand on the chair, tie a rope around one and kick off. She had never thought of suicide as brave. Being a good Christian woman, she had always known it for what it was: a coward's way out. For a person who gave no thought to those left behind, to those who must find the body and bury it and remember it. For as long as they could and then cry when they could not. But now she wondered if maybe it was not so. Perhaps it was brave, she thought, to jump off into nothing, with no idea if there was a fall or stop, what courage it

123

must take to go into the abyss not knowing! She began to cry again, for her lost daughter, for her faith and the surety it had always given her, for her Papaw and his rough hands and warm knees. For a son and husband she understood now she could no longer connect with, for an afterlife that was not only denied her but simply no longer guaranteed.

The next day Macklyn finished loading all the stuff from the shed into the back of Stanford's pickup. She drove two doors down and honked the horn like an impatient suitor, a rude young man, and waited for Miss Jeannie to hobble out. The older woman came after three more honks, looking vaguely hassled and thoroughly annoyed. It took a moment for Macklyn's mind to remember that Jeannie Stone had her own tragedies. Her sadness went as deep as Macklyn's own. She could be turned out of that beautiful house any day now, with her only daughter having totally cut her off and left her destitute, abandoned and forgotten. In fact, Miss Jeannie looked far older than the last time Macklyn had seen her. Much older than her sixty-seven years. Not for the first time Macklyn derided the woman silently for adopting the little girl in the first place at forty years old. It just wasn't natural to raise children alone.

Miss Jeannie made it to the pickup and clambered in, her cane stowed at her feet. Since when had she needed that? The older woman turned and gave Macklyn a very severe look.

"Macklyn." Miss Jeannie said, gruffly.

"Jeannie." Macklyn said, smiling, though she did not mean it. She had called the woman because she intended to sell everything that remained in her booth to her and she needed her there. She also wanted to deliver the stuff in the pickup to Jeannie, but neither of them could lift such things. They were supposed to meet Charles and some of his "buddies" at the flea market. Macklyn, years before, might have been reproachful at the idea, a bit frightened of what kind of low, dirty person or strange oddball her son would show up with, but she found now she just did not care. Miss Jeannie had been taking care of her booth for almost three years now, with assistance from Charles and Stanford.

t would be good to finally rid the herself of the burdens and pass them on to Jeannie. She surmised the old woman had poured her entire life into the flea market. In some vain hope at making enough money she might forestall the bank and keep her house.

"I ain't paying you for nuthin'" Jeannie grumbled.

"I know, Jeannie." Macklyn said, "I don't want your money. I want you to have these things." And she meant it. In every way. She wanted the memories of them gone, she wanted the weight of it on someone else's shoulders. She wanted to be unencumbered and this was the start.

But she would never have told any of that to Jeannie. She suspected the woman might have refused to accept any of it had she known Macklyn truly did not wish to part with it, such was Jeannie's world view since her daughter up and disappeared.

"Well good then." Jeannie said. "Macklyn could tell the woman was about to engage in small talk, as if it were necessary, required by the fact Macklyn was giving her something. They put up some pretense of still being friends. They both knew it was not true. Each had learned tragedy is too jealous and cannot abide the affection of others, each had had no room for each other since their daughters were gone. But Macklyn wished she could somehow silence the woman politely. Some things simply no longer mattered since Cassie died, Macklyn could not remember the last time she had colored her slate grey hair. Or had her nails done. Or bought new clothes or eaten boiled crawfish. She had not lost the innate feeling politeness or its well-heeled veneer must be maintained. She could only lose so much and that was too integral a part of who she was to change it, even had she wanted, she knew no other way to be.

Instead, she just endured Jeannie's prattle.

"Been talkin' with them bankers again and I think they might let me make smaller payments and take sommore of my Social 'Curity. They seen how much I been bringing in from our booths and they told me that if I keeps that up I can keep the house."

Despite the way she talked Jeannie was neither stupid nor uneducated. The woman had been a nurse before she retired. She had been a force in making sure her only daughter had been both brilliant and perfect in everything the girl had tried, though it had aged Jeannie beyond her years to achieve it. Yet she had never lost her bayou roots and to Macklyn, who had not spoken more than five words to her in a year or so, it sounded like she had sunken further back into those roots. Gone deeper country than she ever had been before.

"That's good Jeannie." Macklyn said. Jeannie snorted.

"What do you care? Your house is paid for, your boy is always coming to see you and your man is always workin', ain't he?" Jeannie said, but without sting. Macklyn could only sigh. It would do no good to explain how Jeannie had it all wrong, other than the house being paid for. IT was in Stanford's name though, so it did Macklyn little good except as an idle threat of dividing assets in a possible divorce. But she no longer thought about it. Not since the night Cassie died. Stanford could KEEP the damn thing. When Macklyn didn't reply Jeannie tapped on the door just under the window glass, as if she were impatient to arrive at the flea market.

It wasn't until she neared the flea market that Macklyn suddenly realized what she had intended all along. And it wasn't to go to the flea market. Instead of stopping she pressed down on the accelerator, smiled meanly as the pick-up gained speed. In the bed she heard the heavy items shift and slide backward. Jeannie tensed and cried out. Soft, startled.

"Where is you goin'?" Jeannie asked, her head whipped around to stare at the flea market receding behind them as Macklyn sped the truck down Airline Highway. "The flea market is back THERE!" Her eyes pointed hard.

"I know where the flea market is, Jeannie." Macklyn said, calmly. She was surprised by her own lack of irritation at the older woman. Macklyn struggled to hold back the giddy freedom bubbling up. She laughed knowing there was no reason to hold anything back. Not anymore.

"Well, by damned, turn this heap around and take us back to it! We gots people *waiting* for us, Macklyn!" Jeannie gaped at her and waved a wrinkled hand near Macklyn's face, as though something were the matter with Macklyn's vision and the waving of a hand would correct it.

"Well LET THEM wait, Jeannie!" Macklyn said, laughing, and drumming her hands on the wheel.

"What in damnation has got into you? Where are you takin' us?"

"Somewhere we both need to go, Jeannie."
Macklyn said firmly.

They drove in relative silence after. Jeannie
stared out the window at passing pines, oaks, and
other green things. Her elbow on the window sill,
her head in her hand. Several times Jeannie made
a halfhearted harrumph noise. Drummed her
fingers on the arm-rest. After they reached the
long bridge past LaPlace Jeannie went silent and
still. Macklyn's silence was of a different variety,
bubbly and thrumming with excitement.
Amazement she had waited this long.

Why? Why did I wait this long?

They crossed off the bridge, the gloomy trees
of the swampy, lake-like area of the Ponchartrain
shore falling behind them. Giving way to the
grubbiness of Kenner as cars began to appear
beside them as if by magic. The interstate
widened from two lanes to four. Alongside popped
up signs advertising motels, hotels, IHOPs,
McDonalds and other businesses meant to lure
travelers off the highway. Macklyn paid no
attention to any of them.

She just drove, heedless. Pressed down
harder on the accelerator.   Sped up past the
empty patrol car which sat between Kenner and
Metarie, and usually made everyone slow down
thinking it was an actual police cruiser. Sometimes
it even was, but not that afternoon.

By the time they had reached the French

Quarter it was nearly six in the evening. Macklyn's phone had rang several times on the long bridge and she turned it off rather than answer it. Miss Jeannie didn't have a cellphone with her, because *who* would be calling Jeannie? Certainly not her daughter.

Macklyn parked the truck, no easy task in the tight spaces of the French Quarter's streets. Especially for Macklyn who had great anxiety about parallel parking. Still it was early. The revelers not yet out, their crazy hats and flashy pants veiled.

When she got out, Jeannie scrambled behind her and planted both hands on the edge of the truck's bed.

"What about all this *stuff*?" the woman said. She cleared her throat and continued. "People down here STEALS, Macklyn!"

Macklyn smiled at her. "Let them steal it. I don't want it anyway."

"But you was giving it all to ME!"

"Then stay *here* and *guard* it."

Another harrumph. Macklyn turned away and started walking deeper into the Quarter. She did not look back to see if Jeannie was following her. After a block she knew the woman was. It didn't really matter either way, yet Macklyn was sure the older woman could benefit from this as much, if not more, than Macklyn could. Macklyn at least knew where her daughter was, Jeannie had no idea.

They walked briskly for ten or fifteen minutes. Jeannie's breathing got labored behind her. Macklyn, too excited, did not slow. They reached the place Macklyn had wanted to visit.

She did not know New Orleans well. It had been several years since she had visited the place. Longer since she had come to the Quarter. Yet she had not had to strain her memory too hard to know the place she wanted to go or how to get there. It had been almost twenty years since she and her church group - a gaggle of prim, much older Baptist women, older than even Jeannie was now - had been told of the place during one of the voodoo tours through the Quarter. Those old biddies with their staid *oldness* had comforted Macklyn - had made her feel safe and right. Unlike with her children or the world or her stubborn desire to remain unchanged, traditional. That she was not unchanged, nor traditional seemed not to matter. She liked the idea and those old women, set in their ways, had made her feel this strongly.

...the tour guide showed it to them...he described it as "the most powerful of the witch houses." An old woman asked:

"What do you mean by powerful?" The woman asked, and shuddered, wrapped her spindly arms around her chest and floral-print-blanket of dress.

The tour guide, a young, svelte black man with large, dark eyes, the irises too small and the whites too large, had smiled. His mouth curved upward like a half-moon, his eyes widening in a manner that scared every single one of the old women. Macklyn was scared too, but she laughed it off. It was her place to calm them all, to push the man's foolishness away and keep them from ruining their own trip.

"Cause, ma'am, a witch do live in there. By the name of Madame Ohreally."

Someone scoffed at the name, but the man frowned. "It don't do to laugh at Madame Ohreally, now." He pronounced the name "OHH-ree-alley."

"And how's that spelled, young man?"

"O-R-E-I-L-L-Y." the man said, as if the memory and effort were difficult. The old woman laughed and gave him her correct pronunciation. But the man shook his head and said, "I knows her ma'am and she say Ohreally."

Macklyn disengaged from the conversation. Stared at the wide house, off St. Ann Street. Into one of the curtained windows. No sooner had she done it than one of the curtains swished aside to show a face: black as burnt wood with eyes which looked entirely made of cold, white salt; looking directly at her. Red lips, a pale red, like chewed bubble gum, had moved and said something. Macklyn did not know what, she was too scared, looked away.

"And this Madame Ohreally," the old woman said derisively, the bit between her teeth goading her on.

Barbara!   Barbara Clendon. How could she forget Barbara? She had just seen her....

Barbara harrumphed, "She worships the Devil, THEN?"

But the tour guide shook his head, no several times. "Sure is sure she don't, ma'am. She a good Christian woman, it be God himself gives her her powers." He sounded affronted.

"And what kind of powers does this woman tell you God gives her?" Barbara said coldly. She was a preachy old woman, a strict reader of the Bible and believer of what she was told by the frosty-haired white men who ran every church she had been a member of. None of them had ever said anything about God giving powers to witches. That, Macklyn knew Barbara had been thinking, is the work of the Devil Himself.

"She can talks with spurts. She can find peoples. And she can get rid o'demonics when the 'fflicted be possess-ed." the man said all of this with such calm surety, Macklyn glanced back at the house. Instantly believed it to be the truth. If not the powers came from God, then the powers themselves did exist. And whomever that white-eyed woman had been in the window, if any woman could be called a witch, surely it was her?

Bits and pieces more of that day flitted through Macklyn's mind. Enough to remember what she needed to remember. And now she stood before that very same house. Those very same drapes of dark fabric covering the very same windows. The only difference being the larger amount of chipped paint on the sill and a more weather beaten look to the front door. No tour around, only a few people walking with the stride and nonchalance of people who lived in the Quarter.

"Are you going to tell me what we is doing here?" Jeannie said through hard, sucked in breaths.

"We're gonna find answers, that's what, Jeannie." Macklyn said and squared her shoulders, suppressed the lance of fear which ran through her. She steeled her determination. Hovered on the sidewalk for a moment or two longer, hoping to see a face behind opened drapes, but they remained closed. She saw no one.

Sighing, Macklyn walked up to the front door and knocked hard on it three times.

Nothing happened.

The sun had begun sink quite low. It was getting darker around them, but the streetlight had yet to pop on. The whole area was shady, shadowy - slightly cooler than it had been on the street. Overhead a gable stuck out of the house. Looking at it from underneath, Macklyn saw something had made a nest in there. A bird perhaps.

Grunting, Jeannie made her way up to the door and stood, silently. Macklyn banged three more times on the door.

As she started to turn away she heard the creak of floorboards. The soft smack of shoes on wood. She watched, her breath held, as the door handle turned.

Slowly.

Ominously.

"Can I helps ya?" a man said.

Macklyn looked up and was surprised to see the very tour guide from two decades before. He was older, she must have misconstrued his age all those years ago. Why this man was about her own age! He looked nearly sixty, stooped shoulder and a bald head with wisps of clingy, chalk white hair. Only his eyes had made her so sure it was the same man. The cold saltiness of them was as ragged and hard as it was in her memory.

Before Macklyn could say anything the man looked past her to Jeannie and back to Macklyn. He nodded as though he had reached some decision. "Come on..." he said.

The place was gloomy and poorly furnished. Bare floors under old, ratted sneakers the man wore. Maybe even the same pair he had worn all those years ago. There was no light in the long hallway. None until he led them to a living room where an old sofa hugged a wall and three wooden chairs sat facing it. A space heater was corded out from a corner and a very old sewing machine, Macklyn had an eye for these things from all her antique selling, sat between the corner and the sofa. She saw the two windows on the other wall and knew she was in the room which looked out on the street. The only light, weak as it was, came from a fixture on the ceiling, one meant to hold four incandescent bulbs, and did, though only one worked. Macklyn saw no sign of any one else in the room. She took a deep breath and smelled something musty, like the dusty accumulation from inside a drawer of one of the chifforobes she liked to refinish.

The man shambled into the room, his slow-moving steps making Macklyn think he must be even older than she, perhaps older than Jeannie, possibly nearly eighty. Only vaguely did she wonder if maybe he was the young man from the tour's father or grandfather.

Somehow, she knew he was not. This was the same man.

He slowly lowered himself into one of the wooden chairs, with the practiced movement of someone whose joints pained him.

"Now, I remembers you." he said softly to Macklyn, the sound of his voice echoing in the barely furnished room, though not growing louder. Behind her, Jeannie gasped.

Macklyn moved completely into the room and took a seat in one of the other chairs. She noticed the floor had marks on it, in a layer of dust. Trails. Three sets of them indicating, as she followed the trails with her eyes, the chairs had been drug from the wall recently. She was terrified and justified at the same time, frightened of forces beyond her control. Yet buoyed by their presence. She needed them.

"Now, what brings you here, Miss?" the man asked Macklyn, not bothering to address the question to Jeannie who sniffed grumpily at the sofa before taking the third wooden chair.

"I want Madame Ohreally to tell me about the afterlife. I want to know how daughter is." Macklyn said, surprised at how evenly the words came out. How easily. She had not really dared to think them since secretly forming the plan to come here.

The man nodded several times, so much so at first Macklyn feared he was falling asleep sitting up, but he grunted. "She dead."

Macklyn blinked. Sighed. She supposed it had been a long time and the woman had looked very old even two decades ago. That she might still be alive after so much time had been just a pipe dream after all. The man shook his head and made eye contact with her.

She didn't scream, but Jeannie did. The sound of wood scrabbling on wood alerted her Jeannie had leapt up out of her chair in fright. But the woman did not fled the room, only started towards the door.

"Come ON, Macklyn!" Jeannie said furiously, waving her to follow. But Macklyn shook her head softly. She did not break eye contact with the man, or his entirely white eyes.

"Your daughter dead." The man said, firmly as though he was repeating himself. He swung his head to Jeannie and coughed. "But yours worse."

Jeannie gasped and cried out, rushed towards him and knelt before him.

"What do you MEAN?" Jeannie asked, her voice wavering with obvious fear and need.

He shook his head as if he himself did not understand, as though he were seeing something he did not have words to describe. "She trapped in a bad place, a demon done got at her."

Macklyn started, because at first she assumed he must have talking about Cassie and the man who had cut her up and cooked her. Eaten parts of her, her lover-fiance: Thad. But the man was staring at Jeannie, who had grabbed his hands, held them forcefully in her own.

"Tell me where she is! Tell me so I can help her!"

"You cain't. I cain't. The demon ....whatever it be, it too strong for old people. It only weak against the young." He slumped forward. His breathing went hard, as though he had just sprinted across the yard. He slowly looked up, his face one of anguish as he met Jeannie's eyes again, "I real sorry, ma'am, but she cain't be saved by you, nor me. She gon' have to save herself if she can."

Jeannie released his hands. Sobbed into her own. Macklyn was full of doubt and trepidation and questions.

Why had she come here? Was any of this real? Is this man just toying with us, getting us worked up until he asked for money or something? A huckster?

Macklyn cleared her throat. The man looked up at her. She said, "Tell me if my daughter is in Heaven. Is Heaven real? Is she HAPPY?"

The man clucked somewhere deep in his throat. "Course it real." He sounded annoyed. "You cain't change Paradise to please ya'self now, Ma'am." That had the sound of a quote. Macklyn was sure she had heard it somewhere before. She brushed aside the feeling as he spoke again.

"But she ain't happy, ma'am because that ain't what Heaven is. And she cain't really leave neither, cause you won't let her go."

Macklyn took her turn to sob then, into her hands and palms, though she did not cover up her eyes. The man nodded again.

"See ma'am, that's the demon in you and it it right bad, nah. But she keep it from hurting you, by letting hurt her. Still she too far away to push it outta you. YOU gots to do that. She knows demons, yes sir-ree she do, fought one real good herself! But we's not meant to fight other people's

139

demons and when we does, sometimes they kills us."

Macklyn's sobs started, stuttered, stopped. She wiped at her nose. The room seemed to contract so there was only her and the man. Everything else was yawning empty blackness. They sat together, on a piece of floor, surrounded by the abyss Only the most tenuous of connections kept them from being brushed away into it. The man smiled as if he saw it as well.

"See now." he murmured sweetly.

Macklyn thought it was the start of another sentence, but it wasn't. It was a command. She looked up and cried out. There was her daughter's face, constricted by pain and stretched taut, as though unseen forces pulled at it from every direction. At first was sheer joy, to see that face and know it. To no longer feel terrible she could not remember it. She realized the pain and misery she saw there and she stood up reaching for Cassie before she could stop herself.

Her arms stretched upwards and her body began to float up off the floor starting from her heels so she stood on her tiptoes. Cassie's face strained harder and her mouth moved, but Macklyn did not hear any sound. She *could* understand the words.

"No, Momma! NO!"

Macklyn felt a grip on her ankles, which had begun to float almost a foot off the floor. She saw the dark skinned hand and the body connected to it. The old man, though he had not left his chair, had leaned forward. Dangerously close to tipping out of his seat, his feet still planted firmly on the floor.

Macklyn gave up, let him pull her back down. The room expanded, light rushed in. She was back in her seat staring at the man and Jeannie who still knelt at his feet, weeping in a daze, her head in her hands. The man's eyes were sad now, but knowing. Macklyn did not need to ask if what she had seen was real. She believed it. He had seen it as well.

More, he had saved her. She knew, without doubt, she had been about to die. About to join Cassie in whatever place she was in.

"Ain't your time, ma'am." he said softly. "You go now... and you be with them *demons*..." His eyes rolled upward towards the flickering bulb overhead.

Macklyn saw him look at something behind her. She turned around and saw a pool of shadows hovering behind her. Shadows with clawed hands and vaguely humanoid shapes. The whole mass of it scattered in a split second, a fraction of a moment after she caught sight of it. So fast she could not have been sure she did not imagine it. A wordless howl came to her ears, like a hundred wounded dogs baying at an eclipse, all of them miles away.

"You gots to beat 'em back first, then she can be free, ma'am. That why she sent you here. She wanted you to know she love you and she cain't do it no more, she cain't protect you no more. You gots to do it for yourself. Or they eats you like they ate her."

Macklyn nodded, a feeling of incomplete understanding pervading her mind. The man's breathing increased, came harder and he started coughing. Jeannie looked up from her crying and prayer-like kneel. Macklyn knew it was time to leave. But she wanted to thank him, give him something. Only then did she realize she had not brought her purse with her. It was sitting in the truck.

"How can I thank you?" she asked him. He waved her away. "You cain't. I done made my bed and I done suffered until now. But God he let Cassie send you here so as I could battle MY demons. And now I can rest."

Jeannie moved away from him. He began to change. His skin grew taut and young again. His eyes lost the film of age and his hair grew in steady, crisp even waves. His hands went up and felt his head. He broke out into a smile.

He turned towards the sofa and cried out, "Momma!" Macklyn and Jeannie both turned towards the sofa. Shimmering there, barely discernible was a very old woman with entirely white eyes and a pleased, smug expression on her face. But she too was gone as quickly as the shadows were. When Macklyn turned back to the man he was old again. And dead.

Jeannie ran screaming from the house, but Macklyn did not. She reached over and closed his eyelids, touched her lips to his, whispered.

"Thank you, Sir."

Calmly, unafraid she made her way out of the house and shut the door behind her, not at all shocked to see somehow the sun shone above her.

Chapter 8 – A Clean Smell.

With measured slowness Calvin Courtes adjusted his gun in its Tecron holster. He was not fond of Tecron, he preferred the feel of real leather, but the holster and the gun were issued by Blackrock. His employer. Reason enough to use it. Being a former Navy SEAL did not make a person likely to cut against the grain.. The culture of the firm was such any little deviance could be seen as exactly that: a deviance.

And deviants? They were not only given shittier assignments, if any, they were often given deadly ones.

No, Calvin Courtes; he always thought of himself in this manner, with both his names, *was not going to fail like* that.

He had beaten asthma and poor eyesight to get into the Navy in the first place. Then smashed it all to pieces in order to make it as a SEAL.

No mean accomplishment.

Ahead of him, the asset, a man named Roscoe, this was not his real name, *hell he might not even have been a man*, Calvin thought derisively, you never knew with these people; was being ushered into a large, black SUV. With the war over and funding support eroding, the firm had begun to take on these sorts with more and more regularity. Strange denizens of some mythical corporate world Calvin Courtes hardly understood.

What did a super-rich man need that could be gained in discussions with low-level Syrian rebels? Not natural resources. This ain't Afghanistan. Not any human resources either, this shit-hole ain't Dubai.

No, these ramshackle people in their ramshackle existence were fighting for a piece of nothing in a dusty shit-filled desert. Calvin Courtes kept these musings to himself. No one questioned an asset or questioned others about an asset and remained viable for long. Justice in the firm was often swifter than in an Army movie.

He was the last to pile into the SUV. Slamming the door of the front passenger seat just as the driver gunned the engine. The streets of this fly-speck ruin outside Aleppo were nominally safe now. Supposedly under the control of the rebels after the negotiated peace.

Polite fiction.

Calvin Courtes required harder facts.

Before the SUV had moved much at all he was in his automatic routine: eyes discreetly rolling in the four cardinal directions, searching out and assessing any possible threats or areas which might present a threat.

Those buildings a quarter click distant, that vestibule across the street, or the open-air market a block away. Any of these could conceal a car loaded with explosives. Especially if the pre-sweep detail had not been thorough. It did not happen often, but it did happen. Not that day however.

The trip back to the hotel was uneventful. If wearying. Traveling back and forth from Syria to Israel was an exercise in the hell of military bureaucracy leaving the detail staying in Damascus. Under diplomatic protection from some African Republic Calvin Courtes could neither pronounce nor find on a map. Some days he wondered if it actually existed, or if the whole thing was a product of some egghead's fancy back in the States.

An armchair general of an executive, a computer geek like his old friend Wes Miller. Now that had been one crazy fucker, obsessed with a video game no one played anymore. At the same time Wes was so good at the game you had to give him props for dedication and skill at least. Maybe the runt's assertions the would make a good general weren't entirely unfounded. More than once Calvin Courtes had discovered his fate, his orders, his missions, everything about his life in the military, AND the firm came from men and women who might have once been Wes Miller. Still, he was considerably richer working for the eggheads than he would have been had he followed in the footsteps of his idiotic father or brothers. Mechanics? Painters? Construction workers?

As fucking if.

The detail off-loaded the asset into the hotel

after Calvin Courtes and the others completed a forward sweep of the premises. They searched the asset's suite and gave the all-clear. The second shift detail took over and Calvin was free for the next sixteen hours.

Unlike the rest of his detail he did not go to the hotel bar and drink to excess. Or go up to his room to enjoy the absolutely staggering amount of porn available on the television.

These Arabs. Did they watch anything else?

No, Calvin did what other mercenaries rarely did: he changed into civilian clothes. Not the standard navy blazer and khakis of the firm. A head scarf and white cotton button-down over shorts and boots. He went out into the unsecured area of the city. Despite the war the place did not seem like a war-zone. Trade still took place, people still came outside and hawked wares, whores still beckoned and hucksters still tried to part the strange white man from his very green money.

Calvin Courtes, amused both at the thought of being thought a white man and at such pathetic people thinking they could take his money, paid them all little mind. Instead he went outside the city. Into one of the villages at the edge of town. A place which had been heavily damaged by fighting, where most of the men had died or been taken, leaving behind families and widows and small children. Many of whom refused to leave their hovels, huddling under eaves of darkness in vain hope life would persist and grow again.

Calvin Courtes resolutely made his way to one of these homes. It might have been nice once, by Syrian standards. Gaudily decorated on the inside and with what looked like cheap stucco on the outside. Glass on the windows was single-paned and poorly installed. Appliances were a decade old.   The television large but even older. He did not knock when he reached the door of this house, he simply went inside as though he belonged within. For two previous blocks he had been observing, quite discreetly, to ensure he was not being watched or followed. Comfortable he was not being tailed he had ducked in.

Inside the home was well-lit. Not every home on the block could say the same. Calvin Courtes made sure this one was. A woman, pretty, again by Syrian standards, came out of the kitchen. Her curvy body still bouncy with youth, she couldn't have been even thirty.   She greeted him with open arms. Grabbed at his cheeks, open-handed, lovingly.   Held them firmly. Pressed a very indecent kiss on his lips. She babbled something in Syrian, some benison maybe.   He could sort of understand it. It was Arabic, if dialected from the kind spoken in Iraq and Afghanistan. Loosely it meant: *God has favored us again with your presence.*

She released his face and called out three

names. Two boys, both pre-teens – one thirteen, the other fourteen - came from the back of the house. They had surly, unhappy expressions on their faces and wore rounded hats which labeled them students at a local madrasa.

Topis. That's what they're called the little fucking hats.   They did not approve of their mother's dalliance with Calvin Courtes. For all kinds of reasons. Not the least of which because he was not her husband. Not their father. A white man.

What a laugh!

A foreigner. A mercenary. A host of other imprecations. Calvin Courtes nodded at them anyway. Smiled before he presented them with gold wrist-watches. Both boys froze and goggled at the jewelry. It wasn't real gold, Calvin Courtes was sure they couldn't know that. The watches shone in the light and pinged with the joyous cry of their mother at the sight of them.

Unable to resist both boys scrabbled forward and took their gift. Placed them on their wrists. Uncaring neither seemed to fit. Both were meant for the wrist of a grown man. To the boys this only meant they *were* men in their own estimation, and Calvin Courtes rightly should agree. They said "mamnuun" and paddled off.

Then came Nabya.

She was eight years old. Tall for her age. Still barely above Calvin Courtes' sternum. Unlike everyone else in her household she had fair skin. Not swarthy at all. Light brown hair that in the sun could look blond. Her eyes were the most soft-honey shade of brown, topping a face that was angelic and full; heart-shaped.

Nabya screeched. Flew into Calvin Courtes' arms. She was his favorite and she knew it. He did not ply her with sweets or cheap watches. Pulled out what any eight year old Syrian girl might want: a rhinestone-studded music player. She screeched louder. It had been some weeks since he had been able to visit and this was the nicest gift he had yet given the girl. Her mother, Sunya - in the process of smoothing the girl's hair while Calvin hugged her tight – frowned followed with a smile. She could see no wrong in her American savior. At moments like this she would remember his promises: escape from Syria, a life in America, a car of her own, and a safe place for her kids to grow. Away from war and government oppression. Sunya never doubted those promises.

Calvin Courtes lowered the girl down. Shooed her away to watch television. Grabbing at Sunya's hand he led her to the back bedroom. Their lovemaking was nothing like what Sunya had known with her husband. She actually *enjoyed* Calvin Courtes' hands on her. He obviously enjoyed hers, enough to encourage her to be free and bold. In ways which would have made her husband beat her. After, Sunya would roll over and silently thank Allah. Whispering into the pillow a prayer of thanks her husband had been taken by the rebels. It had brought Calvin Courtes to her.

Later when she had gone to sleep, exhausted by the long day of protecting her family, of mothering and worrying, Calvin eased his squat, muscular body off the bed. The springs of the mattress protested as Sunya rolled over. Grunted in her sleep.

Calvin Courtes paused long enough to make sure she truly slept. Deeply. Satisfied. Safe.

He got up. Crept, as silent as only a man of his training could, down the hallway. Passed the door of the boys' room and reached the last door: Nabya's. It was ajar as it always was. The kid was afraid of the dark.

He eased the door open. Nabya was there. Asleep. Half snuggled into a blanket which was covered in girly things, cartoon characters of young girls fighting a cartoon monkey. All of it pink and red and white. Her long salted-caramel hair was swept behind her.   Her little body rose and fell with rhythms of deep sleep. Calvin Courtes took a measured, hard breath. It had taken weeks and months to reach this point and he was not going to jeopardize it by scaring the girl.

Gently he lowered himself into the bed. Docilely, the girl rolled over and clasped arms over his lap, murmuring in her sleep. Calvin Courtes smiled into the darkness. He gently pulled the blanket down to reveal her cotton nightdress, it clung to her small, damp body due to a light sheen of night-sweat. Calvin Courtes leaned over Nabya and inhaled strongly. The kid carried a clean scent. Not floral or perfumed. Clean. Calvin Courtes couldn't say what about it he liked but he knew he loved it.

Her small arms were wrapped around his waist and lap, her head brushed against the side of his hip. With a nervousness usually reserved for hunkering down behind a pile of stone away from sniper fire, Calvin Courtes looked towards her door. Nothing but soft darkness. Carefully he disentangled the girl and went to close her bedroom door. The moment was right.

Finally.

He made his way back to her bed. She rolled over on her side, turning her back to him. Calvin Courtes laid down next to the kid. Pushed her mane of hair aside. Kissed gently at her neck. When she struggled softly, still asleep, he stroked her head. It was not until a minute or two later she came awake, startled. She did not have time to yell before his rough hand clamped down over her mouth. He whispered softly into her ear, in clipped Arabic.

"Be still. Do no scream. I am your father."

With his hand placed on the back of her head, pushing her face forward and down so she could not fully see him, he bean to undress her, but not totally. He lifted her nightdress up. Wound it in a thick knot around her neck. Rolled it forward. Placed it over her face. Gently, with obvious care, he grabbed her hands and pulled them up. Put them on the wadded up nightdress and whispered, again in clipped Arabic: *"Do not look."*

His Arabic was not very good. He did not know what he actually said was *"do not see."* A subtle difference. One Nabya would never forget. She never knew the origin of the demon who ruined her and would never have let herself see it if she had.

When he was done using her, his seed spent inside and her blood sliming him, Calvin Courtes pulled himself out of the kid. Spit on her bottom. Spanked her hard. With a final look, arch with disgust, he leaned down and whispered his final benediction. The same one he always gave.

"This is your fault. You are bad little girl." His Arabic was practiced this time, clear. Nearly flawless. He required it be so.

Calvin Courtes crept out of her room. Into the bathroom. To clean himself and slide back into bed with Sunya.

The next morning when Nabya did not appear at breakfast Sunya went to check on the kid. Nabya was listless in her small bed, bleeding from wounds of the night. Her tiny lips had the strangest expression frozen upon them. Dried blood caked the blanket disfiguring the cartoons.

Her legs and buttocks were sticky with the stuff. Sunya shook Nabya in her arms. Cried. Pulled the kid to her heaving breast. Screamed in a ululating manner in Arabic.

"Who has done this? What has done this?"

Calvin Courtes tore through the house, face tight with anger. Movements precise. He rushed into the room, gun drawn. At the sight of him Sunya's wail went keening. She covered her daughter with her body. Calvin Courtes stroked the coal black hair on Sunya's head. Tried to coaxed her from the brink. Eventually the woman stopped crying. It was quiet enough Nabya's voice could finally be heard.

With hesitancy and a clipped stutter she kept repeating the same thing.

"Baba." She murmured in Arabic without crying. *"Baba."*

Sunya's eyes met Calvin Courtes'. He looked away. His face flushed, as much as it could with its deep brown tan. He was not a white man, regardless of what these people thought. His heritage was Puerto Rican and Colombian. Such distinctions mattered little to these people. He could not have said what he saw in Sunya's eyes. He had seen it many times before. On the faces of dozens of women just like her.

Mosul. Kabul. Islamabad. Mogadishu. And so deliciously in Croatia. And other places.

The war within as those mothers fought off

154

something they had never thought they would face. Not a man with a gun.   A close-handed slap. Rather a demon with a hard-on.   These battles between peoples had raged for centuries. Millenia in some places. But the battle within; of trust warring with doubt, this was not something the women had the ability or willingness to handle. Not a war they could muster themselves to fight. Calvin Courtes knew this. He chose them because he knew this.

  This moment, in all its incarnations, was perhaps as good as the night before, necessary even. When he watched the struggle in some mother's eyes cease. Watched the need, the hope, the luster of trust shove out the truth of doubt. It was victory of the most primal sort.

  Sunya, in broken English, eventually waved Calvin Courtes out of the room. With admonitions to watch for her husband – the man she said must have done this. Nabya had never called Calvin Courtes *Baba* before.

  Who *else* could it have been?

  Sunya said this several times. Each time with more fervor and surety.   As though she could reinforce reality with steady repetition.

  Calvin Courtes left the room. Holstered his gun. Whistled as he walked down the hallway. Nabya's brothers popped their heads out of their room. Hairless faces. Soft pre-teen faces. Calvin Courtes stared at them, challengingly. Wondering

for the first time what the back of a *their* necks
might smell like.

Chapter 9 – It Goes All White.

Ahmed snarled his way through the press of people, many of whom were also wore a ycron mask. A kylar shield was over his head, tucked around the mask. Beneath those he wore cast-off kevlar body armor, some of it quite damaged, but most in good enough repair. It would stop anything but the *real* stuff. He had little to worry about from his country-men. The Americans though, if they cottoned to his purpose and position, would shred him like so much lamb over a spit. With little more than the activation of neurals. As though alerted suddenly to this prospect, Ahmed looked up at the dark skies and tried, in vain he knew, to hear a drone. Juster had said you could hear them. Him and others. Ahmed had never been anywhere quiet enough to prove them right.

Juster was right about most things involving American technology. The man's hate for "American Imperialists" was as strong, if not stronger, than Ahmed's own. Juster's *knowledge* was far more intimate. The man had helped to design much of the American technology. If Ahmed had cared to make the effort he might have tried to get the fullness of Juster's story. The man was clearly an American. But when they spoke of their pasts over surplus Russian vodka, the truly cheap shit, it was about women and war, not America.

Yet no matter how he tried he could not escape Syria. He knew he never would. That Syria no longer existed was irrelevant. He could still remember her in happy times, when he was far, far younger. A bare scrap of a boy, older than Nabya and Hussein. Before the dark tides had swallowed their family. Thinking of his baby sister's name sent the usual spasms through his body. It had been long decades since he had seen her face in his mind. He could hardly remember it as it was. Still he kept a photo of her in his wallet, turned backwards so he did not have to see her face smiling at him.   Nabya and Syria were one and the same. They had merged into an ideal of something pure and innocent, worth protecting, ravaged. And both were as gone as *ams*, as yesterday. As useless as the Afghan police crossing the street.

Those jackdaws stormed past. Their boots so worn they hardly clacked against the stone of the badly paved road. Still with a force of sixty men they managed to push everyone milling about out of their way. The government, such as it was, no longer rightfully controlled them. You could never say what they were doing at any given point or whom they actually served, if they served anyone at all. To see sixty of them together could almost inspire nostalgia in Ahmed. For days when a brink existed in the eternal conflict, when it seemed possible they might prevail.

He no longer held such convictions or hopes. He knew the battle was ultimately fruitless. No longer did he pray to Allah to forgive him for thinking it. Allah did not answer except with more Americans. More drones. More death from above.

Ahmed did not intend to give up. He could draw breath. His hands were as nimble as ever despite nearly sixty years of age. His rage honed into a weapon as formidable as any.

No, he would fight to the last, even knowing he, *they*, had lost. Also knowing the Americans had *not* won. The world was a failed state. Everyone knew it. The intellectuals did not even argue the fact anymore, only the when. When intellectuals were allowed to argue. They did not do so in Afghanistan. Yet another thing Ahmed missed greatly.

His days at Kabul University had been the summit of his life. He had almost topped the darkness. Had almost stood at the apex and saw the sun. Cleansed himself of the nigirities within. He had almost been reborn.

At times he could reflect on what might have been. Rare times. Had he been able to finish his studies, had that been possible. Where would he be now? Where would Hussein be? Or Nabya? Sunya, of course, would have remained where she always was, with their father, and supposedly the Prophet himself. Ahmed sneered derisively when he thought of it.

The police force stomped past, paying little mind to the bowed old man wearing the mask and Kylar scarf shield. He looked like a fool and they saw him as such. They were neither his target nor his concern. Still, if they caught him, if they knew *anything*, they would hand him over to the Americans. The Governor in Kabul would see him sent to the Hole. Along with his plans.

The Americans would reward the police force with more bullets, of use only against other Afghans, or more cast-off dry food goods Yanks turned their noses up at. Afghans killed for these things. Sold their own without hesitation. They would, without doubt, sell the godless Syrian for a tenth of what he knew. A hundredth.

When he made it back to the staging ground - a basement with a flickering bulb half-hanging, half-swinging from the ceiling he was greeted by Juster and Monica Lewinsky. *That* was not her real name. Though Ahmed did not understand the joke, Juster seemed to get it. The other Americans thought her name funny as well.

She was pretty enough. If a bit large in the hips. Ahmed knew she was not to be underestimated nor taken lightly. He had never known a woman more dangerous. Frightening. He wasn't sure she was American - she could be EU. Without
asking, something he would not do, he would never know. She spoke flawless Arabic; though with a

decidedly American accent.

"Ahmed." Monica said curtly. He nodded and removed his mask and shield. The room was dingy with low lighting and a rather bad smell. It was sealed airtight from the outside. Filtered against poisons which floated in the air. Those poisons could kill more people than the bullets supplied by the Americans, despite the nominal attempts by the remaining government to clean up the mess. It was not something generally discussed, however, neither by Americans nor Afghans. The Afghans needed the pittances the Americans offered for work in the mines and the Americans needed the mines. It was foolish to assume the Americans needed the Afghans. Many had discovered the truth: the Americans would replace them if necessary, with Filipinos or Pakis or African refugees. So the Afghans took the work. Took the poor food and low pay, took the bullets. And the specter of protection if they worked the mines. Truckload by truckload, precious metals and rocks and powders left Afghanistan and were taken to processing plants in Kabul. That Kabul itself was no longer part of Afghanistan hardly still occurred to Ahmed. It was as unnoticeable as the color of the sky and as persistent.

"The US approved the charter today." Monica said blandly. This was news to Ahmed. He had just been thinking of Kabul so it made him pause and glare at her. She smirked at him and tossed her raven hair.

Not natural.

"The sixty-seventh State of the Union. Can you guess what they chose for the name?" She was laughing now. Ahmed did not want to play this game. He had not watched a vid in days, they did not have one in the staging ground or his quarters. He knew several options had been on the table, all of them as hard to hear as to accept.

"Ameristan." Monica Lewinksy said, laughing harder. "Isn't that *rich*? But what's in a name?"

Ahmed nodded fiercely. American states had popped up across the entire world. What had once been known as the Third World, the developing world, like wildfires. Plagues of locusts. There was little to stop them. Choosing a name had held up Ameristan in hearings for nearly three weeks. He had shaken his head at that, in stupefaction. What kind of fools spent three weeks deciding on the name of a place which would be abandoned after it was emptied of resources? It might be fifty years before that happened, or five. No one really knew exactly how much the mines contained. It *would* happen, as sure as *ams*.

Ameristan was appropriate. Ahmed supposed. For the Imperialists. They seemed to enjoy irony.

"We're just waiting for Head." Monica said, turning solemn as quick as the blink of a cursor. It was confusing to see a woman do this, even for

Ahmed - who had been outside the Muddle. Had seen women of the US Empire and the EU. They were nothing like Afghan women, or Saudis or what remained of the Iraqi women. Nor were they like Syrian women had been. Even at the height of Syria's existence when Assad was still alive and relevant. Those Empire women were utterly sure of themselves, strong and confident. For lack of a better concept, they were like men. Not for the last time Ahmed felt the horrid ache as he missed Sunya and Nabya. And Syria. It only steeled his resolve, as if it ever wavered, to stay the course.

Ahmed nodded at her and swept past to the meeting area; a large scavenged conference table surrounded by vids bristling with maps and layered displays. It was the most expensive and extensive technology ECO possessed, as far as Ahmed knew. He knew ECO was an American and EU entity. They existed in cells all across both Empires. They operated ruthlessly in both, but did not send much in the way of new tech to places like the Asrah Mine.

He had no allusions.

This mission was important to them as a public relations stunt. A very important stunt according to Juster, who would know. Nowhere near as important as to Ahmed.

This is my life.

If he managed to live past this mission, then he would live for the next, but he did not think he would. Nor did he plan to do so. He never did.

　　Standing by the table peering down at the displays, his hands held behind his back, was MikeDev. Ahmed knew the D was a capital letter because it was tattooed across the cyberian's cheek. Everyone knew MikeDev. How much of him was machine and how much remained blooded human was not something Ahmed knew. Not that it mattered. MikeDev was an ally. It sufficed.

　　"Ahmed." MikeDev said with simulated warmth. His mouth could not smile. It was plated with tiny platinum lines etched across like a circuit board, but his eyes could warm and they seemed to do so. MikeDev knew something of Ahmed's past, as he seemed to know the past of everyone who worked with or for ECO. Every operative except for Head. But that was his purpose as the IO, the intelligence officer. To *know* was his job. Ahmed did not know if MikeDev's perpetual attempts at warmth derived from his knowledge of Ahmed's own past and tribulations. Or from some other place. Perhaps he was one of those cyberians who had a fetish for sex with ordinary humans. Some even liked mid-aged men like Ahmed. It was not unusual to find such strangeness in Americans of MikeDev's generation.

　　They are ALL crazy.

　　But MikeDev was kind. Treated him like a

man. So Ahmed responded in kind.   He reached out and shook the cyberian's hand. Gave a warm smile of his own. Had the cyberian been a Syrian, or an Afghan for that matter, Ahmed would have given him a one-armed embrace.

"MikeDev, why, you're looking positively *charged* this afternoon..." Monica said as she came up to the table with Juster. Juster snickered without appearing pleased. Ahmed knew it for a joke, though he did not understand Monica's humor. MikeDev nodded. He did not seem like Monica at all. She jibbed him constantly because of it. MikeDev preferred males, if Monica's word could be trusted, which in this instance Ahmed did. He had seen MikeDev looking. Ahmed was very good at seeing such things. If only he had been able to see back then...

"Have you been interfacing with the conference table's tera again?" Monica said, laughing, her eyes trailing over the TeraP interface port. No one else laughed. MikeDev's eyes showed him annoyed, but it was the only reaction he gave. Perhaps the only one he could give.

"Enough."Juster said, lightly pushing Monica aside. "Head is here."

The man known to Ahmed as Head swept into the area with the air of command only a cause-driven American could presume to wield. He was halfway to seven feet tall, in fantastic shape and blessed with a full head of still brown, wavy hair.

His skin was a very light brown and his heritage was something Ahmed could only guess at. He was sure MikeDev knew, but Ahmed would never have asked, especially about Head. Unlike Juster, who was American but occasionally spoke like a Dutchman, or Monica who might be Irish but spoke like a Bostoner, or MikeDev who was whatever MikeDev had been - Head was entirely, unequivocally American. More - he was an important American.

One of their politicians.

He took enormous risks in coming to the staging ground. Head never seemed particularly bothered by this. Monica had tried to explain to Ahmed once, a man like Head could do as he pleased *because* he was the man he was. Apparently Americans were stupid enough to let their own betray them without reprisals.

That was what Ahmed took from it. Or perhaps they did not know about Head's involvement with ECO. Perhaps. They knew everything else though, why not that?

I will ask MikeDev.

Head nodded at them all, individually. "I don't have to tell you all how important this Op is. I will be leaving tonight for DC and will not return to Afghanistan. In fact, I will be severing ties with ECO after this Op."

Several gasps sounded around the room. Ahmed looked first at MikeDev to see if he was surprised. It did not appear he was.

Head continued, "If the Op succeeds, *as it must*, I will not NEED to return to Afghanistan. We will have turned a corner and finally be able to move out into the open. ECO will have served its purpose. The next phase will begin."

Ahmed only loosely understood this. He was not interested in ECO's long term goals and missions. Only in the operations aimed at disrupting the Imperialists across the Muddle. Still, he was not entirely ignorant of politics in America. It was hard these days to be so and live near one of their resource centers.

Still he did not know who Head was. Or his place in the American government. The man's skin was slightly waxed, and Ahmed suspected he wore a different face to the American public, possibly even a different body. For all Ahmed knew the man could be two feet shorter and black. The Americans could do that.

"But why?" Monica said, distraught. It pleased Ahmed to hear that tone in her voice. Her face had blanched and her hands had come off the table, held out plaintively towards Head.

Head sighed. "Because. The fight is over. The Join has been approved."

Now there were ferocious gasps, from everyone except Ahmed.

"The Join?" he asked, quietly. He was an operations liaison for ECO in the Muddle. He could rattle off details of situations in most of the world south of the EU and the Russian Waste, west of Chin-ape and north of the Sahara. But he had never heard of the "Join", though it sounded important. Ahmed rubbed lightly at his temples.

What else don't I know?

Head turned towards him. Held Ahmed's eyes hard before he replied. Head was sizing Ahmed up. Making a determination. With the ghost of a nod, Head said, "The US and the EU will finally become the United States of the World."

Monica actually looked stricken. Juster swore under his breath in some language other than English. MikeDev did not look surprised, but his eyes, as much as Ahmed could read, said he was bothered.

"I thought that was tabled! Blocked by the Libs!" Monica said angrily.

Head sighed. "The Liberty Party is over. It capitulated."

Ahmed could only blink in confusion. American party politics was supposedly simple but he had never understood it.

"And France? Germany? They agreed? What about the Vatican?"

Head shook his head sadly. "The Vatican has been neutralized. The Americans have installed and elected a new Pope. A willing puppet of the Senate. As for France and Germany – they were offered a choice by their fellow EU members: join or be invaded and processed."

Ahmed laughed. He knew *that* word.
MikeDev had once called it a "colloquialism."
Though others in Afghanistan had called it a joke. It
was irrelevant what it was called. The result was
the same: the American Imperialists sent in their
corporate military and drone Army. They bled your
land dry of resources. And they did it all "legally" -
using what passed for money to the other
Imperialists and mere abstractions to everyone
else. They purchased every piece of land in
question, forcibly removed every last resource from
it as a right of "ownership." It had been done first in
South Sudan, under the guise of "aid" despite UN's
protests. When UN had still existed independently.
If there was a living soul in South Sudan, Ahmed
knew, they were either near-death or a corporate
slave. American corporations were nothing if not
thorough.

The others glanced at him as he laughed. He
stopped.
But only because he was distracted by something
on the table vid. Smallish dots slowly resolved into
a horde of drones. Red lights flashed all around the
small room.

"in-coming..." a computer voice intoned.

MikeDev began moving in a blur of whirl and
motion. His hands and fingers in un-followable
gestures of sweeping, pinching, tossing and
ripping. Head, for his part, remained calm, even

when security details appeared from thin air to surround him. One of the security guards was a light brown-skinned young man wearing dark glasses, with a shaved head, and so similar in bearing to the Devil Man himself Ahmed reached for his weapon. He had forgotten he was not allowed to possess one in the staging grounds.

Still, Head was not evac'd. He conferred briefly with the man who resembled the Devil Man.

"This facility will be rubble in fifteen minutes. All of you should make peace with your last moments, and say prayers - if they mean anything to you. And remember, ECO thanks you in advance for your service." With that Head was hustled away with great speed, not looking back once.

Ahmed did not move. He stood frozen, until suddenly MikeDev was at his side, pulling at his arm.

"Come on, Ahmed.." MikeDev said.

Ahmed could not reply. He had tasted betrayal many times. *Of course he had.* From he Devil Man himself in the terrible moment when the American man had *broken* Ahmed. While Ahmed's little brother Hussein cowered in the corner. Both of them still proudly wearing those watches. Which they would only learn later were fake.

What time had it been?

He had not expected to taste betrayal again *here*. He had expected to die this day, but not like this.

"Come ON!" MikeDev's atonal voice urged.

Ahmed was pulled along through a darkened corridor. His feet moved, but his mind remained stuck in the past. Held down, face pressed into a rough pillow, while a man of unknowable strength made a woman of him. He could still feel those thrusts. Those calloused hands around the back of his neck. He could still hear the sucked in breaths as the man leaned down and inhaled, pressing his nose just behind Ahmed's ear. Hussein had already been done the same way. Somehow Ahmed had slept through *that.* Hussein had been forced to watch it done to Ahmed.

Ahmed had always known which of the two of them carried the greater demon. He fervently hoped for the first time in two decades his little brother had gotten his wish and found a Heaven.

Ahmed broke onto the surface.

MikeDev's strong arms propelled him forward. Dimly, Ahmed noted the cyberian holding something familiar. A vest with a shimmering vid near the spot which covered the human heart. Ahmed nodded as MikeDev thrust the vest towards him and he shrugged it on. Instantly he felt the surge of power and force the field generator granted. He had heard of these, but had never worn one. They were for Americans.

"You'll only get one chance." MikeDev said solemnly. "I'm sorry I didn't see this coming."

The ground beneath them rocked with the first explosions as bombs were dropped from drones attacking the staging ground. MikeDev looked upward, his processing gaze quickly scanning the skies, assessing threats. Ahmed reached over and grabbed at the cyberian's arm, squeezed it. It was like iron, which it might very well be.

"Did it hurt?" Ahmed asked. He had always wanted to know, but had never been willing to cross that boundary. MikeDev's eyes widened, but he shook his head.

"I assume you mean physically. Physical pain is part of what humans experience. Cyberians choose to be rid of it. But there are other kinds of pain, Ahmed, as you well know. And I still feel that."

Ahmed sighed. He had always known MikeDev knew about the Devil Man. Sunya's death had led to there being an investigation, but it was a sham. The Devil Man had been cleared. Sent back to the US, while Ahmed and Hussein went to orphanages in rebel held areas outside Damascus. Nabya had gone a darker route. When Ahmed found her two years later, after Syria completely disintegrated - before it became the fifty-third US state; at least the parts that were not "aid"ed into "processing" - she was a wasted whore. And not even eleven years old. Addicted to some new street version of heroin and the new kind of meth which just appeared everywhere one day in the late teens. Her scarred face had not known who he was.

Really, Ahmed said, *it WAS a mercy. She had deserved that much at least.*

More bombs shook the ground and MikeDev shouted over the din. "The vest is armed." He peered off towards the Asrah's main entrance. Men stood before it, staring at the sky in amazement, hands held over eyes, shielding them from the sun.

A hyper buzzed away across the horizon, its motion lost against the swarm of drones above. Head would be on it. Across the bare ground, Ahmed could see two white-skinned people, Monica and Juster, running away from the Asrah facility. He watched as fire from above pierced both. They fell, boneless. Dead before they hit the ground.

Something exploded near him. The vests' field did not let it come near enough to harm Ahmed. Why had Monica and Juster not had such? Ahmed had seen both wearing them previously. He knew they owned them. But he did not spend much time thinking about this. Other thoughts occupied his minutes. He did not want to waste them thinking about traitors and Imperialists, even if they had once been allies.

"Go." MikeDev said, as the swarm swept overhead and the cyberian began to turn back. "And remember, Ahmed, in the last moment, look for *them*. Heaven is a place on Earth."

This last had the sound of another American joke, a cyberian irony possibly. Ahmed did not understand. Still, he nodded and shook MikeDev's hand for thanks.

"May Allah be with you." Ahmed murmured, a benediction which had not passed his lips in decades. "Or whatever god services cyberians."

This last he said with a smile. MikeDev barked a robotic laugh. The cyberian was off. Running at a blinding pace towards the distant mountains, ordnance exploding over his head yet never coming close to reaching him. Something blue arced down from the sky and made contact with MikeDev. His body shot upwards into the air, arms spread wide, legs shaking.

Slowly, the cyberian's body fell back to Earth. Smoking, popping, and twitching. MikeDev did not get up. The drone swarm moved off and Ahmed had only a moment or two before they returned. He did not waste time contemplating what could or would kill a cyberian. Instead he ran, as though the wind itself held his feet.

And suddenly he saw *them*.

His father, face clearer and sharper than it had been in real life. The close cropped beard and white teeth a truly welcome sight.

And Sunya, her brown eyes flashing pride. Her hand covering her mouth as she smiled at him. Hussein, shouting, though Ahmed heard no words.

His brother's face was still a defiant teenager's. His eyes those of the tortured man he had been in death.

Nabya.

Laughing and clapping - as an unbroken, beautiful, little girl.

Ams! Yesterday!

She waved at him and pointed upward with one finger. Giggled and covered her mouth with one hand. Looked away demurely. Ahmed laughed and cried out, "Allahu-akbar! ALLAHU-AKBAR!"

A cry he never though would escape his lips again, a blasphemy. He did not believe, even then, in any god. Especially not Allah. Yet he could not deny what his eyes saw. They were all there. Waiting. Patiently abiding until he silenced his last, his only demon. Ahmed ran towards the Asrah mine, pressed him palm to the vid on his vest and flew hands first into the mine's entrance.

The rest was a flash of white.

Chapter 10 - Like a Smile.

"I don't love you anymore!" Rielle muttered to the mirror. "HAH!" Her laughter was edged like the sharp side of a scalpel. She had honed it to a fine point over her years in marriage to Mister James Cornell Devall.

That asshole.

With a practiced hand she took both her hands and pulled back on her skin just below the hairline, tightening her face more than it was already was. The infinitesimally small lines around her eyes had shrunk, but she could still see them. Her large, pillowy lips were pulled away from one another - stretched over her perfectly white, capped teeth.   Her bold chin with its artful cleft leapt out.   The lips had cost nearly twenty grand. The chin fifteen. Her cheeks, orb-like and tilted to a sharp angle, about the same. The last face-lift had only been twelve. The neck-lift fourteen. She could have gotten it all cheaper, but why? Rielle deserved the best. She also wanted Mister James Cornell Devall to pay as much as possible.

It was his own fault. Were he not the obsessed social climber he was perhaps he could have found a way to deny her. But appearances must be kept. At first Rielle had agreed with that, had desired the same things, until it was clear the Mister had also desired younger women. THAT Rielle could not just let go. So began her punishment of the man who would not divorce her; who could not, in good conscience, allow himself to be branded what he truly was: a man of modest means, overly high ambitions and piddling social presence. He required the assumption of more, so a determined Rielle used this to punish him.

As she pulled back on her face she wondered what she would do next.

Perhaps have her eyes altered into almond shapes like a doll?

That she looked rather grotesque already was of little consequence. She no longer cared to be loved by men who wanted her body. Her children had graduated college. Had moved on with their adult lives. Hardly paid her any mind, except to suggest she start seeing someone, "for help."

What a crock.

Her son, Mike, *that flaming queen*, had gently taken her by the shoulders, stared into her eyes with sincerity, and said, "Momma, I'm worried about you! Dad says you keep doing these surgeries and won't explain why and I'm worried about the effect it's going to have on your body...."

Mike with his father's good looks and svelte body melded to her lustrous mane of raven hair and crystal blue eyes was all too easy to go easy on.

It was always the case with pretty people.

Rielle had discovered this young. She had

always got let out easy simply by being the prettiest girl around. Not with Mister though.

Nothing is easy with that douche-bag. Except taking his money. THAT *was cake.*

At first she had felt bad about wasting Mister's money. When Mike had come to her and given her that concerned look. A little more when she had gotten the chin cleft. The cheekbones. Before she had the lips or the face lift. She might have done the neck-lift already, she chose not to remember.

Maybe the boobs, too.

Seeing Mike's sadness, a mirror opposite of her own, had struck somewhere deep. Yet the wound had not lasted, had not been perpetual. It had only taken one more slighting by Mister for her to launch her next attack on her body.

She longed for the day when one of her children would get married. When Mister would be forced to be arm and arm again with the creature he now despised and feared.

His shit-crazy wife.

He'd referred to her that way in one of the emails she'd intercepted. To some whore named Cassie. She could only hope her appearance was grotesque enough Mister broke and showed the world what kind of weakling he truly was, how pathetic he really was.

That bastard.

She let her face slacken and left the

bathroom, left her imaginings.

"Christa?" Rielle called out to the maid. "I need you!"

After letting the woman help her dress - she still could not put on her clothes without help after the surgery last month to remove her two lower ribs - Rielle examined herself in a full length mirror. Her shape was truly hourglass now, a huge bust tapered to an impossibly, narrow twenty-seven inch waist on a five foot nine inch body. Her hips were far wider than her waist, but not enough to suit. She tacked a butt-lift onto her list of pending surgeries. The list was extensive. It would require at least eight more years to complete. As she often did when bored she ran through the list.

Butt-lift.
Second face lift.
New nose.
Ear tuck.
More Botox.
Eye-shaping.
Permanent lip color.

She laughed again, still at nothing. Behind her Christa cringed and ducked out of sight. The maid knew she'd be called again shortly. And she was.

"Christa!" Rielle said lightly, her tone effervescent. "Get the car, please!"

Twenty minutes later Rielle was in the back

seat of the town car, driving through Baton Rouge traffic with Christa at the wheel.

"Ma'am?" Christa said, not unkindly. She was not afraid of Rielle. Rather she was confused and put off by the woman. Once - maybe eight or nine years ago - Rielle had been different. Better. A whole person Christa would say. They had sort of been friends. As much as a maid could be with her employer. "Where are we going?"

They had been driving for ten minutes or so. It was the second time Christa had asked the question. Rielle, distracted by the passing scenery started in confusion.

"Oh! Um, the Home, Christa. To go see my brother."

Christa cringed again. Rielle pretended not to notice.

At the Home, an assisted living facility called Sunset Coves, Rielle swept out of the sedan. She went straight to number 1-C. She knocked lightly and when there was no answer had Christa fish out a key and unlock the door. Mister paid for the place - which entitled Rielle to a key - something she used to know was a violation of privacy, but had since chosen to forget.

"Wessie?" she called out, peeking from behind the door. The sun cast sharp shadows against her waxy skin. "It's Rielle!"

"I'm here." was the sullen reply.

In the ten years since the family had had him

committed, *since he had gone shit-crazy*, little had changed about him physically. He was still smaller than a grown man should be, except in the belly - which every year kept growing outward. It looked like an alien pregnancy blooming under his stomach. His face however had changed as much as hers had. And not for the positive. He was haggard and drawn. His eyes sunken and bagged with obvious lack of sleep. Lips which looked perpetually chapped. His nose was both raw and dry, flakes of caked skin nestled on the nostrils where he had obviously rubbed too hard, for far too long.

Rielle softened, thoughts of Mister fading and rushed towards him. Her manicured hands ran through his very greasy hair. He smelled like grease too, old French fries and stale sweat. But Rielle was not bothered by this. "Oh, Wessie." she murmured, "You look TERRIBLE!"

He looked upwards at her, a blank expression on his face and in his eyes. The medication he was on, which he was required to take if he wanted to remain free of a commitment facility, had that effect on him. Rielle hardly cared about that. He licked his lips and rubbed his nose with the back of his left hand.

"Rielle?" Wes said.

"Yes!" Rielle said. She watched his eyes narrow in recognition. He shied away from her hands and looked at her as though he had not seen her nor heard her voice in ages. It had only been two days.

"You look really weird. " Wes said despondently. Reille sighed. She was used to such comments. They bothered her, how could they not? But it was too late to turn back now. She had a mission. A goal. A purpose in life again. She was not going to let a little bit of criticism deter her. Besides, it didn't really phase her anymore, especially now, coming from Wes. *He was after all, the shit-crazy one.*

She let go of his hair. "When's the last time you took a bath, Wessie?" She went to open the blinds. Sunlight poured in. The place was clean, that was part of the assisted aspect of it - weekly cleanings. It was also sparsely furnished. A plasti-coated sofa, a television, two leatherette chairs and a small workstation with a computer on it. Wes was allowed to play his game, but he didn't seem interested in it anymore. Rielle didn't know if he'd touched his computer in months, if not longer. It had dust all over it. She tried to remember the last time he had spoken about that game, WarShaft or something.

Maybe before the boob job but definitely not the last face lift.

It doesn't matter.

"I dunno." Wes said. "This morning." She couldn't even be sure he was lying.

He might not know what day it is.

"Today is THURSDAY," Rielle said patiently, "Right?"

Wes looked confused. "Oh." He murmured blandly.

"Four days ago then." He said after some long thought. Rielle wrinkled her too-tiny nose at him in mock disgust. "Well then my little boy, I think you're going to need a shower today!" She tried to say it as brightly as possible, as she would have said it to Mike when he was five, or for that matter Wes when he was five. She was much older than Wes. He was only six years older than Mike after all. Rielle had practically raised him alongside their mother after their assholic father had skipped town.

"Okay," Wes said.

"Good." Rielle said. She wiped her hands on his shirt before running them through her hair and checking herself out in the mirrored glass of the banal painting which hung over the sofa. She sat down on the thing, annoyed by the squishy sound the plastic made. It sounded cheap.

"So," Rielle began, "I'm thinking I'm going to get a butt-lift. What do you think?" She asked spritely, bouncing a bit on edge of the couch. Her breasts did not move.

Wes did not look at her when he replied. "But what?"

Rielle sighed and laughed gaily, as though Wes had made a little joke.

An inside joke.

"Oh you silly bear! I'm going to have implants put in my backside, Wes! To give me that Marilyn shape! You know! We talked about it last week!"

And they had.

Rielle had been coming to Wes to discuss her surgeries almost since the beginning. He was safe. None of their other siblings came to visit him. Their mother had passed on. Rielle's children – Wes' niece and nephew - didn't have the time or inclination to visit their mother much less their crazy uncle. Rielle didn't have very many friends left. None whom she could talk to openly about her surgeries. She knew they would judge her. Or worse. Deep inside she gnawed on a secret fear. When she acknowledged the fear it spoke with Wes's dead voice. It grinned maliciously with his blank face. The whole mental image was vaguely demonic. She had found ways of pushing it away. Rather she just talked to Wes - who listened and replied - though neither of them expected him to really understand.

He is still a man after all, even if he is nuts. Men don't GET it.

Even men like Mike who were... Rielle shook her head every time she thought of Mike's *preference*. She couldn't even THINK the word, much less say it.

It was just GROSS.

His father, in the only time Rielle had managed to get him angry enough to hit her, had called Mike a "faggot," but she told herself she loved Mike too much to call him such and wouldn't use the word. But Wes couldn't tell anyone.

"That's fun." Wes replied to her Marilyn comment.

Rielle nodded, fingered the edge of her expensive silk skirt and the knobbly beaded corner of the cushion on the plastic sofa.

"It will be! I can't WAIT to see Mister's face after I have it done! He's going to go SO red!"

She hopped a bit on the sofa, excited and feeling girlish.   "This morning I was looking at myself and I thought, 'Now, Rielle! What about ALMOND eyes? That's got to be unusual, right?' Right, Wes?" She did not stop for a reply. "I don't want to go all cat lady or anything, I'm going to keep it all pretty, because he's *not* worth ruining my beauty over. But, still, I told myself, 'It has to be unusual, Rielle, or he's NOT going to understand what you're doing!' And I think almond eyes are unusual, don't you?"

Wes grunted in reply, shifted in his chair. He stared listlessly out the window. Rielle kept on talking for some time, until a knock came at the door from outside. The door creaked open and Christa poked her head in.

"Miss Rielle!" she gasped, taking the opportunity to look around Wes's apartment, to oogle Wes himself and do whatever it was maids did when they get to see things they did not ordinarily get to see.

"Yes, Christa?" Rielle said, haughtily.

"You're going to miss your appointment with Dr. Tamlen. . ." Christa said, tapping her plastic watch. An old Timex Rielle had given the maid for Christmas
ten years before. She had tried to replace it but Christa refused.

"Of course!" Rielle said, suddenly happy. She stood up. "I'll be right out."

Christa closed the door and presumably walked away. Rielle walked over to Wes and again stroked his hair. Massaged his shoulders gently with full sisterly affection. "I DO worry about you Wessie. You KNOW you can call me if you need to talk, right?"

Wes grunted and nodded, pulled away from her. "Thanks." He eventually said. Rielle nodded, sighed and left.

The car ride over to the office of Dr. Tamlen - the only plastic surgeon in the Baton Rouge area who would still accept Rielle as a client without burdensome additional referrals - was uneventful. Christa made small talk, Rielle paid little attention to it.

Inside the office there were more men sitting in the plush chairs than Rielle had ever seen there before. Four of them. Usually the place was full of women, but there were only Rielle and another, much younger woman this time. Christa had chosen to remain outside, sitting on a bench reading an Anne Rice novel. Rielle eyed the younger woman, and a strange frisson blasted through her.

I KNOW this woman.

Rielle sucked in a gasp of air and turned away, clutching her purse to her chest with both arms. Her breath came in ragged gulps as though something was restricting her air. She was suddenly dizzy, though she did not want to sit down. She wanted to flee. Her inner core, her very Rielle-ness came into play and she stiffened.

Flee? Because of this cow? Never.

Turning around smoothly on one heel, Rielle arched her back and swayed with as much feminine exaggeration as she could manage. She was after all still a size two and wearing considerably tall pumps. The motion annoyed her still healing ribs, but she did not grimace. Proud of her motion she swayed all the way to the seat right next to the woman. She gently lowered herself into it with a superfluous, mischievous grin.

For her part the woman did not seem to notice Rielle or her swaying. She read a glossy copy of Cosmopolitan, holding the covers with both hands at chest level. Her legs were crossed primly at the ankles. She wore an expensive-looking skirt suit, the blazer off and draped over her knees, half folded. Rielle almost snorted as she examined the blazer, covertly looking for the tag. When she saw it she almost clapped with childish glee.

Lane Bryant. This girl, Rielle could not think of her as a woman in any context, *shops at Lane BRYANT. Hah.*

She did not realize she giggled aloud until one of the men in the room looked over at her, grinned. He was older, but his face was smooth and fresh looking. Everywhere except around the corners of his mouth. A notoriously difficult spot to correct, Rielle knew, without permanently altering one's smile. His smile, wide as it was and ready as it seemed to come was likely the reason he had the lines in the first place. She brushed thoughts of the man aside though.

Just another one of them.

She did briefly think of her son Mike, but only briefly and only in the context of worried pretense. She refused to make prolonged eye contact with the man. He soon went back to thumbing through his copy of Vanity Fair.

Rielle put her attention back on the woman. *Not girl. Whore.*

She allowed her mind to drift until she cast upon the woman's name. *Cary.* That wasn't it though. She had some kind of ridiculous double name, didn't she? One that was abbreviated. After a moment's thought Rielle had it.

Cary Electra Dewell. RE-diculous! C.E.! That's what they called her, wasn't it?

It was. Rielle smiled, vulpine and vindictive.

She wondered if the whore recognized her. A nurse came out and called a man's name. The old one with the Vanity Fair all but leapt up and raced to the door lead by the nurse into the back of the office.

Rielle decided to talk to the whore.

"Don't I know you?" she said warmly, in her best church voice. She did not go to church any longer, not since the kids were grown and had stopped being biddable. She maintained the prissy, pleasant attitude she had once presented after a service. It was her idea of being "sociable."

The whore turned to her, lowered her copy of Cosmo and examined Rielle's face, cringed. Not even bothering to hide it. Her eyes ravaged Rielle's face - searching, examining the features and doing whatever it was whores did when they tried to think. Rielle was used to such stares, she endured.

"Maybe?" the whore said.

"Isn't your name C.B.?"Rielle said airily.

The whore's face contracted visibly and she frowned. It was not attractive. Not only was she florid and overweight, but be-freckled and saggy. Rielle wanted to laugh.

Mister slept with THIS?

Of course it was years gone now, the kids had been in high school and the whore had been in college. Still, the whore looked awful. The whore smiled meanly at Rielle, recognition finally dawning on her features.

"Rielle Devall?" she said, though it was a question she did not wait for an answer before saying. "It's C.E., not C.B."

Rielle laughed, facetiously. "OF COURSE! How HAVE you been?"

She thought back several years to the time when this C.E. had been Mister's whore. How had they met? Mister, of course, had never confessed to any of the many whores. That would not be seemly. Rielle had just KNOWN. She had followed him to work. Caught him red-handed, though she had never told him this.

Yes.

This girl was an intern at the office.

The image came flooding back to Rielle's mind. This chunky young whore, wearing a positively indecent halter-top for such a fat girl, bent over Mister's desk. Her purple panties and slacks bunched up, down around her knees. Mister's hands in her long, wavy dark hair. Rielle had thought at the time the hair was nice, before she had seen the girl's face or how chunky she was. She shook her head, annoyed even in memory she had ever thought of CE as a girl and not a whore.

"I've been well. I'm MARRIED now." CE said and she waved her left hand under Rielle's face. A smallish diamond perched there, a tacky thing, likely purchased at Zales, Jared, or some other mall establishment.

Figures.

CE smiled and her smallish teeth and largish gums made Rielle sick.

What an ugly girl!

"Are you?" Rielle said, distractedly. The idea of talking to the whore suddenly did not seem like fun any more.

Married? What kind of man marries this whore?

This question alone kept Rielle from simply walking away.

"Yes!" CE said. "His name is Sam. He's my chubby hubby!" She said this with evident pride. Rielle could not stop the cringe.

Chubby hubby? Who SAYS such a thing? And with pride? Terrible.

"Going on three years now! Not long after I graduated. How's Mister Devall?"

Rielle snorted. "Dashing as ever."

What else could she say, it was the truth. Mister only got better looking as he aged. "He's away on business."

CE nodded and uncrossed her ankles. Fully closed her Cosmo with the force of abruptness which said she meant to say something important. Rielle braced herself, and prepared the torrent of insults and accusations she would hurl at the whore after she admitted to being a whore.

"Did Dr. Tamlen do all that to you?" CE asked

calmly, her eyes taking in every bit of Rielle's face, scorn evident.

This trollop? Giving ME scorn? AS fucking if.

"No. Dr. Tamlen is my *newest* partner." Rielle said, using the word she preferred to use in referring to her surgeon.

CE looked skeptical, then relieved. "That's good to know."

CE seemed about to say something more, but Rielle had had enough of being nice. In her best church voice she lit into the whore.

"But don't worry, dear! She can fix most of your problems. A few lipo-suctions, well maybe more than a few - if you can afford them, some lifting and tucking around your neck, a really good facial peel and *definitely* several rounds of Botox and you can look thirty again!" Rielle said this with great zest and a beatific smile. As much as her lips and cheekbones would allow.

CE's face immediately clouded.

Of course she was not entirely stupid, she could not have gotten her internship if she had been, the fat cow.

CE started to sniff in anger and turn away, but Rielle was not having it.

"And don't fret, I'm sure she can refer you to *SOMEONE* who can do something about those gums. Honestly, I can't imagine what you must have gone through with *those*." Rielle patted the fat whore on the knee.

"I'm not here for any of *that*." CE said. "I'm getting a breast reduction." She sniffed.

Rielle moved back and away. There was contrition in the whore's voice alongside the anger. It seemed distant. CE actually looked down at her knees as she spoke next.

"One of my breasts is much larger than the other, so I've decided to reduce it, so they'll be even."

Rielle let out a relieved breath. For a moment she was sure the girl,

The whore

was going to apologize. Rielle had no plan for that. Softly, distractedly, Rielle pulled back on her hairline. Smoothing her hair down, much as she had done with Wessie.

"I didn't know." the whore said.

"You didn't know what, dear? About all the surgeries?" Rielle said unpleasantly.

"No. About you? That he was *married*. He said he wasn't. I asked."

Rielle was shocked. She had no response to give. Several stuttering barks popped out of her mouth. She looked hurriedly away. Two of the men in the waiting room were watching them with avid attention. As though they had caught a soap opera unfolding before their eyes. When they saw her notice them, they sent their veiled snickers elsewhere.

But CE wasn't done. "You know, it's not my

fault. And if you really want to blame someone you might want to start looking at yourself? I went to school with your brother, you know. If I had known Mr. Devall was *your* husband I never would have..." Something changed in her tone. Conciliatory was gone, so was contrite. "It's women like you who think being beholden to their husband is top priority who cause these things. I mean, why are you still *WITH* him? He *CHEATED* on you, you obviously know that now. But,
I can see instead you just internalize it. That's why you do all of this," the girl waved in the general direction of Rielle's face. "to yourself. Not to mention, *everyone* says you had Wes committed for playing video games. Lady you are *shit-crazy!*"

Rielle shifted in her seat. The room around her swirled with color. Her head went light. She pressed a hand to her forehead. Not that she believed anything the whore had said. Her hands felt her face.

The waxy skin.

The smallish nose.

The huge lips.

Quite suddenly it was as though an alien had taken up residence underneath her skin. Had rearranged details of who she was and flown merrily away. Rielle wanted to scream, but nothing came.

Instead she reached over and with churchly delicacy slapped CE slap across the face.

"Whore." she snarled.

CE laughed.

Rich.

Mean.

"FAT whore!" Rielle said over the girl's laugh.

But the girl seemed unfazed. She just kept laughing at Rielle and the room kept spinning. Rielle stood up and ran into the sunshine outside. She took huge gulps of air, balancing herself against a concrete and pebble pillar for support. Her left hand trailed across her face again and she sobbed. Any tears were absent, dried up.

Where did they go?

The rest of her simply sobbed into the afternoon's uncaring vastness. Rielle hardened, her skin thickening.

She would not go back.

She would not cease.

A great responsive force crescendo-ed inside her. It washed away grimy doubt and insecurity. She embraced it.

Her arms flung out to the open air.

Her heels coming off the ground.

Her head cocked slightly to the side.

She stood on her toes alone, arms spread akimbo. The sun warmed her face.

It felt like a smile.

Chapter 11 – "That's my life, right now..."

"I want to tell you why I didn't call."

"I mean, *I did call*, that *one* time. Right after I got back from segregation. And you said... but really I'm getting ahead of myself.. I *really* want this to make sense... you said, '*That's my life right now*.' After like *two minutes*. We hadn't talked in about three months and *that's all* you had to say to me. And I know I'm not supposed to think in these terms, but really? *Who doesn't?* You hadn't sent me any money since October and it was March. I was sure you were trying to *tell me* some*thing*."

"Not that I didn't have something to tell you. See, I had been writing this ex of mine, a *really great* guy from New York City, an old friend. He started writing me out of the blue just before I went to seg in November. I hadn't heard from him in like six maybe seven years? Definitely not since I'd gone to prison. It was a shock, but a welcome one. But it did something funny to me. At first I really thought, '*WOW! This could REALLY happen. He wants me BACK!* His letters all but said it. How he realized how great I was but only after the fact. Do you know what it's like to hear that? It's amazing. I was floating."

"So the whole time I'm in seg he's writing me and I'm writing him back. I couldn't call him or you, but he was so... evocative in his letters. Honestly, I don't know how to say this without being a prick, but he's *smarter* than you. Cultured. Artistic. Opinionated. So many of the things I always thought I should want, I *should have* in a lover. Things that I really never thought about with you. With you it was just companionship, pure and simple. You never stimulated me, and I know that might hurt to hear, but it hurts more to say it! We just aren't cut from the same cloth, you know?"

"But don't think I consciously chose to stop talking to you. It wasn't like that. After that first call, when I got out of seg, when you didn't seem like you wanted to talk to me or have anything to talk about, I thought to myself, 'OK. I'll call him in a month and see what's going on then. Maybe *I'll* have something to talk about and I can carry the conversation then. Even though the idea of that was bothersome to me... my life is in prison right now. It doesn't change. You *know* this. How can I possibly carry our conversations? And conversations are all we had. You stopped coming to see me, so what else was there?"

"But again, I didn't really decide to stop talking to you. I just didn't call. I figured I would, the next week; except it was always the *next* week and I didn't *feel* like it. Can you understand that? I didn't have anything to say to you. Ironic, right? Hah."

"Still, there was Jonathan. That's the guy from New York City. We kept writing each other and it felt *so good. Right.* To be able to talk about expansive things, literate things, *deep* things. I never felt that way with you. I would tell myself, 'OK, Charles. *Chuckie-boy*. You don't *need* your lover to have those deep thoughts, after all, didn't Tori Amos say: '*What's the big deal about deep thoughts?*', I don't need Mike to have deep thoughts. *I* can have all the deep thoughts. And I have friends, lots of them, who are brilliant, insightful, *amazing*, I can get my intellectual thing from *them*.' That's what I told myself when I was with you. To make it OK we didn't talk about those things, you know?"

"That was before prison. But after I came to prison I had similar thoughts. After I reached out to you, *I swear* I wanted to make it work. I wanted it to be you and you alone, I DREAMED about it. I chastised myself hard for what I had done to you, for dropping you cold so many times and just picking you back up again. For telling you I loved you when I didn't, like that morning outside my townhouse. When we had gotten *so, so high* and done all that freaky shit. I know you only did it for me. So I felt like I owed that 'I love you' to you. That was so wrong of me! And then just before I came to prison, we had started dating again, and it was so comfortable. You falling asleep in my bed, there when I
got back from dealing and partying, I really liked that. Knowing you were there... I *really* liked that. It wasn't love. I don't want to lie and say it was. It wasn't. But it was something *like* it. A reasonable

facsimile and who knows, it *could* have turned into it? Right? Isn't that how it works? You start with something good and build on it, until one day you realize it has become something so much better? I just don't know."

"So I thought about that the whole time in seg. And here I was, right out of seg, only back in general population for two months, smitten with Jonathan, though it was clear by then, yet again, it was a one way thing, all me. He only wanted to be friends. That always happens to me. The friend-zone. I meet these great guys and they only want to be my friend. Sure they might have sex with me, but *love*? *Never that.* So here I was, knowing I should call you, and not able to make myself. Really I felt so terrible about it! You had stuck by me for over two years at that point, two long years of prison, with you coming to visit, you sending me money, you helping me when I so desperately needed it. I honestly would not have made it without you. You have to believe that, because it's the truth. You made it bearable with your support. And you never asked for anything more than I could give. You made it clear you wanted more, you *wanted* us together, *for good*, but you talked about it in such far off terms, you made it OK for me to not be beholden to it. Does that make sense?

"I need you to know I will never forget that support. That's why I called you. That's why I asked you to just listen to me talk, to hear everything I had to say. I had to put it all out there for you. The whole truth. Everything I felt and feel, you deserve that."

"I guess the really interesting part you don't know is right around a year after you stopped sending me money and coming to visit; just about a year after Jonathan and I started writing each other, he stopped writing me. He dropped me cold. You were the first thing I thought of. I actually went to the phone and dialed your number from prison, thinking, 'OK. I really should call Mike now! It's the *right time*.'"

"But I didn't."

"I couldn't."

"I know what karma is, you know? I deserved to feel what I was feeling, I'm not so blind I didn't understand, this was what I had done to you, I had just dropped you, *cold*. No word, no attempt at telling you the truth or how I felt. Just the coward's way out. I just stopped communicating with you because I knew how wrong I was. I *knew* I was just going to use you again. I *knew* I was just going to tell you the half-truths, ones that made me seem reasonable and smart and good. When the reality is, I'm *not* those things. Not with you.
We aren't right for each other, that's like *totally clear* now, but not because of you. It's because of *me*. Because I'm fucked up, because I need more and was willing for so long to just take and take

and think, 'Well, Mike has *some* of me, shouldn't he be happy with that?' But what if, right? What if that's what Jonathan was saying, I thought that and it made me feel so terrible. Just *wretched*. I actually sat in my bunk, with my arms over my face, half pouting, half crying over you. Because I had done you so wrong. And because I knew I couldn't ever make it up to you. I couldn't ever give you what you wanted, I couldn't ever give you me. And the understanding, Mike, it's horrible. Because I knew. That's what Jonathan *felt*.   For me.   That's why he stopped writing, why he just went from being this great friend, this distant hope, this necessary presence, to nothing at all. Because he *knew* it was going nowhere, knew I could never satisfy him and I'd always want *more*, regardless of what I said."

"Not that I wasn't OK with just being friends, I really was, but I would have always hoped for more. Some day. That somehow the things about me that aren't good enough for him could grow or the bad things wither as needed. That we would get older and find the *need* for each other outweighed the differences. But surely if that could work for me and Jonathan, then it would work for me and you, right? Don't think I didn't have *that* thought, because I did. I just rejected it. I *knew* it wouldn't work. With you I would always look back and wonder what could have been What kind of *star-crossed love* had I missed out on by being with you? What great, inspiring, world-turning love had I left aside to be *good* to *you*? Good for you? I thought about it those terms. And with my writing, I thought, 'Well, Mike doesn't *add* anything. He doesn't inspire me at *ALL*!' As if anyone else had, you know? But I hoped! I hoped to find someone I could be intellectual partners with, whom I could *share* my dreams with and have them reflected back at me, with something more than just '*that's great*', '*amazing, you're so talented*', or some shit. I need that, I can't be great without it. And what if I was? What if by some miracle it all worked out and I became famous for my writing and I was with you? Unhappy? *Unfulfilled*? I would've just ended up leaving you again, only this time it would be far worse, because you were there when I wasn't famous, when I wasn't successful, when I was nobody! I'd have that whole thing famous people feel, that everyone only likes them because they're famous. I don't want that at all."

"Mike! I really *hope* you under*stand*. I don't know what else to say. I don't know how to make this better. I want to be friends with you, you deserve that, you do. But it has to be for *real*. Which means I had to be completely open and honest with you. About everything! The reasons behind why I did what
I did. If you still want to be friends, then I'm here, I'm ready *now*. Just tell me what you *want*."

Chapter 12 – Neither NOR

"No to ROE! Ab-*OR*-tion is *M-U-R-D-E-R*!" Karla chanted, in unison with the others. Seventeen other people to be exact. The clinic, outside Baton Rouge, Louisiana was the last one in the whole state to perform abortions at all. It was housed in nondescript building of gray brick, no sign out front, nothing to indicate the horror that lay within. A narrow sidewalk and a chain link fence surrounded it. Uneven grass grew between the building and the sidewalk. Quite narrow between the fence and sidewalk.

By law, Karla and the other NORers could not pass the fence. 'No On Roe' was a charitable organization, but they could not protest inside fence lines, that was considered harassment. As if those few feet made some real difference.

Typical of these people, Karla thought.

To find a difference between six feet and a fence. To find a difference between six weeks and nine. A baby was a *baby*, it didn't matter when! Why couldn't they see that? Five hundred feet or five, what did it matter? As long as they could save another baby...

"Karla?" Morton. said softly.

He was much younger than Karla, well, only seven years, but to her that was a lot. He was tall, kind and he had a true heart about the right things. Among all NORers he was the most ardent, the most faithful and the most forgiving. He never shouted horrible insults at the girls and women who came to the death houses. He never threw things at them, or screamed in their faces. Never got angry, he just got sad and cried. The crying, that had been the thing that drew her to him first. She had needed to comfort him, make him feel better, to know a kindred spirit. Not feel so weighed down by the deaths of those babies.

"Yeah, Morton?" Karla said, hefting down her heavy placard-on-a-pole. It read, "Abortion is MURDER!" above a full color graphic of a late-term aborted fetus. She smiled coyly at him and he brushed his hands through his bushy hair. He did not make eye contact with her. His toe kicked lightly at the ground.

"You're so ...brave, Karla." Morton said. "You never give up."

Karla blushed at the compliment. "I could say the same about you! When I really don't feel like doing this, some days I don't, I just don't! I think of YOU! And it gives me the spirit to come out."

Morton's head raised and he looked at her. He was not typically handsome. He had tattoos. She was sure he had a past as checkered as her own, but they had not known each other long enough yet to get into it. Only two months. But she hoped.

Past or no, Morton was a gentle soul, and Karla knew it. He was nothing like her father.

Nothing like her first or her last, the only two men she had known. In the Biblical way.

Not that she was very Biblical, somehow that seemed
irrelevant. She had strong notions her need to do good was based on something ineffable inside of herself, not on vague hope of salvation, threat of punishment. The idea of a set of laws and beliefs made up by old white men two thousand years before she lived guiding her?

How silly.

Yet in the fight against abortion the closest allies were people who held such beliefs. At times it was very hard for Karla to surround herself with such.

legs in a set of stirrups, the slosh of something wet. Everything washed in the color of blood. A scream trailing off into the distance.

She had little hope she could escape the memory.

How does one undo a memory? Scald it away clean, burn it off, lance it?

She did not know, but she knew she could fight against anyone else ever having to experience the same. If that required her to partner with crazy religious people, she would.

"I don't understand why they can't see that it is *murder*." Morton whispered to Karla in a break between chants. No one had visited the clinic in hours, not since the employees had arrived. The other sixteen protesters were several feet away, signs slanting towards the ground, some leaning against them, some holding on to them with white knuckles and fierce expressions, ready for anything.   Karla's sat against the fence, delicately set aside, waiting.

She smiled at Morton, flipped her shoulder-length, red hair. The particular shade, Nutrisse Applecherry was her favorite.

It would shine brilliantly in just the right kind of sunshine.   Her eyes trailed upward, but clouds, fat and puffy lazed a way across the sun, dappling her in shadows.

"Some people are just blind." Karla said, her eyes glancing back at Morton, then at her fellow protesters. "But that's why we have to keep on, if we don't stop eventually they *will* see."

Morton nodded and smiled, his uneven teeth showed. His back molars were missing on both sides and they had a patina of yellow on the edges of the incisors.

Years of smoking and drinking coffee. Karla thought. *He must have started young.*

She hadn't seen him smoke yet, but he was always nursing a takeout cup of Starbucks. Some girl kept bringing them over, from two blocks over, refusing to take any money for them. Saying she supported their cause before she hustled away covering the Starbucks insignia on her apron with her hands over her stomach.

Morton downed the last of his coffee. Shifted out of the wash of sunlight, towards a fence post. He was also now much closer to Karla. He smelled nice.

Some essential oil, vaguely orange-y, and something vanilla-y. Pipe tobacco maybe.

Her father had occasionally smoked the stuff, one of the few times the habit had seemed tolerable to her. Versus Karl's constant, suffocating cloud of cigarette smoke. A disturbing image came back to her.

riding in her father's pickup on the way to school, the entire floorboard of the passenger side covered in ash which had spilled out of the overflowed ash-tray. Her feet hovering over the ash as she held on tight to the oh-shit handle, wincing when Karl cursed and sped up.

Angrily she pushed the image away.

"Are you okay?" Morton asked.

"Yeah." Karla murmured. "Sorry. I was somewhere else for a second."

"That's okay. So. You're from South Carolina, right?"

They had talked about this before, but only when they first met. She knew he knew the answer. Part of her enjoyed watching him struggle to come up with things to make small talk about.

"Yeah." Karla said, grinning.

Something about Mort was dichotomous. His tattoos and teeth. The cock-sure walk. His lean, handsome-ish - if not quite really – face. It all spoke of someone who had great confidence in his ability with women. Or maybe with girls. Men might not know the difference. Karla did. Yet he was hesitant with her, like a teenage boy.

always testing, always looking for signs of approval

Karla found that she really liked this. She let him squirm.

Silence.

"I've never been there."

"Lucky you."

"What makes you say that?"

"Because you haven't been there."

Laughter.

"No really, were you not happy there?" he asked.

"What is happy, Morton?" Karla asked, intensely. He was stumped. His body folded in on itself: shoulders slumped forward, hands clasped and reached towards his knees, fingers stiff. Karla let the moment hang. She hadn't intended to go all philosophical on him. Only to stall. See what he came up with. As he silently considered her question she did the same.

What is happy?

Happy is red hair in the sunshine, strong hands around her cheeks. The waft of fresh air, free from cigarette smoke. The moment you fully enjoy something before realizing you need more.

The time between memories you can't erase and won't talk about.

Morton finally nodded to himself. Smiled crookedly at Karla. Clouds shifted and he was covered in shadow again,   *How had she ever thought he wasn't handsome?*

His cheeks were high and tilted. Angular. Over a square jaw right out of old Hollywood. His skin was smooth, on his face at least. Speckled with just the slightest growth of dark brown facial hair. It was clear he could not have grown a fuller beard. A nose which should have been too long, but was thin enough to be just right.

And those eyes...

They were not one color, but three. Green, brown and gold mottled together in flecks which sparkled at her when she wasn't looking to see it.

"Now. Happy is now." Morton said triumphantly. "Happy is being with someone who makes *now* worth prolonging."

Karla snickered.

A good answer...

Though it was tinged with morbidity, perhaps he couldn't see that, but she could. She looked upwards at him, tucked a lock of hair behind her ear. Ran her hand lightly down the chain links of the fence.

"Are *you* happy, Morton?"

A loaded question.

But she owed him the chance to tell her what

he obviously wanted to say. Clouds still hovered above. Sudden shouts caromed off the open space around the pair of them. A car door opened and slammed shut. Footsteps on gravel.

Karla's head swiveled towards the parking lot. There was a girl, *a teenager*, her hands hovering protectively over her midsection, though it did not show yet. Behind her was another girl.

It took a few seconds for Karla to realize it was not a girl, but a very pretty boy. A man. An obviously gay man.

The girl, Karla examined her in brief, was slight. Mousy. She had a chin too large for the size of her face. Otherwise she was pretty.

Even with that shocked and scared look on her face.

She wore baggy yoga pants, a hoodie and dark-colored sneakers. Now Karla could see her better she wasn't so sure the girl wasn't already showing. The clothes were too baggy to tell, especially with those small arms cradling the girl's stomach area.

The man, though polished and pretty, was bulky with corded muscle. He wore a t-shirt at least one size too small. It showed the shape of his large arms and chest as if he wore no shirt at all. The shirt was powder blue, the same color as his tennis shoes. His cargo shorts had the look of casually expensive clothes Karla associated with brands like Abercrombie and Fitch. Though the man was pretty enough to be a model, his bulk was off-putting, it made his effeminate gait comical. His head looked too small and his facial expression cartoonish. His lips were pursed in womanly anger as he stared down his very straight nose at the group of protesters who had bounded towards him and the girl.

Karla sighed as she reached over to grab her sign. Morton was right behind her grabbing at his. They moved together. The other protesters having made a gauntlet of sorts at the opening to the fence. Their stares of anger, condescension, and outright rage were suddenly cast into brightness as the clouds parted.

"Leave us ALONE!" the man said, his voice matched by his stride, not his bulk. It was high-pitched and squawky. He held out a hand to brush Doreen aside and Karla saw the fingernails were painted. The same color blue as his shirt and shoes.

"No to ROE! Ab-OR-tion is M-U-R-D-E-R!" Doreen shouted at the top of her voice along with sixteen others.   The protesters paid no attention to the tears flying off the girl's face or the girlish half-shoves the man directed at them. Karla looked at the girl again and revised her opinion.

Not a girl. A small woman.

Though she had a girlish air about her she could have easily been in her thirties now Karla saw her up close. The small woman would not make eye contact with any of the protesters. Karla had seen this before. So had the other protesters. They knew their roles well. Shame the woman enough and she wouldn't go through with it. Make her cry and she might not even go inside. Morton was standing right next to her, but he was not shouting. His sign was upside down, the placard turned towards him and loosely held by his right hand. For a moment the girl and the gay man no longer existed for Karla.   Only Morton.

His face had gone slack with pain. Recognition. Fear and wide-eyed sadness. Tears welled up. The gay man was shouting something, but Karla didn't hear. Even the other protester's shouts hardly reached her ears except as noise. Morton's mouth hung open, his tongue pressed over his stained bottom teeth touching his lower lip, like he was about to begin panting. Or maybe vomit. Karla dropped her own sign to the ground, stepped on the placard, as she pushed herself between Morton and the three protesters in front of him. She hovered there, taking up his field of vision, though he looked through her, past her, unmoved.

"Morton? MORTON?" Karla said, "What's WRONG?"
Slowly, Mort's eyes trailed down to her and his face followed moments after. His tears tracked the hard angles of his cheeks and pooled under his chin before dropping, drip by drip, to the gravel.

"It's *her*." he said softly.

Karla didn't know much about his past, certainly not what he meant by *her*. Her own image of terror came flying in: *legs in stirrups, the blood, the sloshing sound.* She gasped. Her head turned back to see the muscular gay man push Doreen aside as though the fat woman were nothing. Two men, Terrence and Joseph, both of whom had beards and thick necks stepped into the path - something they were forbidden to do - the expressions on their faces clear. Their intentions obvious. The gay man pushing Doreen was offensive to these hyper-Christians on too many levels. Karla thought she could actually hear one cracking his knuckles.

But it was no use.

The gay man simply bulled through them as well, pushed them into each other and to the ground with a huffed shout. The woman, her arms no longer hovering over her mid-section, wailed and leaped over Terrence as he scrambled to climb over Joseph and get back to his feet. The whole thing was about to turn very ugly. Then the woman was clear of the gauntlet, behind the fence and running as quickly as her small legs would allow towards the door of the clinic. Two nurses waited there waving her onward. Karla noticed a third, holding up an iPhone, filming the whole incident. Someone inside had undoubtedly already called the local police.

The gay man did not make it clear of the gauntlet. Ten or so hands grabbed at him. Terrence pulled at the man's uncovered legs. The gay man went down to the gravel over Terrence. Sounds of fists hitting muscle echoed as more clouds passed overhead, blotting out the sun and dimming the brightness of the morning.

A look of shock on her face, Karla turned. Brought her attention back to Morton, only he was gone. She stood up on her tip-toes and craned her head around looking. Karla could not see him. There was no point in staying for what came next. She did not want to spend a night in jail in Baton Rouge.   Sourly, she started to lower herself when she saw Morton, running towards the entrance to the clinic. Heedless, not taking the time to examine why, Karla ran after him. Behind her she heard the shouts and wails of protesters. As well as more thuds announcing blows landing on the gay man. Karla had a moment of doubt over not helping him, but as though on some kind of autopilot of necessity her brain changed the man. Encoded him. Not as the gay man she had seen, but as the man she and her friends had tricked into getting them pregnant.

Back when they were teenagers in South Carolina. Though she studiously could not remember his name, that was tucked away quite deeply, she could somehow still picture his face. His mop of orange-ish hair, the broadness of his features, flatness of his nose. All things which both in real life and in memory had suggested slowness of mind and touch. With ease she pictured *him* beneath the flailing blows of those righteous Christians.

Karla smiled with relief, thankful.

Then she was at the door of the clinic. A nurse stood there, or just a woman in scrubs. The nurse had her arms crossed over her chest, her expression blocking the way into the clinic. She was middle aged. Squat and strong-looking. Wattles of fat lounged under her chin and around her upper arms, but surprisingly little around her waist, which curved inward. Her hips and thighs were positively enormous - giving her the rather comical look of a human-shaped gourd.

"You ain't 'llowed in." the woman said in a thick Louisiana drawl. It was wholly unlike the drawl Karla had known back in South Carolina. It was slower, longer, harder on the roof of the mouth. And the woman's chins wagged distractingly as she spoke.

"I'm not .. ." Karla started to say, but what could she say? She realized she had been about to say, "*I'm not one of them!*"

The same thing she had said years before to her father after her friend Joyce Conners had broken down and told her own mother about the pregnancy pact. And the orange haired man they had tricked was arrested. Karla's father had

pounded her with questions. Requests for denials. Pleas for
her as his little girl, all begging for her to give him what he had needed so much. Nearly as much maybe as she had thought she needed that baby.

So she gave it to him.

She had lied.

Said she wasn't part of it.

But she was.

It had been *her* idea.

Now she couldn't do the same. She couldn't force the words off her tongue and out of her mouth. The woman snorted and shifted her feet. Took a harder stance. Waited for Karla to try something physical. Instead, Karla did the only thing she could think of: she aped her father. S

She begged.

"Ain't no way, girl." the woman said. "The doctor said ya'll wasn't comin' in... and he already done called the *po*-lice. So, you and them out there is in a heap of trouble!"

Karla reached out and grabbed the woman. Not in anger. Not to harm her. She grabbed at the woman's hands. Pulled them away from the woman's chest. But the woman was far too strong. Her arms hardly budged.

"Please!" Karla said, "My..." But the words wouldn't
come again. How could she describe Morton to this woman? She herself didn't know what Morton *was.*

Not to herself. Nor in any larger sense. Karla had just barely caught the expression on his face.

recognition and loss.

She knew she needed to understand what had caused it.

It can't wait.

"Sister is in there." Karla lied.

"Then why was you with *them*?" the nurse said, her eyes narrowed.

"I hoped to scare her out of it." Karla lied.

The nurse looked full of doubt. Her head and wattles shook slowly from side to side. Maybe a sign of indecision. Maybe a form of denial. Her eyes softened. The nurse glanced over Karla's shoulder - she was short and had to stand on the balls of her feet to do it. "Come on then, before them crazies pulls out a gun or sommin'."

Ushered inside, the woman shut the door behind Karla. Karla had not been inside one of these places in nearly ten years. For some reason part of her, a separate analytical part, expected them all to look the same. Why she expected this she could not have said. Would not if she could. Who would she have said it to?

Instead she took the place in: the industrial grey carpeting. The beige walls. A hallway which opened to a sitting room with obnoxiously comfortable looking chairs and a flat screen TV on the wall. A area in one corner was obviously meant for children to play in. It had toys and small plastic seats, but radiated a sadness and quiet loneliness which choked Karla up.

The TV was tuned to MSNBC and the volume was softly describing election coverage for the coming Presidential contest. It was nothing like the place she had gone to in Greenville.

Alone.

With a fake ID!

And six hundred dollars in cash she'd gotten from stealing crumpled bills out of the senior trip collection box.

She still cringed at *that* memory. Still expected even now someone was going to come and arrest her. Punish her and repudiate her for all of it. Stealing the money had never left her, but it did not haunt her as viscerally as the abortion itself did.

Her head turned reflexively backward as she walked down the hallway.

"Don't worry, hon." The nurse said. Up close and with her

arms no longer crossed over her chest Karla saw a name embroidered on the scrubs shirt, just over the left breast.

Trish Chenevert.

"They ain't gettin' in *that* door, it's reinforced! This place used to be a Navy building, it's real tough." Trish said with obvious pride.

"Ok." Karla said, distractedly. She turned back around to the waiting area and processed the fact it was empty. The only sound quiet admonitions from the television claiming a sure victory for the Republican guy and the woman sitting behind the counter opposite the television talking into her iPhone with clear, nervous energy.

"They already went to the back..." Trish said, pointing to a nondescript door next to the counter. A placard on the door said, "Incoming."

Trish saw Karl 's eyes take in the sign on the door. She laughed, her chins waggled. "S'pposed to say INTAKE, we just remodeled and they got it wrong. Ain't got round to changin' it yet."

The receptionist hung up the phone. Changed the channel. She leaned out over he counter and said, quite loudly, "TRISH! Look, we on Channel 2 again!"

Karla and Trish both turned their heads to the television
as the receptionist laid down the remote control. Bright sunshine caused glare on a moving camera which showed, from a distance, the fence-surrounded clinic. The mass of people thrashing the gay man who superimposed with the orange haired man who had gotten Karla pregnant.

Karla heard sirens, both on the television and from outside. Police had shown up and were wading into the mess, trying to separate people. Karla stared in disbelief. Nine years she had been participating in NOR protests and never had one gone *this* way. She had been at clinics when some *crazy* shot at the staff or a patient, but those had always been people not associated with NOR. People who had used the group's presence as cover.

Twice Karla had spent the night in county jails, being questioned afterwards.

"Well, I'll *be*!" Trish said, laughing. "There's the damned Sheriff hisself!"

A gray-haired, white man with a stern face and brownish uniform was visible with what looked like a small army
of other brownish-clad men. Pulling at the NORers. Handcuffing them.

Karla watched, strangely pleased, as they pulled the man who had impregnated her, up. *That bastard.* They cuffed him too, drug his limp body to a waiting squad car.

"They tore tha' poor thing up!" Trish said excitedly, "Put up a helluva fight for a sissy though, I have to say."

Karla stared at Trish, blinking in confusion. A sissy? Karla's head swam precipitously. But that wasn't it, not entirely. Something was weird about Trish's voice now. Her cadence and accent. As though she were affecting a deeper drawl and poorer language than she actually possessed. Karla didn't have much time to think it over before her mind drifted back to why she had come inside.

Morton.

"Can I go back?" Karla asked. Trish shook

her head "no," She bit her lip as she did so.

"Patients only." Trish said.

"Listen, girl." Trish said catching Karla's fallen expression. Her voice *had* changed. It confirmed Karla's earlier errant thought. "You ain't 'llowed back there and I'm 'bout tired of dealing with you, so sit down and wait. Your sister will be out when the doctor is *done*."

Trish waddled past and went through the door, swaying her hips like a thinner, sexier version of herself. She even tossed her head and laughed when the receptionist met her eyes. Though Karla could not see Trish's face, she could imagine the expression it had shown, '*Can* you *believe* this girl?'

Karla sat down and watched the television. She bit her fingernails, something she had not done since high school. The protesters were herded into vans on TV. Their arms bound in front of them with wire-ties, signs left abandoned on the ground. A vaguely Asian woman reported on the scene,
her hair flapped the in the wind. The changing pattern of clouds overhead altered her skin color from pinkish red to an orange-ish yellow and back again.

"and that's all we know for now, but it looks like the Sheriff's Office has the disturbance under control, Candace."   The Asian woman pressed a finger to her earpiece.

"I'm being told that the Leifwitz Clinic has been attacked four times in the last ten years, prompting the owner to move to this location - in a formerly secure Navy depot building - here by the airport. We'll be back with more, live from the scene, now back to you Candace."

The screen flicked to an amiably older white woman with very short curly hair and a bemused expression.

"Great reporting, Judith Lee. We'll be right back with more Live at Noon after these commercials."

Karla sighed and looked at the toys area from of the corner of her eyes. She didn't want to look at it directly. Slowly, as if her eyes were pulled by insistent hands of an unseen person: small, furtive, sticky hands. Her head turned and she saw a small boy playing among the toys with an angry, petulant expression on his face. He would slam the toy cars together with a loud noise, followed by a wail not of satisfaction, but snarling disaffection.

Karla gasped, then blinked. Her eyes misted up with tears. The boy was gone after she blinked, the toys still and forlorn as they had been before. Behind her the receptionist raised the remote and changed the television channel. Her head tilted to the side, considering.

Sometime later, Morton came out of the back. He stared into space, not noticing much, including Karla. He walked past her.

"Morton?" Karla said.

He turned and stared, dumb-faced at her. Morton wiped his nose with the back of his hand.

"Karla?" Morton said, obviously confused. "What are you doing in here?"

"I came to looking for you." Karla said, trying hard to dispel the lingering sound of the small boys snarls. Without any further words she pulled Morton close to her and folded her arms around him. There was no need to talk or try and draw words out of him. Words simply began to spill out, amid sobs and half coughs.

"I couldn't...tried...make her stop, not again. She shouldn't....and all I could think...but wouldn't listen. Then I saw him..."

Karla froze. Morton pulled away just enough, still wrapped in her arms so his eyes met hers.

"You think I'm crazy?" Morton said.

"Because maybe I am. I've been seeing him for years. My son. The one she killed."

Karla began to cry. She pulled Morton close and unfroze her stiff posture. Morton thawed against her, his body loosening into hers. Her hands rubbed against his back - surprisingly taut for such a skinny man. Karla's hands found the back of his neck and before she could think it over her mouth found his. She wasn't sure how long this kiss lasted.   The only thing that brought her out of it was the receptionist's loud call.

"Um, if you two don't mind..." she said,

"Could you go do that elsewhere? People come here to get rid of that kind of thing. This neither the time nor the place for that."

Morton grabbed Karla's hand and beamed down at her before pulling her out the door. She started to tell him that she had seen the boy too, playing with the toys, but he had dragged her to the door and opened it.

Sunshine blinded them both.

Chapter 13 - f******ck

Julie Dewell sat down with her slightly older sister, CE. They had not seen one another for months. But Julie had heard second hand CE had purchased a house.

That was a big deal...a big event...

She decided it was good enough cover to try and be sisterly again. Julie had texted CE. They talked amicably enough before CE suggested they meet for brunch. Julie hadn't really wanted to go. She had little, if any, real desire to see CE in the flesh. Julie's only expectation was any actual meeting would turn sour. As it always did with CE over the past couple of years.

Or longer. But CE bought a house.

Julie hadn't wanted to just let that go by.

CE looked different than the last time Julie had seen her. She was smaller, yet fatter at the same time. Her face was still freckled and round as ever, her perfectly aligned teeth a stark contrast to Julie's own. Once they had shared the same gap between their front teeth, but CE had insisted on getting hers fixed, while Julie had kept hers, thinking it lent her a separateness, a beauty. She still felt that way.

As she looked CE up and down she noticed her sister's breasts were far smaller than they had been. Julie's thoughts were interrupted by the arrival of the waiter.

"Can I get you ladies something to start? A drink perhaps?" he said, smiling. Julie was certain he knew CE, since she worked at the restaurant next to this one, the steakhouse. They were owned and managed by the same people. It was only as she saw his smile Julie got an itch between her shoulder blades telling her CE had an agenda in choosing the place, other than the supposed quality of the seafood.

CE ordered an Irish coffee. Julie had water, no straw.

As CE drank her Irish coffee several people visited the table and spoke kindly to her. Most did the whole social butterfly thing, laughing too loudly, gesturing too much emphasis. The redness of CE's face only getting brighter as she drank and verbally glad-handed. Then came the second and third Irish coffees. The two mimosas. Despite, they were not having a bad time.

"So, Saul and I got the house on foreclosure..." CE crowed.

Julie sighed and inwardly thought, "How apropos: you profited off the loss and destruction of someone else's life." But Julie said:

"That's great, CE, when do you move in?"

They talked about decorating schemes. Occasionally having moments of mutual laughter over the disaster that had been their home growing up, with its sprawl of detritus and accumulated layers of bad taste and useless junk.

They talked about their days in high school. Having only been separated by one year, they knew many of the same people.   Julie pretended shock when CE brought up Wes Miller, but that was old news.

Everyone knew he had gone crazy and been committed.

CE ordered two appetizers. None of which Julie touched. CE attacked them both. She laughed a lot. CE called people over and made unfunny jokes with them. Only occasionally bothering to indicate Julie was present, never that she was her sister. Without the gaps in their teeth to match them the only thing that could obviously show they were sisters to those who did not know was their voices.

On the phone it was all but impossible to tell them apart. Quite easy by listening to content, in Julie's opinion, but otherwise, difficult. CE, in fact, looked rather like a female version of their father. She had his broad features, wide nose and thick lips. CE *had* been pretty. Years and years ago, before she had gotten so fat, when they were both just starting high school.

Those days were long gone. No one in honesty ever called CE pretty now unless they wanted something from her. Julie suspected even the married man CE had once had an affair with at the accounting agency had been more interested in her relative age and easiness than any inherent attractiveness.

Finally, they ordered actual lunch entrees. After they ate CE called the waiter over for yet another Irish coffee. She leaned in, conspiratorially, and said, her face florid with drink:

"You know, I was this close," she held up her left hand, her thumb and index finger separated by half an inch, "to having CPS take the baby away from Kahne. I had it all setup. One phone call and it would have been done, but I decided it *couldn't* be my problem. Not with the house and everything."

Julie sighed. She hadn't wanted to talk about Kahne, though part of her had known they would. The very mention
of their much older sister, whom Julie got on with but CE hated, would usually send CE into hysterics.

I have not seen CE in months and months, almost two years actually Maybe she's changed?

But she had not. CE's face constricted with what anyone but a sister might have thought was contempt, but Julie knew it was jealousy.

"At the very least there should be an *investigation*, you know? She's *totally unfit* to be a mother. Knowingly having a baby with a crackhead? C'mon that's grounds for all kinds of shit." CE said, downing the last of her Irish coffee. It was well past two in the afternoon and Julie was quite ready to leave. Julie was an anxious creature though, she wanted CE to like her.

All in all, the lunch hadn't been THAT bad. Perhaps we can end it on a good note?

Julie did not make the required comment about Kahne's inherent unfitness to be a mother, despite CE's urging. Because she did not feel it was truth. Kahne was as invested and loving a mother as possible. Their older sister was devoted and caring and reasonable to her son in a way wholly unlike the manner in which Kahne treated everyone else in their family, including Kahne herself.

If such devotion was reason for being unfit then how could CE possibly think anyone actually deserves to be a mother?

Julie said none of this, she only hmmm'd and sipped at her coffee, black with one sugar, no Kahlua.

CE's eyes narrowed, her cheeks puffed out and her nostrils flared. As though she were an obese hound, sniffing out a fox.

"You don't think so?" CE barked. "Her arrest record and drug use alone is enough! Not mention that the kid's father is a *crackhead!*"

Julie sighed. She carefully set her coffee down and repeatedly told herself:

I will not have this argument with her today.

She had seen the expression on CE's face. She knew it for what it was, what it was always was with CE about Kahne. Jealousy.

When CE wasn't trying to covertly ape Kahne

she did her best to lambast her. Demonize her as if it were obvious Kahne was the most horrible and careless of people. And though Julie could easily admit Kahne was not the easiest person to love or live with - at times Kahne's craziness made her impossible to be around - this was not the source of CE's scorn.

Jealousy, pure and simple.

Because despite all CE *felt* she had personally achieved - more effectively, with more grace than any of her sisters, no less - *she* had not been able to conceive a child. Despite having been married and trying for nearly three years. And yet Kahne, in typical Kahne-ness, had simply gone out and decided it was time to have a baby. Picked a thoroughly pathetic, much younger man to enact the deed. The whole of the situation was guaranteed to drive CE bonkers. And it did.

"The fact she LETS the *crackhead dad* around the baby, that's reason enough to have the baby taken away!" CE said.

Julie sighed and inwardly seethed. She had reached her limit. She waved at the waiter. "Can we get the check?"

"I've got to go."

CE's cheeks sucked in and her nostrils flared further. She was scarlet-faced; huffing in Julie's direction. Worse, even drunk and clueless, she seemed to have uncanny ability
to see past any pretense Julie offered. She could

somehow know what Julie truly felt. Wished to conceal.

"See, that's *your* problem, *Julie*. You're so selfish and self-absorbed. You think *everything* should be about what *YOU* want. Just like Rob's wedding. When you brought that *supposed*," CE made air quotes around the word supposed, "*boyfriend* despite being told not to. Despite knowing how rude it was. How inconsiderate was *that*? *Everyone* said so, they were just *so* offended, but did *you* care? Did *you* notice? *No*. Typical Julie! so into *yourself* that what other people want doesn't matter. I mean, it was *ROB'S* wedding. Not *YOURS*. You knew it was for family only! And you brought some *black guy* you're in an *open relationship with*. It's not like I don't KNOW about it!"

This was news to Julie. She had not spoken to CE about the nature of her relationship with Jason. She had blogged about it. But she had not given out the location of her blog to anyone, especially not CE. Yet it was clear from the tone of CE's voice - the derisive sureness - somehow CE *had* been reading it.

What ELSE did she think she knew?

"It's just *disgusting* is was it is. Sleeping around with whomever you want and shoving it in all our *faces*. Even Nana was offended when you showed up to the wedding with *a black boyfriend*!"

Julie blinked away tears. Crying was her

normal reaction to being accosted. She always cried easily. It was an exorcism. A way to channel out pain and hurt, to literally wash it off her face and send it away. Once the cry was over she usually felt better - she could move on at least.

What she could not do was bottle it up. Hold it in. Just *TAKE* it and not cry. This made other people think of her as weak, effeminate, ineffectual, weepy. But she was not. She had explained it to her close friends. And Jason. Charles. *They* understood. Yet CE had nothing but scorn. Would not have believed no matter how true Julie's words might be.

"When are you going to grow up? Just because you *can* do something doesn't mean you *should*. That's what got Kahne into the mess *she's* in! Just up and deciding she wanted to be a *mother*, that she *NEEDED* to be one!"

Deep, hard disgust infected CE's use of the word 'needed.'

"And here you are *defending* her! You're just as bothered by it as I am, I'm just *honest* enough to admit it."

Like everything else CE said, there was always a kernel of truth behind her words. Only twisted – changed horribly - given a Kafka-esque treatment until it resembled nothing like the original intent, instead mirrored the faulty internal compass which guided all of CE's truths.

Julie thought - unbidden by anything but

desire to think of something *other* than what CE
was spouting - of their father's assertion CE would
have made a fantastic lawyer. That comment had
been bandied about a great deal when they were
younger. Even once it was clear CE neither wanted
to be a lawyer nor was capable of being one.

CE must have taken Julie's quiet musing for
permission to continue. She barreled forward.

"And *you* work at that anti-abortion clinic! You
SEE all those women who come through there,
with all those 'mistakes!' You should under*STAND*
all of this! I shouldn't have to keep pointing it out to
you!" CE swizzled down the last
of her Irish coffee.

She leaned in, her expression feral and the
tiniest indication of a frown twisting the corners of
her mouth downward. The waiter hovered just past
their table with the check in his hands a perplexed
tilt to his head showed this was a side of CE he
had never seen.

Pleased, Julie waved him away. She was
pleased when he only retreated far enough to
nudge several other employees, all of whom began
to covertly watch as CE continued to speak.

"I don't even *KNOW* you anymore! And you
wonder why I don't want anything to do with you or
the rest of the family. Because the Julie *I* know
would not have some black 'wannabe' boyfriend.
SHE wouldn't wear an inappropriate dress to a
family function. *EVERYONE* thought so. And the

Julie *I* know wouldn't be content to let our sister *ruin another human being's life! MY Julie would agree with me!*"

CE seemed about to pound on her chest. Julie leaned back in her chair and saw her sister clearly, perhaps for the first time, beyond the standard family anecdote about CE...

...a much younger CE, not much past five or six years old sitting with her little back to a large window of a restaurant, which one long since lost in the telling. The rest of the family sat facing the window and could see clearly out of it. Julie, her father and mother, her older sister Kahne and even one of their multitudinous "working" uncles, Dane. All of them could see the ambulance as it roared by. It drew attention the way ambulances always draw attention - sirens blaring, boxy bulk weaving around traffic, the hurry of slow-motion emergency. But CE did not, could not see it. Nor did she turn around, though she DID register the sound of *a* siren.

"That's a firetruck!" she said, exuberantly, with gap-toothed zeal. Aquiver with the strength of her convictions and necessity of her knowledge, CE had beamed at them all.

Even as her father jovially said, "No, CE, that was an ambulance."

Julie, though she was only four or five, remembered the event with such clarity it was hard to believe it had been nearly two decades before.

..the tacky, hard feel of the leatherette covering the seats; the thick wooden table, laden with breads and fried potatoes, steak and sodas...

Mostly she remembered CE's face as her father told her it was an ambulance. Julie and CE had always been incredibly close, they were little more than a year apart in age. It had been natural for them to bond in such proximity. She looked up to both of her older sisters. Kahne was much older, a distant twelve. Her pretty face - so unlike CE's or Julie's - plastered with too much make-up, her hands gentle in comparison to her stern voice. But it was CE Julie had idolized.

CE had such confidence!

It was clear when contradicted by her father something integral had snapped in CE. It had terrified Julie to see the snapping. Already slight and short for her age CE had sunken in on herself - her hair, waist-length and a terribly pretty raven color, rattling - as her head shook from side to side. Her little pouty mouth creating synchronous gaps between the lips, a perpendicular to the gap in her teeth. CE had turned a shade of deepest red.

"*NO!*" CE had shouted. "*IT WAS A FIRETRUCK! I KNOW BY THE SIREN!*"

In a helpful tone their maudlin mother, so often lost within herself, had said: "But dear, it *WAS* a firetruck!" She had even reached out towards CE, her exquisitely manicured fingernails not yet gross in comparison to the mammoth amount of weight the woman would gain in place of her lucidity.

CE had jerked away as though some poison lurked beneath those nails. Perhaps it had been foreshadowing. And this Julie remembered clearest of all:

CE's eyes landed on ME. Occluded olivine green raging with inner fire.

They had gotten wide, those future-hate-blaring green orbs, softer and kinder than the friendliest of puppies. They had pled with Julie then.

Believe ME! Take MY side!

There was surety there. Of all the people in her life Julie was the closest to CE. Surely *SHE*, Julie, would confirm to the others what CE already knew:

She, CE, was *right*. It was a *firetruck*!

TELL them Julie! TELL them it was a firetruck!

But that is not what Julie had done.

She had blurted out just one word. Then rushed from the table to go cry alone in the bathroom. Kahne had followed, came in to soothe her, with her scent of too-strong perfume, and enveloping hugs. Her bangs peppered up vertically over her forehead.

Julie had said, "Ambulance."

The rest was a blur, as Julie only knew of it in the telling, since she had been in the bathroom. CE had apparently broken down into hysterical tears. Claimed she was unloved because no one believed her, tossed away any reach-over attempt at comfort until she was spluttering and spitting. The family left the restaurant in hustled shame.

All the while Kahne had soothed Julie, as if their older sister by her choice of giving had said:

"This is where my love NEEDS to go, so it WILL."

Julie could not have thought this then. She wondered now - as she sat across from CE who was leaning over the table - if that very night was the reason why she could find reasons to love and value Kahne when CE would not. Even at her worst. When all CE *would* see was the worst. Even when it was such a clear reflected projection of CE herself.

Because who had led CE down those dark paths if not Kahne?

Their mother had lost her mind less than a year after the night with the ambulance. Kahne had been forced to become more of a mother figure than she had already been inclined to be. When the next round of siblings were born during a brief, silent lucidity a year or two later, "Mom" was more of a creature to visit and dawdle with than any kind of figure to whom one owed authority. With "Mom" so indisposed and their father so often away "on business" it had been Kahne who mothered CE through first crush, her first period, her violin lessons, her decision to cut her hair for the first time in her life. Yet even then it had been Julie who nestled against Kahne and found comfort there, instead of being offered it.

But perhaps it all went back to *that* night. To a mistaken
firetruck, to a real ambulance careening down the highway with someone's real emergency inside. Somehow forgotten by the family amidst CE's invented trauma.

CE will always see what she needs to see to make that ambulance a firetruck.

With this new-feeling understanding of her closest sibling, Julie leaned away from CE. Julie could see down CE's v-neck shirt, to the exquisitely pale, freckled breasts nestled in a pale, pink bra. Without doubt much smaller than they ever had been. Julie met CE's green eyes and said with a smirk , *"Firetruck."*

CE's mouth quivered in shock. But Julie didn't have anything else to say.

Whatever damage exists inside her - it's beyond the pale. Deeper than the flesh. Only CE can fix it. Not me. She will always see that firetruck until she decides not to. Even when looking at me. Even when claiming somehow it's ME who's different and not her. CE will always see the firetruck.

The word was guaranteed to make CE go apoplectic. She did not disappoint. It was a bygone word in their family, oft accompanied by rolling of the eyes, to indicate when someone was being obstinate in the face of all evidence, but CE knew it differently. She always took it as a personal attack on her, as though she were still that little girl her back to a window, unable to see, unable to believe her sureness could produce anything but the unshakable truth. CE had not changed. She had never left that restaurant.

"Fucking bitch!" CE said.

Hearing CE call her a "fucking bitch" might have once made Julie cry. It would always be her first line of defense: cry, then move on. This time though, she laughed. A hard laugh. Full of mirth. CE was incensed.

"You can't laugh at ME!" CE spluttered. "You're a LOSER! You *and* your black boyfriend! Everything you do is a JOKE! Everyone thinks so! They just won't tell you! I'm so sick of you thinking you're better than everyone else, well you're NOT! You're worse and they *all* say it behind your back."

Again these words might have once caused tears or even Julie's secondary line of defense: a panic attack. A loss of breath until Julie was bent over, huffing in a paper sack, while CE or their mother or Kahne or someone else screamed at her to stop.

There was no panic attack this time. No tears.

Julie shook her head, truly sad and full now

of only pity for her sister. CE could not see behind her, where people she worked with shook their heads in startlement. They all knew CE.

the reason she had chosen this restaurant likely...

To show Julie lots of people in fact DID like her. They would never see CE the same way again. It was no use telling CE though. The ambulance would pass her by again and again. She would hear the wail approach, see the lights and *know* in her heart of hearts it was a firetruck.

Always a firetruck.

Julie stood up and dropped her napkin on the table, walked over to the waiter, took the check and left. She did not look back. No matter what CE yelled at her. She didn't even hear the words as words. Only as noise. Someone's emergency passing her by unremarked – unnecessary to the continuation of her happy life.

Chapter 14 - MamaDew

The bottom of her purse had a distinct smell. Slightly acrid. Like cheap leather. Sweet as well. As of abandoned candy. A powdery feel of all kinds of things left behind. Things meant to change only on the outside and be seen coated by the dark inside and thus darkened themselves.   She dug around for a cigarette. She knew was in there. It was her habit to not smoke. One she made sure to break only once a day. When things with Toby became too much to handle. She never smoked around her son. Or in the house. Unless she had to. In the house that is. Never around Toby. The car she had once used as her smoke haven could no longer be so. It carried Toby too often.

Her grasping fingers found the cigarette. She pulled it out. Dusted it off. Wiped her fingers against her sweatshirt. With slow zeal she flicked her lighter. Lit the thing. Inhaled deeply. Leaned back against the wall of the building. Around the corner she heard the sounds of other mothers laughing. Most of whom would be going back to their husbands.

And real house lives.

They were her sisters. Sort of. From her La Leche League group. This would be her last meeting.

When the cigarette was done she carefully

rubbed the butt out on the heel of her sneaker. Wrapped it in an old napkin. Also fished from her purse. Tossed the whole into a garbage can on the way to her car. Several mothers greeted her, waving. Calling her name. Smiling. Nodding at her. Some
had disapproval in their smiles. Kahne paid them little attention. She knew she would hear about it later. She was already imagining the post:

NatureMom31: Does anyone else think that maybe it's not the most natural thing in the world to be SMOKING outside of a LLL meeting? I mean, ladies,
all of us are MOTHERS. We have children to think of and we all go back to them after those meetings! Those meetings are supposed to be SAFE places! NOT places where you pick up the carcinogens from second-hand smoke, which you can pass on to your BABIES. Right ladies? I'm just saying. Peace out, bitches!

Scowling on the inside, Kahne beamed on the outside. An expression she had perfected in her days going to raves. And gay bars. She had learned from gay men how to project a persona.
Never let it drop, Miss Baby.
It was a life lesson for her. Though she didn't think about it like that. She just did it. Naturally. They had all loved her too. She had been

enormously popular in both scenarios. That was a long time ago, though. Before she went crazy. Before the Bad Seed. Before Toby.

She couldn't stop it. Didn't want to. Her outer smile reflexed inward. Aired out the dark place which had been about to choke her from inside.

Toby.

Her son. The light of her life.

Especially since Charles went to prison. Her gay best friend. Her titular first husband. Life partner. Oft-times nemesis. Charles had been so much to her. Now there was Toby.

She pushed aside the last memory of the LLL hags as they drove away. In their late model Passats and Town & Country minivans. Kahne popped a breath-mint. To ease the taste of the smoke from her mouth.

She hadn't even pulled out of the parking lot of the YMCA when her cell buzzed. Part of her hoped it was a call from Charles. She looked forward to those. More than even she knew. They eased her like few things could. Hearts fonder in absence and shit.

It wasn't Charles.

It was Aidan.

She stared at the phone in her hand for a few moments. Her eyes came unfocused. Instead of seeing the characters spell his name, form his number, she saw only fuzzy-edged dots in strange, undulating groupings. The result was a calmness of thought. A smoke break for her mind. After the fourth or so vibration of the phone she sighed. Focused again. Gingerly pressed the green talk icon.

"KAHNE?" Aidan slurred a half-shout. She held the phone away from her head. Sneered at it. "I WANT..."

She sighed. Loudly.

"I HEARD THAT." Aldan said. He sighed. His voice came down a bit. When he spoke next. It was surprisingly deep for such a small man. He was not halfway to six feet. She was rather close to it. "I need to see you."

"About what Aidan?" Kahne said.

"About our SON. About US. I'm tired of.. ."

She cut him off. "Where are my *Lortabs*, Aidan?"

The silence from the phone was itchy.

"*I* didn't take them."

"Yes *you* did. I KNOW you *did*. You *KNOW* you did." Kahne said. Unable to keep the weariness from her voice.   This was not the first time they had had this exact discussion. She loved everything about her son. Had tried, to love everything about his father. It hadn't worked. Sure he was a former crack user. Maybe still was. He still went to meetings. When he needed a dose of self-righteousness. A claim to touch something between them. Or actually touch her. THAT at least he hadn't attempted in some time.

Aidan laughed crackly. "So what if I did? It's not like I have
a problem! I *NEED* them for my back because I'm WORKING all day to support OUR son!"

Kahne's right foot slammed down on the accelerator. Though she had yet to start the car. She snarled. As if she didn't want to work! As if Aidan worked to support them! He spent most of his money on who knew what. Not on her. Or Toby. She got most of her support from her father. A fact they both knew. He was always quick to mention support. To hold out his working. As if it were something forced upon him. Something sacrificial he was doing for others. Therefore deserving of indulgence. She knew the trick well. She had used it herself many times. In many ways. She did not think of it like that however. She was not so self-aware.

She had given paid to his lie before about back pain. When she had allowed him to have some of her Lortabs. This left her feeling partly responsible. Like she had opened a door. Or something. How could she condense a week's worth of counter-arguments into a conversation of minutes? He wouldn't listen even if she could.

"I'm WAITING." Aidan said. "Are you coming home?"

In the background she heard Toby call for his father. He was not yet two. Didn't speak much.

But he could say a syllable similar to "Dad." Aidan loved it. The imprimatur of fatherhood. As much as she loved being a mother. But for a different reason. "Not Really." is what she would think every time Toby said "Dad".

What irony! Neither one of them knows it, but it couldn't be more appropriate to call him 'Duh' and mean 'Dad'.

"Yes." Kahne said. Her jaw clenched. She exhaled sharply. Not a sigh. A true exhalation. Minty smoke coming out of her mouth.

It was important for a boy to have his father. She truly believed this. And she *had* loved Aidan once. Maybe still did. She should just try harder. Spend more effort being good to him. He would see a reason to change.

"I'll be there soon." she murmured. Almost sweetly.

"Good." Aidan said. He hung up.

The moment she was inside the door a toddling Toby careened into her legs. He garbled some toddler speak at her. She hefted him up. Allowed him to nuzzle her. She gave herself over to intense pleasure of his scent. A clean, dusty aroma. His warm, light body invigorated her. She was laughing without trying.

Aidan's feet stomped closer. She could see his face. Behind Toby's struggling body. The boy wanted down. She slowly lowered him.

"Why do you even GO to those meetings?"

Aidan asked. "You're not breast feeding anymore!"

She blushed. She still breastfed. Sometimes. She lied. Said she wasn't. It was such a great feeling. She hadn't been able to let it go. "That doesn't mean I can't be *involved*, Aidan," Kahne said patiently. Smoothly. "It doesn't mean I can't *share* my experiences with new mothers or spend time with my mom friends."

Aidan rolled his eyes. Oddly, smiled wide at her. "What's *UP*?" he said.

He hadn't asked her that in months. Not like *THAT*. Not when he wanted *THAT*. She blushed again. Smoothed down her hair. Straightened her baggy sweatshirt. It hid her bulk. Her baby fat. Mass. "Mom weight." Aidan had never made her feel sexy. Beautiful. He had clearly enjoyed fucking her.

That had been enough. He moved in close. She could smell him. His musk overpowering the lingering hint of their son. She smelled the smoke on him. And something else. Something indistinct she could not place. She could not think much on it. He began kissing her.

Toby pulled at her pants leg. Jerking her jeans a bit. They fit too tightly to come down. She disconnected from Aidan and laughed. Aidan scowled. Noticed Toby. Grinned. He grabbed the boy. Swung him into the air to many giggles. Ran through the house with him. Both of them screaming. Kahne's father was not home.

The screaming would have driven him nuts. Kahne wended her way through the baskets of laundry. The boxes. Chairs. Following. Aidan flew Toby into the Sun-room. The family-apartment sized addition her father had added to the house. When her last two siblings were born. She set her purse down on the coffee table. Sat on the sofa as she watched Aidan goof around. The pair of them so adorable together. It made her heart leap and ache. After ten minutes Aidan grew up. Sighed. He told Toby to get ready for a nap. Winked over Toby's head. At Kahne. Get ready. The wink said.

She went to her bedroom. Where Aidan sometimes slept. Pulled off her sweatshirt. Avoided looking at herself in the mirrored doors of the sliding closet. Struggled out of her jeans. Her green silk panties half coming off with her jeans. She listened. Without processing the words. As Aidan settled Toby into the playpen for a nap. Toby wasn't resisting. Kahne pulled off her bra. Fell back onto the bed.

Aidan fucked her and she hadn't come. That hardly mattered anymore. She was full of him. For a few minutes. That was enough. He rolled over. Went to sleep. She pulled on pajama bottoms. A t-shirt. Went to go check on Toby. He was zonked out. She gently lifted him up. Settled him on her chest and stomach. Sat on the sofa. Where she fell asleep herself. While Toby snored lightly against her heaving chest.

Hours or minutes later. Who knew? She woke up with a start. Toby was no longer on her chest. Kahne panicked. Screamed out his name. She saw him. On the floor. Drawing on baseboards with a crayon.

"No drawing on the walls, Toby!" she crowed.

His smile lit up at the sound of her voice. He waved crayons at her. She walked over. Pulled him away from the wall. Kissed the top of his head. She was smoothing down his hair. Noticed her purse was no longer on the coffee table.

Eyes narrowing. She set Toby down in his play pen. Went into her bedroom. The only sign of Aidan was a small indentation in the memory-foam where he had been lying and wet spots on the fabric of the knit comforter. Trying not to scream she pulled at her hair.

Going over to her iPhone she called his.

No answer.

She left a voice-mail. Called six more times. Barely kept herself from throwing her phone at the wall. Crying. She wished Charles would call. She needed him so bad. He wasn't there.

Why was I am always alone? When I need help?

She knew from experience after experience she would neither see nor hear from Aidan. Until the money and Lortabs he had taken from her purse ran dry.

She got online.

Bypassing the alerts of a new post to the LLL message board. She logged into Facebook. Navigated to his page. Saw a new photo there. The one of Aidan, her, and Toby had been replaced. With a candid shot of Aidan laughing. Obviously taken from a cell phone. The tip of one well-manicured fingernail on the edge of the photo.

His status said: "Partying with the bros and Erica!"

Kahne snarled at her monitor. She mouthed a word. One she would say over and over again. For years to come. *Skankasaurus.*

It had little meaning that first time. Besides referring to this Erica in abstraction. She wasn't sure he was actually sleeping with the tramp. But she definitely thought it. As she sat there her view of the monitor twisted and flexed. Like she was suddenly seeing through a lens. A fishbowl. One of those awful filters on Instagram. It filled her vision. The photo larger than everything else around it. Disproportionately so. Glaringly so. Hatefully so.

Smiling, one arm loosely draped around him was Erica. The Skankasaurus. Like Kahne's little sister Julie, Erica had a gap between her two front teeth. Though unlike Julie Erica's gap was obscene. In the manner of difference between Madonna in the videos for "Like a Virgin" and "Justify My Love."

A slut's gap.

She reached towards the keyboard to send him a message. Her hands froze above it. They curled in mid-air. Fingertips facing those from the opposite hand. Forming the rough shape necessary to throttle Aidan's neck had it been between them. Kahne pictured exactly this. Try as she might she could not hold the image in her mind of Aidan's face and neck there.

It kept sliding backward in youth. Until it was Toby's face. Gurgling. Choking with accusation. Emotions inside her twirled about. Not an uncommon occurrence. She knew she was crazy. Had been on some form of medication for nearly two decades. When she wasn't conscientiously objecting. Two stints inside psych wards. One voluntary. One not so much. Had made it clear to anyone despite any evasions. She was always *potentially* crazysauce.

Kahne knew people loved her despite this. Usually that was enough to draw her back. From whatever brink she hovered over. Usually. Sometimes it took longer. Sometimes no time at all.

Staring at that picture on Facebook. Seeing her son's little face between her choking hands. Was almost more than she could bear in the same passage of moments. Those emotions did something they had not done before. They hardened inside her. Like arterial plaque of the spirit. She felt the hardening inside. A constriction

between her breasts.
Not near her heart. Behind it. Deeper. All her
uncertainties about Aidan surfaced. Questions she
had asked herself. All of it came back to her.
Flashing in photographic stills through her mind as
the blog posts they had been recorded as.

KahneDew: Does it matter that he is so
much younger than I am? Who knows? Julie
seems to think so and I talked to Charles the other
day (as if HE has
the grounds to talk about it, but hey, I digress, ya
know?) and he really wasn't into the idea. My dad
thinks I'm cray, not to mention CE (but she really is
cray) - so what am I supposed to think? if being
crazy were the criteria I used to make my
decisions, then I wouldn't make any. I AM crazy
folks (funny, since no one is going to read this, it's
like I'm calling myself folks!) But I'm not getting any
younger and I know lots of brainless chicks use
that as an excuse, but where IS my life heading?
Don't they understand I need THIS? I might be
nothing without it and it's here. What if it never
happens again? It can't be ALL that important he's
twenty-two and I'm thirty. Besides, isn't it better to
have a grounded more mature Mom? My mom had
ME when she was younger and she went even
crazier than I am, so what does THAT say? And
my dad (gotta love the fat bastard) he was younger
than HER and HE managed alright. No one is

EVER going to think Aidan is like Ralph Dewell, but maybe if I try hard enough he can be close? We CAN make it work, because it has to. Because I want it to! More than I've EVER wanted anything! This isn't like moving to Houston or New York City folks! This isn't like buying a Jetta! This is a BABY! I need this, I'm ready for it, hell, I was MADE for this! I was mother in everything but name to my four sibs wasn't I? I shudder to think what they would be like if i hadn't been there! Aside from CE hating me ... three of four isn't bad for a teenager whose womb didn't do the bearing, right? I guess I have my answer. I'm DOING this.

KahneDew: Can I let another drug addict into my life? Especially in this way? He's in rehab, so that's a good thing, but it's not the first time. Still, it IS the first time since he found out he was going to be a dad. He's CHANGING people! I can SEE it. He goes to work now, he doesn't STEAL anymore! He STOPPED smoking CRACK! But I can't let the idea go that drugs took Charles away, and as much as I love him, he is NOT the father of my future baby. Although we DID talk about it, OMG like forever ago. We planned for it. It was going to happen, I can remember when we saw that awful Madonna movie, and we PROMISED each other we'd NEVER do that. I wish I had asked for a different promise. But Aidan ISN'T Charles. He is TRYING, Charles.. . .well, he just got swallowed by it. It consumed him and he couldn't come back, cuz they sent him to PRISON. Aidan has a chance, and he's taking it, so I'm going to swallow my doubt and try it. Yay to the baby! ;)

KahneDew: I know he took those pills from my purse. I can't say which ones, because really, this IS the Internet and anybody COULD be reading this, though I know they aren't. I haven't told ANYONE about it, but that doesn't mean..... better safe than sorry. he's in enough trouble as it is. But rehab is ALMOST done. I told him that he had stay sober if he wanted to be part of our son's life. And he's trying, but there were BOUND to be mistakes. I can forgive that, can't I? I'm SO not perfect, especially since I had to stop taking the Paxil and Abilify. Because of the baby. I'm moody and mean and I actually cried at Charles the other day when he called from prison. But he just took it, he let me yell at him, something he didn't really do before. Maybe he's as changed as he says, I dunno. Maybe Aldan needs prison. But then my baby's dad would be gone for who knows how long. No. I just have to let him know that I know. about the pills, and that if he doesn't stop, then he's gone. Besides, there's ALWAYS
the chance he just wanted to sell them for money, but really after what happened to Charles that's almost as bad.

KahneDew: We went for our first family pictures today! It was so nice to sit there, well, Toby was laying, but whose arguing? Hah! And Aidan was so THERE. He was loving and caring and these PICTURES! OMG! We're both looking down at Toby and he's SO BEAUTIFUL and PEACEFUL, smiling up at us. I don't think I've ever seen anything like it, the LOVE there, it is SO strong. I can't believe I ever questioned it. Does that make me a bad wife to be? That I questioned? That I doubted? I don't think so, and if anything this picture proves that I was right to question and STICK with it. With Toby. With Aidan. With my FAMILY. It doesn't MATTER what CE said or thinks, we ARE working and MAKING it work. Aidan is doing SO well! I just. I don't have the WORDS for how happy I am. Maybe Charles could come up with something, for me, I think this picture says it all.

KahneDew: He hasn't been home in two days. I can't leave anymore messages. My THROAT IS KILLING me from crying. Toby is sleeping FINALLY. I don't know where to turn or what to do. I have this wonderful son and sometimes this wonderful fiance. SOMETIMES it is SO GOOD it hurts, and other times I just have to wait it out, close my eyes (metaPHORICALLY! Charles!) and imagine it as it has been, as it should be, as it will be again. I'm not even on any meds and I can still find that bright side. I've not gone crazy since before I met Aidan, what does THAT say? But now...I know he's been taking more and more of my pills and I know he's not selling them, and I THINK he's on something else too. And that girl who called him last week ...He said they just work together at Papa John's and i could TELL he wasn't lying, but that doesn't mean he's not holding shit back, right folks? I've done drugs, so I KNOW what it's like, but they never got me addicted, not like Aidan.. Not like Charles. I just want my fiance back. I just want the father of my son to be HERE. With us! Is THAT so much to ask? Am I so WRONG to want THAT? This is what drugs do they make such a simple question, such a stupidly easy one all fucking complicated! He SHOULD BE HERE WITH US. But I have Toby. He's the best thing that ever happened to me, even though every time I see his face I can see Aidan and I get so scared, what if Toby grows up and gets hooked?: I can't even LET myself THINK about that. Not with this bullshit going on, not with Aidan staying out all night after work, not paying our bills, taking pills from my purse... all is not well folks.

Her life had crumbled. Until all she had left was Toby. Charles wasn't coming back for years. And years. Aidan was out with the Skankasaurus. High on who knows what. He wouldn't take her calls anymore. Her father was pressuring her to get a job.

Start supporting yourself!

Toby was just over two years old and even he wasn't the perfect being he had been. Her sisters either hated her. Pitied her. Found her irrelevant. Her mother was gone. Moved away. Distant. Her brother was at college. Growing into some other person. Kahne hardly knew him anymore.

It was just all crumbling. She had pinned so much on Aidan sticking with her. Getting through it. Lasting. *BEATING* his addiction.

Now *THIS*.

She had not counted on Skankasaurus. Wrenching it all up. The hardness inside her created a frisson inside her. All her uncertainties rose up. The hardness merged into a totality. A sudden, irresistible force of change swept through her. Like

how X used to make her feel. Before the psycho meds. Before Charles got on meth. Before raves became all *meh*. When the X would still give her stomach butterflies. She KNEW the high was coming. The music about to roar inside her. Mesh with the high. With the spirit of caring and mothering within her.

It had been her nickname then. *Mama*Dew. Long before Toby. Because of moments like when her URGE to care became a high. She spread it

around her like a glowing, pulsing, dancing blanket.
A sense of righteous separateness. A new
wholeness outside what she had always felt.
Stripped of doubt. Insecurity. Uncertainty. Totality
of moment. Self and love. It was like that.

But not euphoric.

It hurt.

It clenched around her chest in a spot behind
her heart. Just kept hardening. She could no
longer see the difference between what her
fantasies of hope were and what reality was. They
were equally unreachable. She could not grab at
them. Could not fix them. Could not go back.
Rearrange it all.

Her hands relaxed. She smoothed back her
hair from her face. Wondering how long she had
been sitting that way. Her body hunched over.
Lost in the hardened frisson of her not-X moment.

It didn't matter.

She smiled viciously at the monitor. Clicked
the "Unfriend" button on Aidan's Facebook profile.
She vaguely remembered a question Charles had
once asked her.

"When do you leave? When do you choose
the moment that makes it all force you into action?"

It had been about something different. Some
other boy she could not remember. The question
she COULD remember.

And now she had the answer.

Her alarm clock was visible.

The little green lines showed 6:58.

Kahne stood up.

Called out softly to Toby. Her voice full of a now less effortless spring. Her son's name rang like an enchantment from some Harry Potter book. Loosening the hardness inside her.

Levitating it up.

Away.

Chapter 15 – Burning at Both Ends

A wheezing chill drummed across the skin of Thad's forearms, raising goosebumps across the whole surface of his skin. He reached out and pulled his arms back towards himself, wrapping them tight around his chest. The persistent cold was unusual for late March in New Orleans. It had not lifted for nearly a week. He was not deterred though. *Cassie* was waiting for him. He could be warmed forever simply by the *thought* of her.

Under his feet the cobbles of St. Ann rang against his shoes - patterning out into the cold, Tuesday night. Few people were about. It was too early in the night. Too late in the season, too far away from the hubs of Bourbon and Canal streets. The apartment he shared with Cassie was several streets over, off Burgundy, in a rather quiet, rather gay part of
the Quarter. He certainly did not mind the location. It had been Cassie's idea, along with input from her brother Charles. A *bona fide* fag.

Thad had shrugged and said, "Sure thing Cassie." And he meant it.

When he ran into the strange, homeless-looking man he was not thinking of anything so much as getting back to the warmth of his apartment, to Cassie. To whatever she had concocted for dinner, to whatever she had chosen for them to watch on TV. Reruns of Gilmore Girls

on DVD or maybe, just maybe: Buffy the Vampire
Slayer. His initial hesitance over the latter had
quickly faded as Cassie prodded him to keep
watching until he now, furtively, looked forward
to the nights when she felt like marathon-ing four or
five episodes. They were almost through Season 3.
Maybe tonight they would finish it.

The man hobbled over from a poorly lit
pseudo-alley formed by the gap between a large
brick wall and a much smaller three story
townhouse. The space between was not more
than four or five feet wide. The only light washing
into that alley came from the street light on St. Ann.
It penetrated enough for Thad to see the way
ended sharply at another brick wall, darker than the
others with a thin, narrow door recessed upon it.

At first Thad assumed the man was one of
the homeless vagabonds who wandered the
Quarter at seeming random. For the kind of city
New Orleans was these people were surprisingly
rare and out of sight, especially in the Quarter.
Thad supposed they were not good for tourism or
the image of the neighborhood. Young, homeless
punks and queers and queens were another
matter: most of these could be seen without trouble
on major street corners. In front of bars and cafes
and open-air restaurants; hotels with easy
bathroom access. Truly bedraggled, cracked-out
homeless people were rare.

It took a snap moment for Thad to realize this

man was not one of *those*. He was black though. Thad instinctively missed a step.

"Say" the man said. "You believeded in God?"

Thad blinked in confusion. It was, possibly, the last question he expected to be asked at such a moment by such a man in such a place. He easily could have expected something along the lines of "Wanna hookup?" or "Want some hard?" first.

Thad was a striking man. Tall and thick, fresh-faced and younger in appearance than he actually was. Though he had put on some weight since partnering up with Cassie he was still muscular underneath. He wore clothes which made it obvious enough. Fags were always coming on to him in the Quarter. A situation he had, after initial creep-titude had worn off, gotten used to. Even been flattered by, in a gross way.

And drugs... those were *everywhere* in the Quarter. Someone not using them, buying them, or selling them was rarer among the constant population of residents than the random vagabond he had assumed this man to be. But a *Jesus* freak? That was *TRULY* rare. Outside of festivals.

"*Um..*" Thad stuttered, unsure what to say.

The man sidled up closer. Now he was under the light Thad could see him clearly. Stoop-shouldered, fat and older, with a jowly face and bug-eyes. He was quite ugly. But his skin shone in the lit dark, a deep, lustrous black stark in contrast to the unseemliness of his features. He was at least sixty, possibly older. Yet his voice sounded young. The word which popped into Thad's mind was *spry*.

"I axed if you believeded in God?" the man repeated. His smile was a mass of white teeth, straight and large. Almost too large for the size of his face. Intimidatingly large. "It ain't no *hard* question, son."

Thad was an atheist. He liked to think of himself "an atheist's atheist." He believed all religion to be mummery and chicanery, at times serving a useful purpose. Most often not. Religious texts to him were just that: texts. Books. Fantasy novels. Fairy tales. Magic realism of the worst sort. He
had read actual fantasies as young man. Dragonlance novels, *Harry Potter*, that sort of thing. It had inspired him to become a writer, or to try at least. He had never found religious texts resonated in the same way as those fantasy fictions had. It bothered Cassie he was an atheist. He knew she wanted to *turn* him.

She's a Unitarian after all.

It was not surprising to her or Thad he always replied, eventually: "NO." *Emphatically.*

The man snorted. He moved closer, steps jerky and strange, like he was being moved as opposed to moving on his own. A smile stayed plastered across his face, inviting yet weird. The man reached out a hand, gnarled with longish fingernails glistening under the street light. Pale against the darkness of the stranger's skin and gently curved around each finger; the tips just starting to point downward. Thad had never seen nails like them on a man, not even a drag queen.

"*He* believed in *you*, though."

The man was too close now. Near enough Thad could look down on the top of his balding head, curled wisps of white and black hair tight against the man's scalp, the rest shining black. A well-formed head, all in all, as if to spite the face it bore. But he smelled funny, like vanilla pipe tobacco and dust. Thad got a deep breath of it and sneezed. For a brief moment he lost his sense of place during the sneeze, with his eyes closed for a microsecond. When he regained equilibrium the man had moved again, back towards the alley and the shadows.

"He done chose *you*, boy. Remember that when it happen, cuz it *gon'* happen. And when it *do*, you best be thankful of Him, cuz nothin' make God madder than someone who takes his gifts and don't says *thank you*."

Without another word the man melted into the alley and went inside the door. Thad watched in startled amazement, heard sounds coming from inside the door, the slam of something he thought was a domino on a table maybe. Laughter, rough and raucous, and aggravated yelling. A plume of smoke whirled out of the door before it slammed shut. A half-second later the street lamp exploded sending a shower of sparks down on Thad. He screamed and covered his head with his hands.

Moments later, breathing hard, Thad looked around and saw he was still alone. The street was dark between street lamps and he shivered as he pulled his arms back down.

"Quit being silly Thad".

"Just a coincidence. He's just a crazy old man and street lights DO explode."

After that he felt better.

Cassie!

His steps hurried towards their apartment, his hope for a Buffy marathon coming back to mind. He was almost there when he heard the first unusual sound. On Burgundy a small group of people were a couple of yards ahead: two women and two men. Beyond them, three teenagers wearing caps and low-slung jeans. Further ahead, far down, maybe ten full blocks, were a pair of headlights from an oncoming car.

Bang!

A solitary gunshot rang out. Much as he had when the street lamp exploded, Thad covered his head with his hands and arms, this time he also ducked down. Only the sound of laughter brought him back up.

The two men and two women were looking

directly at him. Pointing, snickering. He had yelled and not realized it. The three teens had turned as well. Their expressions were too far off, too ahead in the darkness to be clearly seen.

"What a dumbass!" one of the men snorted. "Place is full of them. Freaks, crackheads, losers, you know..."

One of the women, blond and perky laughed. A twittering sound.

"Totally. It's why I don't come here much except during Mardi Gras. How far IS the restaurant Trish?"

A larger, robust woman in her mid-thirties with a sour mouth said: "Two blocks over, come on, leave them crazies alone."

More laughter and the four turned away.

Thad, breathing hard, looked around in poorly suppressed terror.

I HEARD a gunshot!

But how was that possible? Clearly the other people around had NOT heard it. Thad shook his head. Tried to clear it, get his bearings back. Maybe the old man had unsettled him. Maybe he was just tired from a long day of dealing with his family back in Metairie. They disapproved of his decision to quit UNO; to write full time. Despite his recent acceptance of a short story to the New Yorker.

THE NEW YORKER!

He wanted to shout at them. He had *made* it

yet they still disapproved.

Idiots.

He needed to get home.

Cassie!

Pushing his body back upright, ignoring the cold wind gusting down the street, Thad started walking again. Careful to stay on the opposite side of the street from the foursome and the teens. Far enough back he would not have to interact with them. Ahead the twin lights, like numinous square eyes crossed the next intersection down the block and slowly approached. For a second the lights hypnotized Thad. He slowed nearly to a stop. Shaking his head again, rough and more insistent this time, he leaned against a high stoop for some deep breaths.

Calm the fuck down, Thad. Damn!

Then he heard *it* again.

Bang!

A solitary gunshot. Only this time it was followed by screams. The squeal of tires. Loud music. A very small, distinct thud. Slowly; everything felt so slow then, his first time ever experiencing such a long, drawn moment.

He had tried, unsuccessfully, to write such a moment, to adequately detail the sussuration of sensation, the periodization of bits of information like what he had just felt. Each detail hit his brain distinctly. Clear and carefully enough Thad could have labeled each individually, examined them at leisure, like photographic stills.

The car was now even with him. Occupied by four people, none of them looking in Thad's direction. The interior of the car was very dark, as was all the clothing Thad could make out. Bass thumped like a slowed heartbeat from the car. Between beats he heard the men inside, they were definitely men, laughing. Thad was frozen as the tires spun, kicking up flakes of asphalt and rubber which seemed to float through the late night air like dust motes.

Across the street the foursome collapsed in on itself, huddling around the man who had called Thad a dumbass. That man was falling to the pavement, a gentle flutter disturbing his hair as he drifted downward. Not more than a step away the three teens were flying, arms stretched forward into diving positions. Each one aiming to land behind a massive and high concrete stoop.

Trish, the brash and chunky brunette, had her mouth opened mid-scream. She fell inward, arms stretching outward, hands opening, reaching, for the falling man. The perky blond had a similar expression on her face, but her mouth hung lower. Her shock seemed greater judged by the wideness of her eyes: the rime of white around blue irises bright in the night. The fourth, another man, was in the process of catching the falling man, or attempting to do so. Everything sped up again.

Squealing tires squelched out all other
noises. The image of the man, fallen, a pool of
blood spreading out beneath him overcame all
other sights. Once Thad reacted the car
had already turned on Rampart Street, hauling ass.
The three teens ran in the opposite direction,
pulling at their baggy pants or comically holding
down their caps as they ran. Thad looked over at
the foursome and caught the eyes of the blond
woman, also frozen: in confusion and terror, as she
looked at him.

"Help US!" she shouted. "He's been SHOT!"

Thad fumbled for his iPhone. Dialed 911.
Told the operator what had happened. He did not
move closer to the group. They hardly seemed to
notice. The girl had gone back to staring down at
the man, presumably her boyfriend. Wailing in
grief. Thad sat down on the stoop to wait for the
police, lost.

The commotion of the police ratcheted up,
the questions startled Thad each time. Causing
him to shake his head in confusion. As though he
had seen lips move but heard nothing that made
sense and required a repeat.

"Uh, what?" he said several times. Annoying
the detective taking notes.

"Christ, kid! Are you *slow*?" the man drawled.
"Was the car a Cadillac or not?"

"I don't know. It happened so fast... I..." Thad
stuttered. The detective waved him off lazily. He

had taken Thad's information down but Thad knew the man would not be contacting him. If his expression was any clue. He had given no useful information. His stuttering responses had made nothing clear. Other than the fact that he had heard the gunshot *before* it happened.

Hadn't he?

Thad shuddered to remember it. Moments, maybe even a solid minute or longer before the car had rolled past and shot at the people on the street. He *HAD* heard a gunshot.

But it's New Orleans! It's the French Quarter!

Gunshots were not such rare things. Maybe he had just heard a *different* gunshot, a farther off one. Because *that* would make sense.

Except he could remember the moment so clearly.

The foursome laughing, the teens lolling forward, none of them aware of the first gunshot, the distant one. Was it possible they had somehow NOT heard it, though he had?

He knew it was *possible*. No matter how many times he told himself that it *must* be so - as his feet slowly steered him towards his apartment - he did not believe it.

I HEARD it. Before it happened.

This refrain kept disconnecting his attempts to rationalize what he knew was not possible. Then, almost as an afterthought, he remembered the strange man who had stopped him on the street. Who had asked him about God. Suddenly Thad was running.

He saw flashing lights ahead. Turned down a different street. Eager to avoid being seen running. Stopped for further questioning. The man who had been shot was gone. In an wailing ambulance. His friends huddled together in the dark distance. Whispering fretfully.

Thad caught only that slight glimpse of the remaining scene before he whisked down a cross street. On, towards the corner where he had been asked about God.

The circuitous route complete, Thad stopped. Huffing, under the busted street lamp, he looked up at it warily. He was not a fanciful person, not anymore.   Though he was trying to be a writer. He did not write fantasy novels, or magic realism or fairy tales. Serious attempts at literary fiction, sometimes surreal when the mood struck him or after watching a good episode of Lost or Buffy, these were what he tried to write. He did not *BELIEVE* in fanciful things.

In magic. In ghosts. In God. In the supernatural.

He was not willing to accept the busted light overhead could mean something, that it might be connected, however tenuously, however strangely, to the man who had asked him if he "believed."

Yet here he stood.

Nervously hopping from heel to heel under

the busted lamp, staring at the pitch black door, knowing he would not be able to rest until he had at least tried to find out.   He sighed loudly, startling himself by the strength of the noise he made - there was no one else around - only the sound of an occasional car a street or two over. Thad strode forward into the dark alley, towards the door. He was hazardous in his steps, taking each carefully after he had passed the edges of the building and the large brick wall.

Once he was encased in shadows he turned his head backwards. Stared at the street beyond. Which from the alley was garishly bright and well lit, even busy. Two people walked past, a gay couple, holding hands, oblivious to his presence.

Thad turned back toward the door. His night vision was balked. Everything was the darkest of blacks. He thrust his arms out, knowing the door was not much further ahead.   Grasping with his fingers, each digit flexing and jumping in near singularity, none of it visible to Thad, he moved forward.

Just as his fingers brushed against something solid his face was flood by light. He nearly toppled forward.

The door had swung open from the inside. Memory of what had been happening there earlier:

the sound of dominoes crashing hard against a table, raucous laughter, billowing smoke...

These things all came back to Thad. He

expected this to still be the scene. But it was not.

"What in'na hell you wont?" a round-faced, toothless black man asked.

His cheeks were large and pressed upwards against his eyes making them look slitted. Furrowed, precise rows of arching skin began halfway back from his bushy eyebrows. Descended past where Thad could see.

An arm held up against the brightness of the light, Thad saw only bits of the man at first. His arm blocked the rest. The man's head turned. He shouted, "Some crazy white kid done showed up."

Laughter from behind. Though Thad could not see anyone else. He blinked furiously, hoping to clear his vision. To excise spots flaring up across his field of vision like insects. He waved at some of them, vainly. More laughter followed this.

"Boy? Is you ra-tarded?"

"I.." Thad started, but his mouth snapped shut.

What was he going to say? What was he going to ask? Oh by the way is there a guy in there who somehow gave me the ability to hear a gunshot before it happened?

The very silliness struck him forcefully. He was standing in a strange doorway, looking utterly foolish. About to ask the most ridiculous questions. Of a stranger!

"Sorry. Wrong door." Thad said, looking away from the fat, bald man.

"Ain't no wrong do's here abouts. You here fo' sommin?" The man said and smiled. His toothless gums, the first Thad had ever seen, seemed grotesque. Like tiny appendages on an octopus or slug. Still, Thad had no idea what to say.

"Get on then." the man said after a long pause. He shut the door leaving Thad with the echo of the laughter from within. The smell of smoke from Kool cigarettes. In the dark, Thad stared at the doorway for some time. His thoughts unable to coalesce, before he finally turned and walked slowly away. Several times he was sure the door was about to open again.

The man from before, not the fat bald man, but the other man, was going to come out. But that did not happen. Thad even stood under the busted lamp again, alternately staring up at it and then at the door. Waiting. He saw no sign of the man from earlier, though several more groups of people did wander past, including a trio of gay men. One of whom whistled, cat-called at him.

By the time Thad made it back to the apartment, Cassie was in a near panic. He was hours late. Had left his phone in the apartment. She had clearly been worried to distraction. Her curvy, thick body crashed into his as soon as he was in the door. Wrapping around him with warmth and squeezing arms.

"I was SO worried!" she said.

Thad held her. Leaned down to smell her

hair. It was fruity and smokey at the same time, from her shampoo and whatever she had cooked. In the other room the television was on. The sound was too low for him to hear. Cassie sobbed, halfheartedly against his heavy chest. Their bodies, for the moment, heaved together in safety.

All Thad wanted was to tell her about the gunshot. Cassie was exactly the kind of fanciful he was not. She was trying to be a writer as well. This had drawn them so tightly together in the first place. Yet where he wished to write the *real* and make it grand, larger, more *emphatic*, she wanted to embellish and draw in. Grasp the mystical and the unreal, the numinous. Make it seem cleverly, simply: normal. He, if only admitting it to himself, did not particularly like her writing. More specifically what she chose to write. YA fantasy. Dystopian worlds. Off-kilter romances. Most shrouded in the fanciful and fantastic, the supernatural and luminously spiritual. Though he did not know for certain, he suspected she felt the same about *his* writing.

Still, he might have known - of all people he could confess to - Cassie would be the most understanding. But he did not confess.

"I got...caught up." Thad said. He described the gunshot. But not his warning of it. Otherwise in detail. He did not talk about the man who asked him if he believed in God. Nor the exploded street lamp. The possibility Cassie would believe him bothered him more than the opposite, that she might think him crazy. Or a liar.

As he held her he made a decision. He *HAD* heard that gunshot *before* it happened. Not some other, different gunshot, but that one *exactly*.

Later that night as he tried to fall asleep, Cassie's heavy warmth next to him, Thad kept hearing the gunshot until he dreamt of it as well.

Four days later, Thad walked with Cassie through the Marigny. An adjunct neighborhood of the French Quarter, full of New Orleans character: cafes, bars, restaurants and lots of homes. Two hours after sunset the streets were full of revelers.

Unlike the Quarter, the party always began earlier in the Marigny. In fact, many of the party-goers in this part of the city were locals as opposed to the swarms of tourists in the Quarter and off Canal. A club ahead was opened to the. street, its four sets of shutter doors swung wide to let the thumping music of a live band filter out into the streets. Small groups of people with plastic cups in their hands moved in and
out of the opened doors. Thad, his arm around Cassie, walked toward this club. People they knew, if not well, smiled at them. Some said hello, but they did not stop for more than simple pleasantries.

Once they had reached the club, Thad relaxed. He had tried hard over the days since the gunshot to think of anything but that night. For the most part he had succeeded. Outside of his dreams at least. He and Cassie had not spent a night home after that first, except to return for sleep when Thad was exhausted enough he would not lay awake. A hostage to his doubts.

Ordinarily Thad would have done some writing at night. It was his routine as much as Cassie's was during the early morning after breakfast. He could not focus. Did not want to be alone with his thoughts. Even watching television shows didn't help. He dreaded the coming week when he would no longer be able to avoid writing: he had pieces due for the Times-Picayune. Would soon have more. His week's worth of vacation had likely piled up the work as well.

Cassie, who did not work and lived off a monthly stipend from her mother and step-father, was a full-bore writer. She was committed to writing as a career. Her family was behind her: they believed and expected she would produce a best-selling novel. A new *Hunger Games* or *Twilight*. She believed it as well. Humility usually kept her from outright saying so.

Daily effort was not something she lacked. She had not yet let Thad read her latest iteration of her novel, so he couldn't say if he thought as she did. Their vacation had not stopped her from writing but she had noticed his stoppage. Thankfully, she had not said anything about it.

Thad relaxed to the music, some kind of jazzy ska. Some hipster-ish young people danced on the sidewalk, others leaned and preened. Still others sipped drinks. A pair of shaggy, baggy homeless-looking teens even leaned together against a wall smoking a joint. A smiling, tall man with a precise goatee wore a hat with a pinwheel and bubble machine on it. The whole scene calmed Thad. Conventional in an unconventional way.

Over the last four days he had been sure to choose such places, places where he would *NOT* hear any gunshots.

"This music is...different." Cassie murmured. She smiled as she said it. "Want a beer?"

He nodded and she left. Thad took a seat at one of the high stools just inside the open shutter doors. The band hardly held his attention: a group of thirty-ish men swaying and jamming with sad, earnest effort. When Cassie returned, she slammed two bottles of Corona on the table. The sound was so much like a gunshot Thad jumped off his stool and nearly fell to the floor. Cassie laughed and rubbed his shoulder in consolation.

Most of the rest of night passed in easy laughter, cold beer and gentle head bobbing for Thad. Cassie also appeared to have a good time. She even ran into her friend May - the bohemian girl's mottled hair cut into a ridiculously short, overly boyish style. Thad smiled at May, though he did not much like her. She struck him as a user. The kind of person who lacks any fundamental sense of self and purpose. Who sponges off empathetic people like Cassie who are both driven and needy. Still, he smiled and joked with her as well as the tall, skinny oddball of a boy-man she had with her. Thad did not bother trying to remember his name.

May danced: an annoying forward toss of her hips and crass swaying of her arms evocative of her quasi-Goth mentality. Thad had seen this exact dance any number of times by any number of utterly replaceable May-Goths. He found it revolting.

That could have just been because it was May. Cassie danced with her for a time. The boy-man having disappeared to do whatever it was such men did.

Cassie came back, sweaty and giggly. "This *is* good music." she said, taking a sip of Thad's warm beer. "I'm glad you suggested it!"

Thad smiled at her, genuinely pleased she was enjoying herself. He titled his head to the side and considered, glad she had found the music to be good. "May might come back to the apartment with us... if that's OK with you." Cassie said, almost as an afterthought. She took another sip of his beer. It was almost gone.

"OK." Thad said, knowing there was really no other response. He and Cassie did not fight much. May would always be a fight though. She would likely end up staying with them for *weeks* maybe *months* before the rootless bitch got bored and moved on. He looked over and saw May flirting with some bull-necked older man who looked as though he could not decide if she was worth the effort of indulging. Thad snorted, full of understanding.

He had just reached over, to grab his beer, finish it off when he heard *the* sound. Soft, as though from a distance, but clear, easily identifiable.

A gunshot.

Followed by several more in quick succession. Thad could not count them. He dropped his beer to the ground. It smashed into curvy pieces of brown glass at Cassie's feet, drenching her toes. She shrieked. For a brief second Thad thought heard the gunshots before he realized it was just because her toes had suddenly gotten wet.

"THAD" Cassie said, long-suffering. "Are you drunk? Off BEER?" She laughed. Flung her foot to toss off the liquid.

He sat on the stool in stunned silence, turning his head this way and that, searching for some sign the sound had been heard by others. When that was obviously not forthcoming he counted as he looked for the source of the shots. With dread. Which increased on each whispered number. There were no ominous headlights. No scary predators. No gang members.

May had just wandered over to their table. A bemused and desultory expression on her wide-mouthed face. If he had not been so preoccupied he would have yet again thought how much she looked like a fish. His counting reached eight. Nine. Ten.

Gunshots.

People screamed. Thad's head whipped around to the source of the noise. It was not close. He jumped up, started running, not away from the noise, but towards it. Behind him he heard Cassie cry out: "*THAD!*"

He was four blocks away from the club when he stumbled across Frenchman street. Turned first one way then the other, confused and out of breath.

And there it was.

A man lying in a steadily spreading pool of blood sun-setting across the pavement. Thad just stared at him. The man did not move. Neither did Thad. People peeked out of their homes and nearby restaurants. The only club on the block was farther down. The loudness of the music must have drowned out the gunshots.

"Somebody call the cops!" Thad heard. A door opened somewhere behind him. He was tackled to the ground before he knew what had happened. A large weight held him down. There was more shouting.

"Don't move!"

Thad, rather large himself, snapped out of his reverie and struggled back. Eventually throwing the weight off. It was the bull-necked man from the club. The one who had been waffling over May. Thad blinked. Realized it was not the man, he only looked similar: large, fat and bald, with the aging bulk of a former body-builder gone to seed.

"Why you shoot that man?" the tackler shouted as he got to his feet, his beady eyes searching Thad's hands for a weapon.

Thad, brought out of his doubts by anger, shouted back, "I DIDN'T, ASSHOLE!"

The man blinked. Tilted his head to the side, considering. It was obviously difficult work. "Then who did?"

Thad shrugged, defeated. He wanted to run away, but for some reason didn't. It was confirmed now: he had heard the gunshots before they happened. A kind of despair settled over him. He tilted on his feet, woozy.

"Whoa fella..." the tackler said, coming over to steady him, "It's just some damn blood. Didya see who dunnit?"

Thad shook his head no. After another glance at the dead body, another down the street he heard the sound of sirens. He shoved the tackler away. Starting running. No clear direction in his mind. Other than away.

He ran like this until he was winded. Could run no longer. He found himself leaning against a wall, heaving in deep, hard breaths. His side hurt. Feet on fire. Distantly he heard more sirens over his panting. Hands on knees a police car came into view and zoomed past in the direction of the gunshot victim.

Once he caught his breath, Thad looked around. He had run into the French Quarter. It was nearly midnight. There were people about, some of whom gave him appraising glances. Others who cast suspicious glares at him. Thad tried to ignore them all and focus.

Cassie.

"Shit." Thad said and started running back towards the Marigny and the club. Two blocks away he found Cassie. With May. Walking away from the club and towards the direction of their apartment in the Quarter. No sign of boy-man or bull-neck. Just Cassie.

And May.

"Thad!" Cassie shouted and trotted towards him.

"Are you OKAY?" she said, tense.

May hung back and just watched them. Thad put her out of his mind, already trying to forget she was around.

"Yeah. I'm..." but he didn't know what to say. He gulped. "I'm OK. Really. I just freaked out."

"Yeah! You and everyone else! After those gunshots people just kinda froze, then some guy shouted, something, something about a gun and people started running." Cassie said, somewhat breathless. Her face was flush with blood. May finally strolled up, leaned against the wall, alternately looking one way down Bourbon, then Rampart, methodically.

"You *saw* the gunman?" Thad said, confused.

Cassie shook her head. "No. But people were saying something … like maybe somebody did. I dunno. Where did you *GO*?"

"I went..." Thad started. He decided not to lie. "To see what happened." Concern washed over Cassie's features. May snorted.

"What did you see?" Cassie said, her voice steady. Not at all morbid.

"A dead guy. Blood. Some asshole tackled me and thought *I* had shot the guy." Thad said. "Then I just freaked. I ran away. To find you"

"Wow." Cassie said and released him from embrace. "We should go home. This is what? Two shootings in a week you've been around? Man! New Orleans is just crazy violent, right? May?"

May sidled closer. Nodded. Laughed. Meanly. "People get killed in the voodoo city, you know it!"

Thad wanted to sneer. He was emotionless towards May now. She was not from New Orleans to his knowledge. Not Louisiana! Though he did not know where she actually *was* from he found her voodoo comment to be insipid. Cassie rolled her eyes.

Later, after they had gotten into bed and May had gotten settled on the sofa, Thad lay awake, unable to sleep. Staring at the ceiling. His mind whirled recounting the night, re-counting the seconds between his initial hearing of the gunshot. The period between what he was thought of as a "pre-echo" and the *actual* shots. For long minutes he would muse he was some kind of super-hero in the making. With this ability he could save people! He planned the logistics of it. How to hear and respond. What he could do and not do. After a while these plans became horribly stupid. They fell apart.   He despaired. Instead of thinking himself a hero he decided he was cursed. He longed to share the secret with someone. Anyone. But could not. He could not bring himself to tell Cassie. She fell asleep and slept soundly. Sometime after 2 A.M. he got out of bed. Went out of their bedroom. Restless.

The living room was dark. He didn't see May sitting up on the sofa. Her arms wrapped around her knees. She was invisible until she spoke.

"*Something's* weird about you." May said, in very May-like fashion.

Thad froze. He scowled. "Leave me *alone* May."

He started to call her a name, but held back. She laughed. A trilling, grating sound.

"How long are you going to stay *this* time?" he asked. Not really expecting an answer only wanting to be mean. Remind her of her frequent impositions on him and Cassie.

"As long as I *need* to *Thad*." May said. "*Cassie* said it was OK." She laughed again. Thad sighed wearily.

"Whatever, May. Just leave me the hell alone."

"Fine, Thaddie-cakes." May said, In a falsely seductive tone. One she had used before. The first time she stayed with them. When she had tried to seduce him. Thad had vehemently told her *no.* Even as she promised it would be the *filthiest, most amazing sex* he had ever known. May clearly thought this would intrigue him into cheating on Cassie. It only showed how little she knew of him or Cassie. How much Thad loved Cassie and she him.

Faithless.

That's what May was. Even if Cassie couldn't or wouldn't see it. Partly to escape May, partly to walk and think, Thad left the apartment. Wandered the streets of the Quarter. People were about, leaving bars on Bourbon for cars parked down side streets. Swaying drunkenly. Singing and carrying on, some doing more. Thad paid little attention to any of them.

He had wandered across the whole of the Quarter and reached Canal before he stopped and looked around. Canal was more brightly lit than the rest of the Quarter. Busier at than any other street aside from Bourbon. Thad lost himself in the small crowds, weaving between people. Hardly noticing them. His feet kept him wandering until he had passed out of the brightly lit area into the more residential, tree-shaded area of Canal street. Full of row houses. Law firms. The occasional McDonald's or Burger King.

Still he kept walking until he was about to cross a major street. He was not sure which one. His thoughts had again been circling the pre-echo of gunshots and what it meant for his belief system.

Did it mean there *was* a God? A Devil?

Was all of that supernatural nonsense true?

Or was there some logical, albeit strange physical explanation? COULD there be one? He was wrestling with this very question when overhead another street lamp exploded into darkness.

Thad stopped and looked up. There was nothing to see. Just a darkened light. The falling residue of sparks. He made his way back to the apartment just as it was beginning to get light outside.

May was awake. Eating cereal from a huge metal bowl. One of Cassie's precious mixing bowls. Thad, not surprised, noted it was *his* Crunch Berries.

"Cassie hates when you do that." Thad said.

May snorted.

"I figured it out, you know." May said.

"Figured out what, you leech?" Thad said.

May unwound herself from the sofa. The blanket she had wrapped around her lower body fell to the floor. She was wearing only a tank top - one of Cassie's which fit her thin frame in billowing folds - and a pair of black panties. May's legs were stick-like. Scattered with drawn scars, in obvious patterns, as though she had attacked herself with a razor blade. It was not at all attractive to Thad. Still, he did look, and May saw it. She laughed.

"That you're evil." May said, and she moved closer to him.
As she moved one of the straps on the tank top fell from her shoulder. Sending the whole thing cascading down to her ankles. Her bare breasts, mere pointed lumps of pink-topped flesh, both curved downward on the side near her armpit giving her chest the look of a frown below two pink eyes. Thad snorted in disgust.

Flushed, whether by excitement or anger, May shimmied the tank back up and rested the straps on her shoulders.

"I know all about that kind of stuff, I'm SENSITIVE to it." May said, too matter-of-factly. Not quite off-hand. But close enough.

"What the fuck are you talking about? God! And put some clothes on!" Thad said harshly, through clenched teeth. He made a point of moving away from her, putting a chair between them. In case Cassie came in.

May's head tilted to the side. Her eyes narrowed, a devious look, as though she were deciding whether to let him in on a secret. A terrible secret. Thad's insides twisted. He had to put a great effort into not grabbing at his lower stomach. Even still he grunted.

What did she know?

"You've got a *demon* in you, and I can *SEE* it." May said, with sure confidence. She slithered closer to him so only the chair's breadth separated them. Leaned forward, pressed one knee on an armrest, both of her hands on the chair's back. The tank draped forward and exposed her thin, bony chest, her barely dangling breasts. Thad coughed in discomfort.

"But don't worry. I won't tell Cassie..." May said.

"Tell her WHAT?? You whore-troll!" Thad countered. "She doesn't believe in that shit anymore than I do!"

May snorted. Adjusted the tank top, hid her breasts. But otherwise she hardly moved.

"She'll believe *this*. We *are* best friends, you know. She *knows* I can see things sometimes. I've done it for her."

Thad was intrigued despite himself. He hated the idea of bringing May into his confidences. She had opened a door he could not close though.

"It's not a demon." Thad said. "I can...*hear*...gunshots before they happen."

May's head tilted to the side again.

"*That's* it?"

"Yeah, like ten seconds before it happens. I hear it. It sounds like a weird pre-echo. Then it happens. It's happened twice now."

May stood up straight. Her face clouded and distant
it almost looked like she was about to fall asleep. Eyelids softly fluttering towards closing. They snapped fully open, eyes wide enough her entire iris was surrounded by a chrysalis of white.

"I want you to hear *death*. I think you will listen to me more now." May said. Her eyes went back to normal. She shook her head gently.

"What?" she said in obvious confusion.

Cassie came into the room. May saw her and ran toward her giggling, "Mama Cass!"

They hugged. Chittered. Talked nonsense until Cassie noticed Thad and came to hug him as well.

"I was worried. I woke up and you were gone." Cassie murmured into his chest.

He stroked her head lovingly.

"It's OK. I just needed to walk. I couldn't sleep." Thad said, looking over Cassie's head with a warning glance at May. Hitching up the tank further against her chest she exposed the top half of her panties and grinned.

"Well, let me see about breakfast then." Cassie said. "You hungry?"

Thad nodded instinctively. Cassie went into the kitchen. May plopped back down on the sofa and wrapped the blanket around her lower half.

"Don't." Thad said harshly. May made a locking motion around her mouth. But her eyes sparkled with meanness. Thad knew it was only a matter of time before she told Cassie about his secret. Probably before the end of the day. The first time he left them alone.

Thad growled a sigh and went into the kitchen. Cassie was moving from fridge to stove. Pulling eggs and milk, butter and jam. "Eggs and toast OK?" she asked, looking over her shoulder at him, beaming. He did not smile back. Cassie picked up his mood. Shut the fridge door. Turned to face him.

"What is it?" Cassie said, "Is it May? She doesn't have anywhere else to go. I *know* it bothers you, but..."

Thad shook his head "no."

"Then what is it?" Cassie said on the verge of a pout, chewing on her lower lip.

"I have to tell you something." Thad said, trying not to give the pronouncement the air of finality it ended up having anyway. Color drained from Cassie's face.

"You're not...*leaving me*...are you?" Cassie said. Crestfallen, frozen against the fridge.

"NO!" Thad said, a touch louder than he might have wished. Cassie winced and pouted fully. "Sorry." He moved close, wrapped her up in his arms, his hands just above her ass. His forearms pressing against the soft fat of her waist.

"Something *fucked up* is happening to me. And I'm *scared*. And I didn't want to tell you about it, but I can't hold it in....and I don't know *HOW* but I think May *KNOWS* what it is."

Cassie's expression was bewildered. For the first time in terms of May, obviously suspicious. Cassie knew well Thad did not like May in *that* manner. He had been quite candid about what constituted an attractive woman to him.

Thick and curvy, intelligent and kind. In a word: Cassie herself.

"It's not what you think." Thad said, registering where Cassie's thoughts must be going. *She* thought she was too fat. Too dumpy for him. He knew she would always think this in some manner about herself. She had mostly kept it to herself before. He would never have known she felt this way, if not for May. And his innate desire to understand people as a writer.   Still, he had never let on he knew this about Cassie. "The other night..."

Thad related the whole story. From the moment the man asked him about God. The busted street lamp. Everything that had happened since. Cassie listened intently, not interrupting once. Not even moving much. She brushed hair from her face twice, but little else. When he was done Thad heaved a sigh of relief. A weight was lifted now he had told Cassie.

"And May thinks this ... demon? She wants you to hear death?" Cassie asked, slowly.

Thad nodded.

"She's definitely into all that stuff, you know. She reads Tarot. Practices witchcraft and rituals and stuff. Or at least she used to. I don't know if she does much of any of it anymore. She did a lot when we were kids. Once she gave me a book on candle burning rituals so I could make a boy at school fall in love with me....I left in my sock drawer. I got my Mom to buy the candles. I did the ritual. Then my mom found the book. She *burned* the book in the backyard. After I told her May gave it to me she wouldn't let her come over again." Cassie said and laughed weakly.

"Maybe she's just messing with your head?" Cassie offered. "She likes to do that. People give off vibes. I'll give her *that.* And she is really good at picking them up. She plays on it. Mostly to scare people. You shouldn't take it seriously."

Thad gaped at her. It was as if she had missed the whole point of the story. He got annoyed.

"This ISN'T about May!" Thad half-roared. He loomed over her, menacingly. He was not aware of his looming, nor had he intended to do it. He just did it. Cassie shrank back and away. The fridge behind her kept her from being able to move very far. Thad hardly noticed.

"I can *HEAR* these gunshots before they happen, Cassie! Something is *REALLY* wrong in my head and it's *terrifying* me! I don't care that your whorebeast best friend thinks it's a *demon*. I just want it to *STOP!*" He yelled at her.

Cassie shook and began to cry. May came in from the living room. Put herself between Thad and Cassie - using her thin, stick-like body as a flimsy shield. May's eyes held only reproach. She smoothed and stroked Cassie's head. Exactly as Thad had done only minutes before.

"Dammit, Thad! What the *fuck* is wrong with you?" May said. Cassie was sobbing hard now. Thad realized he had never yelled at her before. An overwhelming shame crested inside him. His jaw worked in unsaid remonstrations before he could squeeze words out.

"Cassie! I'm SO sorry!" Thad said, rushing forward. Easily brushing May aside. He shoved her out of the kitchen. The thin girl squawking and batting her fists at him uselessly. Cassie shied away from him at first. Eventually she stopped resisting and collapsed into his arms, sobbing hard. He stroked her head and murmured apology after apology.

Finally, Cassie moved to gently disengage. She kept his arms around her as she looked up at him.. Her eyes were still wet with tears. "I know. You were so scary! I've never seen you like that!

And I was thinking about what you said May said. About death! Because you know I've never had anyone die on me and I broke up with.. ." she gulped and tossed her head defiantly. She never said her last boyfriend's name. Ever. "*him* because he couldn't understand how much this bothered me! That as a writer I had no knowledge of death! Of something so *IMPORTANT* to life, so *INTEGRAL*. And just now .. ." Cassie gulped again, taking in giant breaths of air "....was sure you were going to *kill* me."

Thad squeezed her hard into himself. "Never. Never. *NEVER!*" He kept on repeating it until he was crying. "I'll love you forever, Cassie."

Outside neither of them saw May lighting carefully arranged candles in the living room and chanting under her breath. Her head cocked to the side. Eyes wide in the flickering orange flame-light. Her puffy, wide-lipped mouth occasionally smiling at nothing in particular, especially not the two of them.

Chapter 16 – The Players

"Ain't nobody gon' beat Miami this year..." Trump said, his sunken lips wrapping the words in a drawl. The swirl of cigarette smoke undulated around his bald head and fat, dumpling body as he hustled away from the door. The strange white sucka forgotten. Strange white suckas knocking on that particular door were not a common occurrence.

Trump had been in mid-point about Miami's prospects for the coming college football season. He did not like being interrupted mid-point, even though he hardly ever had anything new to say.

"Who was at tha do', Trump?" Kools asked, not looking up from his dominoes.

Trump trundled the last few steps and frowned. He puckered his lips at Kools, made a snort-like sound. Trump had been about to explain about the sucka at the door before Kools asked. Heaving his fifty-seven year old bulk down on a folding metal chair, Trump lifted a lit cigarette from the Harrah's Casino ashtray. Took a drag and leveled his best steely gaze at the other three men in the room, resting finally on Kools.

"Some sucka white boy." Trump said, flicking ash into the tray and taking another pull.

"Damn Kools, ain't you heard?" T-man growled. "Trump just SAID it were some crazy white sucka. Whatchu goin' deaf 'gin?"

Kools, himself somewhere between fifty and sixty, glared at T-man, went back to stroking his dominoes. "I ain't payin' no 'tention to y'all bull."

Trump flicked more ash down. "Cain't pay with something when you ain't BEEN paid..."

Everyone laughed, but Kools.

"Fuck you, Trump, old toothless sucka." Kools muttered. He lifted a domino in a flash and slammed it down on the table. The other bones rattled, causing a near deafening clang to echo through the room.

The fourth man, Laws, blew a proud gust of breath out of his nose. "You boys need to get right wit Jesus. All this cursing and what not, it GONNA come back on ya."

"Aw DAMN, Laws. Go bother somady ELSE wit tha' shit!" T-man said. "You always rassin' folks bought theyselves, when you SHOULD know God don't like tha. He like you to be MEEK. It say so in the Bible." T-man paused. "Sucka."

"Sho do!" Trump echoed, flicking ash at the casinos' logo, but also in Laws' general direction.

Laws' bug-eyed face and jowly cheeks quivered with suppressed rage.

"Sides," Kools snickered, "You *too* black to be preachin' no how, LAWS. Inside *and* out. Sucka!"

Laws bristled as he gently laid his domino down and scored ten points off Kools' slammed mistake. "Black is beautiful, that in the Bible, TOO."

"No t'aint!" T-man retorted. "Only in that fool's Bible you and them Blackies be readin'. The one say Jesus was Black and God Black and Mary Black and the Holy Ghost prolly Black too!"

They all laughed. Laws was laughing at the others, not with them. T-man set his domino down. Took a drag on his own cigarette.

"You think Pittsburgh goin' all tha way this year?" T-man said, looking at Trump as he spoke, obviously hoping to change the subject. He did not believe in the same things the others did. When they went off about religion it was
hard to shut them up or keep them from fighting to the point the game became unplayable. Trump, was nominally a Baptist. Kools a Jehovah's Witness. They did not actually go to church except when forced by a family member. Laws however did not miss church, not on Monday nights, not on Wednesday nights and definitely not on Sundays. Tuesdays and Fridays had become regular nights for dominoes, spades and gambling amongst the foursome, a tradition which stretched back to childhoods spent together in the 9th Ward of New Orleans.

Laws was part of a smallish church. Run by a fiery young preacher out of South Carolina, everyone called Bishop Mack. The church was officially called the Nubian Congregation of the Covenant. Around the area they were known simply as "Blackies." Laws preached, at times constantly, to his friends trying to convince them of the rightness of his beliefs. They usually ignored him or made fun until he moved on to football or basketball or endless re-hashings of spades and dominoes games they had played. The Blackies, aside from Laws, were an aloof lot in the neighborhood. Trump was rather sure they did NOT know Laws played with the others on Tuesdays and Fridays.

"Pitt ain't shit." Trump said. "I likes Indy this year. That new white boy gon' come up. *Watch*."

"What 'bout San Fran?" Kools said, his cigarette dangling from his lower lip as Laws placed a domino. Five points.

"They good." Trump said, a smug turn to his sunken mouth. Trump was an idiot about everything else, but blissfully unaware of it, though he DID know football.

Kools, who had gotten a college degree in prison, was by far the smartest of them. Even though he was also at times the one who least appeared so. T-man and Laws had been in prison as well, as had Trump, all four of them had served time on the same federal case for dealing crack-cocaine in the eighties. They had spent the entire time doing exactly what they were doing now: smoking and playing dominoes or spades. "But Indy better"

The conversation continued in this vein for

ten minutes or so, until T-man laid down a bone and shouted, "DOMINO!"

The others groaned.

T-man had won, again. "Damn, sucka, you on a streak tonight." Trump said. "Get them cards, less play spades."

"Sore loser." T-man said, with a warm smile.

"How Ja'neice?" Kools asked Trump.

"Bad. She small, and them girls up there fuckin' wit her." Trump said as he lit another cigarette. His daughter, Ja'neice had just been sentenced to fifteen years in prison for holding her boyfriend's stash of guns and drugs and refusing to point the finger at him. Amongst his friends Trump towed the
line and expressed pride in her decision, but to her and to himself he had encouraged her to tell.

"It AIN'T worth yo' life gurl." Trump had told her. "Don't be no sucka! Ya momma don' deserve this, not over some sucka ass fool who gonna leave you soon you go in."

But Ja'neice had been unshakable. Trump had been right. Her boyfriend, LaCharles had already gotten one of T-man's sister's daughters pregnant. Worse, there were rumors LaCharles had been seen with AppleB, Kools' punk son.

Everyone knew AppleB had the AIDS. Trump thought it only a matter of time before LaCharles got it as well. He had thanked Jesus Ja'neice was in prison then. *That* way she was safe from

LaCharles and the AIDS.

"She gon' make it, Trump. She strong." Kools said, shuffling the cards. "She ain't no sucka."

"T'aint like it was for us." Laws said. "Them womens prisons nasty - they crazy like nuttin' you ever seen! Tonya tell me sturies sometimes an' it scare the Holy Shit out me what them bitches be doin'!"

"Is your Holy Shit black too, sucka?" Trump said, laughing around his cigarette. T-man and Kools snickered. Kools let Laws cut the deck. The devout, dark-skinned man frowned at Trump before cutting the cards.

"T'ain't funny." Laws muttered, handed the deck back to Kools.

Kools dealt. Laws and Trump bid first.

"What Tonya went in for 'gin?" Kools asked as T-man said, "Board. Damn."

Laws sighed. "She stabbed tha' sucka nigga in the thigh when she foun' out he had a baby by that cluck ho from the Fourth." Tonya was Laws' oldest daughter. Now an ordained minister and wife of Bishop Mack. She made Laws seem tame when it came to preaching. Of all the Blackies, Tonya was the most ardent. Nothing was ever good enough for her.
Her brand of fire and brimstone held nothing back.

Suddenly, his eyes peeking upwards from his cards, Laws seemed to realize something. He glared at the door. "Hey sucka." he said, slowly.

"You said that was a sucka white boy, ri'?"

The others paused, confused. "Befo' sucka," Laws clarified. "A crazy white boy came to the do'?"

Trump ashed his cigarette, "So?"

"When I went out earlier to get smokes, I seen some white sucka just outside the do' on the street. Lookded like he was all fulla demons! Like them faggots over deeper in the quarter. I axed him if he believeded in God and he just look at me like I'm crazy. I wonder if it the same one?"

"Whatchu think some white sucka watchin' us, Laws? One of them punk white boys?" Kools murmured.

Laws glared at Kools. After all Kools' was the one with a punk son who walked around swishin' like a female and callin himself AppleB. Getting his face all messed up from injections and wearin' women's clothes. Kools never called the boy a faggot to his face though, but Laws would and did.

"Naw. Jus' weird is all. Two white boys in the same night at that do'?" Laws murmured, "Don't nobody ever come to tha do', 'specially not no white sucka we don't know."

Nods all around. It was simple truth.

The cards played out. Laws laid black spade after black spade down. Pulling eleven books. "Y'all set like jet!" Laws trumpeted. "See that's Jesus talkin' right there! The BLACK jesus!"

"Sucka, the only *black Jesus* in here, right

here." T-man said, grabbing his crotch. Laws choked on his cigarette smoke.

"You crazy for tha' T-man. Takin' HIS name in vain like tha'! Blasphemin'! I knowed a man did tha' an had a demon get 'em, back at Beaumont."

T-man laughed and waved a dismissal. Trump and Kools both took long drags on their cigarettes and looked away. Laws took the cards. Shuffled angrily, then let Kools cut before taking the cards back to deal.

"Y'all some triflin' suckas, ya know tha'? All y'all gonna be laughin' right good when tha' fire burn yo' ass in *Hell*. Gon' be *screamin'* for some *Black Jesus* then."

"Hell I be screamin' for some black WATER." Trump crowed.

The others cawed with laughter. Except Laws, who sighed and finished dealing the cards.

"Just you watch," Laws said over his cards. He put them into place in his hand by suit and rank. "Someday you fools gon' see I's right. Wha' then? Huh? 'Oh Laws, help us get right wit God', 'C'mon Laws, tell us bout how Jesus really was a black Egyptian man!' *Watch*. It *GONNA* happen."

"Sucka would you shut the hell up and play?" Trump said, his cigarette stuck to his lip. Three cards had been laid. They were all waiting on Laws. Laws' jaw quivered and he made a sound like a bee flying too close to the ear. He was quite used to the attitude of his friends about his religion.

It had been the same when he became a Muslim in prison and before that when he was a Pentecostal. He knew what he knew. He laid down his card, a two of hearts. A losing card. It was all he could do not to smile though, he held nothing in his hand but spades after that.

"Y'all gonna see someday. God as my witness, his blessing is on me, just like i tried to give to that crazy white sucka earlier. Watch. The Black Jesus dun gimme the spirit now!"

A few moments later Laws looked up from the table just in time to see Kools' great-uncle Josephus come toddling in from the outside door. The old man was stooped with age, he was well past eighty, rounding on ninety. Old Joe lived in a house across the quarter with his grandson and daughter, both of
whom participated in the sham of a voodoo tour the old man had run for years. It irritated Laws to the extreme, because Old Joe claimed to be a man of God despite his obvious blasphemous forays into the realms of occult and voodoo. Laws made a half-growl, half-resigned sigh, a dying bumblebee. "What's that, boy?" Old Joe said, smiling his toothless smile.

"Nuttin', Unc." Laws said. Even if Old Joe wasn't a good Christian to Laws, Laws maintained the form. Old Joe was *old.*

"Is this all you boys do?" Old Joe said, the hint of a sneer obvious in his tone.. "Play dominoes,and cards and smoke? Ain't y'all got something *WORTH* doing, sides games?"

"At least we ain't busy playin' wit the devil, old man." Laws spit out before he could stop himself.

"The Devil, huh, boy?" Old Joe said, hobbling closer, leaning over him. Rheumy white eyes blinking in the dim light Old Joe murmured: "The Devil here all the time, he's a *player*, just like you. And he *win*." Josephus flicked a gnarled old, finger at Laws' ear. "Sucka."

Laws ground his teeth. Kools looked nervous and uncomfortable as if he held back a laugh. Trump's lips quivered and his eyes shone. T-man actually laughed behind his hand as he pulled out a cigarette to light. Laws glared at them all.

Josephus wasn't done.

"All you NIGGUHS," Old Joe said this word with ultimate disdain. Old Joe hated the word and it was clear. 'do is *play*. Sit around and pretend to live while you plays *A GAME*. Life *ain't* no game, boy. God *know* that. But the Devil don't. *He* think he can win and he got a *team full of demons* on his side. Just cuz *you* cain't see them don't mean they not there. I knows 'bout demons! Me and God been on speaking terms longer than you been alive. So keep playin' the game boys. But don't kid yourselfs." Old Joe coughed and cleared his throat. "Now. I only came over cause that idiot boy of yours done gone and got in trouble again. He called the house again from the Parish."

Laws sucked at the remnants of his cigarette, realized it was just filter. He pulled the nub from his mouth and ground it out in the H of Harrah's. He laid down his last card.

"Your move." he said to Trump and pushed himself away from the table to go home and see about bailing Junior out.

Chapter 17 – mms

A gentle buzz was the only sensation MikeDev felt as the mm downloaded. It was no longer new. This ability. This service however was new. He had begun implanting himself with cybernetics when he was just out of high school, long before the law allowed. Right after the North Korean War in '19. Back then mm-ods were just talk in magazines. On the web.

Everyone had said it was coming. Labs at Universities had tested it on mice. Monkeys. Pigs. Elephants. Eventually humans. The process had taken nearly forty years. Those years did not lie heavily upon MikeDev. His body was seventy percent machine now. He didn't think he *could* die a natural death. A walking experiment. One of millions around the world.

The mm-od began to slowly propagate through his mind. Sharp neural connections snapped together. Like the tingling of skin in cold air. The way a mm spread through the brain, how it leeched into separate areas, hooked around individual neurons, connected to neural nets, still left MikeDev with a profound sense of wonder. One of the few things in the world which still could.

As if in response his brain ticked off a mechanized list of locations. Each tagged with an emotional response. Syria. Afghanistan. Iran. North Korea. Egypt. Mexico. China. And most recently,

Argentina. He had been to each one, had embedded himself in the middle of conflict prone areas. All in the name of business interests who needed enhanced on-the-ground i-tel. His quadrillions of data points equated to tens of billions of dollars in income, yet hardly mattered to him anymore. What mattered was experience. He *craved* it.

WRD had ran a story about mmods and those who used them. Roughly ten years earlier. "mjkz," they had called the story. And people *like* MikeDev. But the articles dealt with *people*, not hybrids like MikeDev. Full cyberians. Society had since accepted some of its members were now part or mostly machine. Laws had been passed. Others repealed. The ebb and flow continued in debates. Cyberians had other more pressing concerns. They did what they did because they could, because they must. They could afford the long view.

Not all cyberians were so called "mjkz"; some were "rtjkz" - they actually needed to *live* events. Not just have the mm of them encoded within their enhanced brains. But those cyberians were a tiny minority. Most were closer to MikeDev. They ate mms like fine meals. Experienced what was to be experienced neither wanting nor desiring one over the other.

To the truly enlightened mind there is no difference. Experience is mm and vice-versa.

Such was wholly out of the grasp of the unaugmented mjkz.

But this was new. Open to anyone who could resolve the address. Not an easy task.

The marketplace of mms.

Some humans jokingly called it 'iRemember,' a pun on the old time service which once sold music over the web. The laugh was cheap. APPLE's censors were not fond of jokes about their history. They had discovered popularity and money were phantoms. Guns, lasers, fields: these made one an *entity.*

As any cyberian knew.

But APPLE had not embraced cyberian technology along with the guns, lasers and fields. Had refused for years to legally allow its products to be implanted. It had been the first sign of its impending fall.   The marketplace would be the first jolt in the incinerator.

The marketplace was decentralized. It did not even have a name, aside from joking. Cyberians thought of it digitally, a series of numbers demarcating a cluster of ceep.

On a whim, MikeDev ran the term "ceep" through his processors wondering where it had originated.

Ceep: A term made popular in the late 2010s to refer to cloud space and the data servers populating the Earth's information networks.

MikeDev would have smiled at the mm if his

mouth were capable of the movement.

That the marketplace was not illegal anywhere in the world did not mean it was actually legal. A fine distinction, but easy enough to grasp. The cluster of servers changed every few days, or less. Yet it could be found by any cyberian with the GAPI. Or variant thereof.

MikeDev was one of the former who as a matter of principle was also one of the latter. He had the money to own every branded piece of cytech he wanted. The skill to craft the kind favored by hacktivists. So he used both. It was the kind of dualism cyberians found either necessary or impossible.

There was little need for the marketplace to be regulated. Cyberians took care of such themselves. Though there was always worry of vifec, most were sufficiently protected before they reached the ability and functioning level necessary to access the marketplace. If they were not then, perhaps, they were only getting what they deserved.

As such just about any mm could be had in the marketplace. Cyberians and scientists. Doctors and doctoral students from around the globe all contributed. Normal humans could use it with the aid of devices. Most found it too immersive and yet not enough. Only a cyberian could truly integrate the mm and make it part of itself.

Still, this widespread appeal brought in

hacked mms from every walk of life. Every vice and virtue, every war and porno. Every moment of ecstasy and bitter loss. MikeDev had particular preferences, of late. After nearly thirty years in conflict torn areas he had little need to experience more of war, fighting or other macho driven mms. His sexuality was firm and frequently in practice. He had little need for the insuperable market of porn mms. Much had changed in the world since his first implant but whores were still cheap. And loves even cheaper. Mms cheaper less so.

What MikeDev preferred to experience was trickier to find. Harder to quantify. Quite beyond the purview of most other cyberians. He wanted the supernatural. The religious fervor. The ineffable touch of the ultimate. The numinous something.

Enhanced, he could see a great many things otherwise he would not. But not spirits. Demons. Gods.

There was a cyberian of every stripe somewhere in existence. If it could be imagined someone had implanted themselves. Became it. But for one large exception. No cyberians held on to religion.

It had been the great awakening in many senses. Those who had been truly devout had discovered after being implanted wonder had been a base emotion. Something intrinsically fleshy. Not replicable in binary.

Cyberians quickly released what belief they

may have once had. In god. The devil. Demons. Angels. In the whole realm of the spiritual. In the or any *after*life.

Who needed an afterlife when I will never leave this one?

An urge from something external, unidentified made MikeDev want to snicker at his own thought. His mouth did not, could not even twitch though.

Cyberians were functionally immortal. The advent of mm transference had only made it certain. Yet some small few found they yearned for the very thing: that sense of wonder they had parted with. Most cyberians of MikeDev's age had unknowingly embracing their tech. It had then yet to be fully quantified, tested and probed. The newer, they dove in knowing what they would get. Some of the worst violence against cyberians had occured because of this. Around the world they had been termed 'godless', 'unholy' and 'demonic.' Of course the irony of the last did not often escape the cyberian mind.

MikeDev did not need to close his eyes to relish to sense of wonder which came with the mm. It was not a pleasant mm. But the *wonder!* It was beyond anything MikeDev would have imagined. The mm itself had come from a convict serving a life sentence for killing, dismembering and eating his girlfriend. The particular mm had been taken from the convict, now a rote procedure, at his death, along with a host of the man's other mms.

Social Networking for Demons

To be examined by the vanguards of social science, those who sought *still* to understand crime. Those who still wondered: *why* does this person do *that*?

    The convict whom the mm had belonged to had claimed he was possessed by a demon. Yet another reason MikeDev had wanted the mm. He did not really believe the man had been possessed. Yet the man had sincerely believed himself possessed. Sometimes there was no difference between the two. Much searching had resulted in many failures before MikeDev found this convict and his seemingly sincere mm. MikeDev couldn't know beforehand. He may have been the first to purchase this particular mm. Mms did not settle in instantly. They took hours. Sometimes days. Sometimes the brain required a shutdown. A period of sleep or several, to integrate the mm. MikeDev knew this would be one of those mms. It would come on slowly. Bit by bit he would relive aspects of this convict's experience. Amalgamate the convict's mm in the process.

    No smiles but his eyes were still able to widen. Brighten. They did so as the first tendrils of the mm took hold. He tasted the air. It was humid and less smokey than his own mms of air in this part of the world. His banks remembered the taste, vaguely from his youth. There was another taste in the mm as well, stronger than any other. It made MikeDev's banks catch. They had not come up empty in a very long time.

It would have been a gagging to a human. It took some time to process and understand the reason why.

The taste of human flesh.

It was not repulsive. Only horrible. Perhaps that made it worse, that it did not inherently taste awful. A humor GAPI in MikeDev's brain unleashed a torrent of tX. Making jokes about a machine which could finally describe what it was like to eat the meat. Other, worse, culturally relevant jokes and comments came out. All immediately flash-posted around the world to be consumed by other cyberians, the occasional human, and the aggregators humans used to discover things they were supposed to obsess over. Eventually MikeDev switched the humor GAPI off. The mm needed priority, he decided.

Not shared.

Other things began to hit him in digital wisps. A woman's fat flesh under his fingers as he caressed it. MikeDev was entirely enamored of the archetypal male figure. He had never wanted nor needed to touch a woman in this manner. But the mm's owner had *loved* the woman he consumed. Supposedly.

The first bits of love were seeping in, little flashes of touch and sensation and colored emotion. Beyond was something else. Something MikeDev's GAPIs could not easily process nor quantify. They were all kicking it back for further examination at a later date. Assuming not enough information had yet been gathered.

The remainder of MikeDev's brain remnants tingled with possibility and the very thing he had been after: wonder. It grabbed at the *something* else and sucked in. Drew the sensations and data points into itself. The color black was prominent amongst the data. As was the color red. In thousands of shades. But nothing more distinct yet. It would come. MikeDev knew it. He remained still. Content to wait.

Outside his stayroom something crashed. MikeDev's enhanced reflexes responded. Gently, effortlessly lifting him upright. Turning him towards the noises. Small, indescribably small nanoparticles, like pigment cells in an octopus, began to coalesce in his hands, arms and feet. His face descended in shades from a tanned white-brown to a steely, dead-looking gray. His eyes were covered by a protective film, as were his nostrils and ears, all invisible. There was no need to cover his mouth: those systems were always in place, the world's climate being what it was.

More sounds crashed outside. The reinforced door shuddered. MikeDev's defense mechanisms were fully engaged and everything visual was tinged with warning reds. Muscles and carbon fibers flexed in unison. Dtics verified weaps were online. Then, suddenly, the racket ceased.

Without the need of moving MikeDev's sensors engaged. Connected to the necessary security networks. Viewed all camera angles approaching his building and stayroom. Spread out to the street beyond. Tested the air again. Looking for molecules which could identify and clarify. The only sign he was at all agitated were his fingers - which every ten seconds gave a slight, hardly noticeable twinge, and his skin coloring.

Data was compiled and results fed to his cortex. There was nothing unusual out there. MikeDev's head tilted to the side slightly, confused. His human brain remnants were given more oxygen and blood and small, slight electric shocks from the cyberian devices to speed processing. Had he been human he would not have been able to easily remember when the last time he had had to do this was. But he did.

Twenty-six years, forty-three days, eight hours and seven minutes, fifty-nine seconds.

The first thing his brain registered was amusement at the arrangement of numbers: no digit was repeated. His cybernetic processors tried to make larger sense of this. They could not so they fed more oxygen, more blood, more shocks to the brain remnants. MikeDev's body shook from the juice running into his nervous system.

The first result his brain achieved was quite simple.

Imagination. You imagined it, nothing more.

This sent the cybernetics into loops of processing, examining incoming sensory data. Splicing it. Searching for degradation in the signals. Hints of apparatus failure, negative feedback loops. But this was done quickly. All results negative.

The sounds HAD happened. The door HAD shaken and rattled.

Undeterred, MikeDev let his brain remnants remnants continue to investigate. He strode over and opened the door, peered around, though there was nothing invisible to sweep of the cameras. He was again amused by the subtle differences in experience when he viewed the world in what cyberians thought of as "analog" mode. Colors were just so slightly different. Blue-shifted for some reason. Sounds were just a shade richer, fuller. It was not something his cynetics could quantify It was rejected as noise by the devices, but not by the brain remnants. The brain remnants accepted, revelled.

Peeking around the hallway outside, MikeDev left the stayroom. Shut the door behind him. His ambulatory systems in control, his brain remnants only accepting sensory data from the eyes and ears and mouth. Curious, his brain flipped on the feed from tactile sensation as well. Instantly, small titillating eddies of air rustled against hairless skin on the arms and neck and little bumps were raised. Yet no air was detected as moving across the skin.

Strange

Intriguing.

MikeDev wandered the hallway. Made four circuits of it before deciding there was nothing new to learn. Yet he found, oddly, he did not wish to go back into the stayroom. His brain wished to remain in full control of the sensory data for more bits. Even suggested travelling outside.

MikeDev's systems steered him outside. His protective mechanisms shielded him from the glaring sun overhead and from smog in the air. The streets outside were quiescent, calm. Overhead, transports hummed past at regular intervals. Some occupied, others not. Not many people still lived in NOLAMetro. The majority of the population were cyberians. The place had lost it tourist appeal after repeated floods in the twenties. Its final charms sank after oil and gas fires in the thirties damaged what remained of the outlying area. It was not a problem for cyberians or humans with the money for the necessary gear. Only the most desperate of the latter remained without such protections. And all of *them* lived in the semi-protected area which had once been the French Quarter.

MikeDev's feet were already heading in that direction before his brain remnants made the decision to do so. His GAPIs were hovering against what his brain remnants would have called intuition. It was esctasy.

The area was surrounded by a large lake and a huge levee. Covered by a shoddy dome. It was not far off, ten minutes by transport, an hour on foot. Making his way to the nearest access port MikeDev loaded into a transport and let devices input his desired location. Soon he was flying through the air with only the distant sound of rushing outside as company. Cyberians never travelled with company unless forced. MikeDev was no different.

Ten minutes later, almost exactly, he was disgorged from the access port at the top of the French Quarter dome. He was fielded down to the street below. The air tasted funny: humid and dank. Cobblestones beneath his thinly covered feet were almost a new sensation after so many years in full cyberian interface. It had been almost as long since he had ventured to the French Quarter. Far more people were about here than in the area around his building. Cyberians, too.

The cyberians varied in appearance wildly, except for an utter lack of obesity. Skin colors, hair colors, facial shapes, body types; all were on display in the French Quarter. Most of the variation was human in nature; cyberians tended to average towards the mean in appearance. They simply lacked desire to express themselves solely with their bodies.

Still, MikeDev saw several of those strikingly new visual elements. One was most disconcerting with his brain remnants in control: transparent skins. He saw only four, but statistically, it meant a great deal more he could not see. The trend had exploded in the few years since it became widely available. The sight of human muscle and bone and cartilage, in varying colors and shapes beneath a layer of what looked almost like thin plastic was strange, even to MikeDev.   He pushed such thoughts away.

Only then, watching the melee of human and cyberian life
wandering the streets did MikeDev's brain remnants begin to ask itself:
Why did I come here?
As if in response more of the downloaded mm bled into him. In spurts, stronger and faster than before. Something about the place was activating it, drawing the mm out, forming and shaping it. MikeDev's brain remnants tried, and failed, to slow the process. He could only stop it by giving control back over to the cybernetics and then the mm would be arrested. Back to the merest of experience when he was feeling so much more. Needing so much more.

Two human men, quite tall and both swishingly blue approached.   Their skins changed shades and depths with each movement, so they looked like one being with two sets of disconnected parts responding to the other naturally. They noticed MikeDev and walked towards him.

Sensing no threat, MikeDev did not re-activate any defense mechanisms or switch over guided control. He let them approach.

"Hi hnsm!" A tXX appeared across MikeDev's field of vision moments before the pair was close enough to speak. MikeDev looked them up and down. Found his human body was attracted to the leanness of their figures. The hardness of their shapes, accentuated as they were by the roiling-wave like coloration of their skins.

It was quite beautiful. As if they knew this, both of them smiled at once. MikeDev tXXed back. A standard response of appreciation and mild interest. His body shook with further effects of the mm.

MikeDev knew from the looks on their mirrored faces, each bearing the exact same expression of hesitation, they assumed he was malfunctioning. A malfunctioning cyberian in the French Quarter was not a terribly unusual thing. Older models, of MikeDev's age, ones created with less care and precision often ended up in places like the Quarter.

In response MikeDev ran a dtic and posted the results to his site, tXXing the basic data and availability of the rest seconds after. Their smiles returned. The pair was now standing before him.

Up close he saw subtle differences in facial structure which spoke of extensive plastic reconstruction done to make them seem similar.

The kinds of things only enhanced eyes would see. Slight deviation in the length of the nostril on one, slighter dip in the eyelid of the other. MikeDev found these differences compelling. He allowed his cybernetics to tXX his appreciation. More smiles before they both spoke, at the same time, their voices slightly different in pitch and intonation. Just enough to enhance the sound, to beautify it and deepen it, to add what musicians for centuries had called "color." Not surprisingly the "color" made MikeDev's brain remnants think of blue.

"Would you interface with us?" they asked.

MikeDev's brain remnants responded. Funneling attraction for their bodies towards his genitals and glands. The only way he could stop now was to give back control. The mm was coming on stronger by the millisecond. He did not want to lose the sensation. Enhanced as his brain was, he could divide the tasks using quantum-threaded processing, paralleled and simultaneous.

He could not do this with too many things at once, but he could handle at least three rt narratives without much strain. MikeDev nodded at the pair. They turned, separated and stood one each on the side of him. Their hands pressed against his. Electric signals raced between the receptors.

MikeDev's body stiffened as GAPIs processed the data and made a determination of sexual compatibility. The pair both shivered in excitement. Deep lust for cyberian sex obvious in their expressions.

MikeDev had little choice then. He could not let his brain remnants remain in control, not fully. Lancing probes of the convict's mm caused him to be unable to focus on anything else. Sensation overloaded his parallel processing.

The pair before him would demand total attention. Realizing this MikeDev changed his mind. He sent tXX to the pair he could not meet them until later. They registered disappointment with a darkening of skin color until they were almost navy skinned. Nodded in unison and transferred a detail of contact information and a request MikeDev respond when available. His cybernetics filed the information away allowing his brain remnants to keep control over his thoughts. But his parallel processing was incapable of doing more. He collapsed against the wall to his right side.

The pair hustled away. MikeDev stood there for a minute as the mm overrode his thoughts. As if he were stepping into a vid, everything around him changed. An overlay had been thrust across everything, so though he knew it was still a brightly lit day, the shade of night lay across everything. In a way, it *was* night.

Phantoms of people still walked around, sometimes walking through others who were actually present. Ghost-images of long dead people from a New Orleans well over fifty years gone. MikeDev reveled in the sense of wonder. His arm raised up to touch a beautiful man walking past. He was shocked, truly shocked, for the first time in nigh on thirty years, when the man responded as if MikeDev had actually raised his arm to an actual person and not one in a mm.

It took a few moments of single-threaded human thoughts to realize this must have happened in the mm. MikeDev flowed, his legs moving at the speed required by the mm. Though the phantom night around him was clear enough his enhanced eyes still picked up distortions. Differentials that at first he thought might be corruption in the mm. The more he walked the more he knew they were not distortions at all. They were *sensations* of the mm. He was experiencing what this convict had experienced.

How random objects had seemed to have a life of their own. An animated shadow of something terrible living in inanimate objects, causing the convict to experience a paranoia unlike anything MikeDev had ever known. He relished the feeling. It was as disconcerting as it was frightening. Immersed as he was in the mm.

He saw shadows that were right to be shadows, only they were longer than physics should allow. Some had faces, anthropomorphological traits: hands, claws, GAPIng mouths. Had he been experiencing this first hand and not as a mm he would have been terrified by it. All the more because his cyberian enhancements would have *insisted* these things were not actually possible and must be somehow contrived. An effect of the mind, a corruption of nerve data. An illusion imposed upon the brain by itself. Yet MikeDev with his human thoughts running the show combined with his enhanced processing knew this was not the case. This man had *SEEN* these things and somehow others around him had *not*.

He walked a normal pace to an apartment building, which in his time no longer stood. Having been replaced by an energy processing tower. Still, the mm was able to transport him inside. He walked up stairs to an apartment and opened the door. A woman greeted him. She was chubby and quite pretty, with cascadingly gentle waves of brown hair around light blue eyes. She had a slight gap in her teeth and the blazing look in her expression which told him she loved him.

The mm told MikeDev the man had loved her as well. He tried to separate his consciousness, to remember he was not the convict who had experienced this mm. He failed.

I am.. I am NOT....

He tried, unsuccessfully, to remember his own name, but it did not come. mms were sold and traded on the open market, but though personal details remained, they were not tagged with actual names, for various legal reasons. He could have found out the man's name easily enough: but it would have required allowing his cybernetics to regain control, connect to various public info-nets and aggregate info until he had a match. That was science fiction!

The sensations coming to him now intensified, the wetness of the mouth as he lusted for *her*.

Ca...

The smell of her: baby powder and sugar and vanilla, intoxicating to the man in the mm. A feel of her softness pressed against him rivalling anything he had felt for hard, muscular men. A familiar taste, unwelcome, but known crept in.

He smacked his jaws as the she turned her back and walked away, as the taste filled his mouth. And the taste, it was terrible, because he knew what it was: cooked human flesh. He wanted it.

All across the apartment shadows lengthened and stretched, grew heads and arms and cawing beaks or GAPIng maws. They shouted inky screams causing him to cover his ears as horrid shrieks pierced the viel of silence and stung his eardrums. Far worse than any sound they had ever heard.

They?

Worse, there were whispered words in those shrieks, suggestions, commands, urges. Lurid, horrible things creating a feedback loop which somehow passed from some other and back. Though a join over the gulf of time. Poles of the same half. Scared out of his wits he tried to...

reassert control

...but failed. Then he tried to turn his cy...
what?
on. Release...thoughts...to ...GAPIs.

But this too failed. Something held him. He knew it. More, it always had.   He understood this now. It was

a function of time that he had to reach this point before experiencing this past, but it had always been his past, just as this moment had always been this man's future.

Nonsense.

Error! Cannot divide by zero.

They were not the same person. I am alive! He had been put to death by lethal injection decades before! I died!

Reluctance bleeding into the him, he walked towards the kitchen. He knew where it lay. Shadows brushed against him. Clawing insects with tiny bites, sharp pangs of bearable pain and unbearable terror. Step by step he covered the distance separating him from the love, the need, the hunger. A name was there now, branded upon her image.

Cassie!

And he knew her. More he now knew himself,

if not the *other* seeing behind his eyes with him. He was in thrall and believed this new presence in his mind simply another part of that.

ME.

They reached the kitchen as Cassie hovered over a huge, steaming pot. A rich smell of gumbo and chicken and sausage wafted into his nostrils. It was delicious and new. Not enough to dispel the taste of human flesh. Another pot sat next to the first, containing only boiling water. Whatever Cassie had meant for it had not yet begun. She stirred the first pot, heard his gentle footsteps. Turned around, her waves of hair making soft motions in the air, fluttering in a breeze of unknown origin.

All around were shadows cast by the overhead light. They lengthened and grew appendages. More faces. They screamed.

Cassie seemed distantly to hear something, her head tilted questioningly to the side. Something startled her. She looked around. Her eyes narrowed to slits. Those blue eyes examined a place where a huge roaring shadow with angry eyes and six-fingered claws grabbed at her, though she clearly could not see it.

His arm raised and balled into a fist. His nanoparticle skin hardened, weaponized. When Cassie looked away from the site of the grasping shadow, he swung. Trying to dispel the horror of it his enhanced fist smashed into her face, ruining it.

Blood splashed across the walls and drenched shadows. Some of which seemed to dance amidst the shadows. Glorifying the feel of it upon themselves. Thad's hand went flat, like a blade, sharpened and on edge. Divided into small serrations, like the edge of a steak knife or saw. He hacked into Cassie. Carved her up. Her screams merged with those of the shadows into a cacophony of sound. A crescendo which filled the mind and drowned out everything else. Numbed as the same time it prodded forward.

Cassie took long minutes to die. Huge chunks of her were sliced and sawed off. Tossed into the pot which had contained only boiling water. After she died other parts were flayed off and added to the gumbo. He sampled both.

A deep sense of despair roared inside him. Held barely in check by remaining echoes of the shadows and their screams. Enhanced by demonic sensory abilities. Given strength and power. From behind he heard footsteps.

He turned slowly, his mouth dripping with human grease, his body slashed in splattered blood. Cassie's chopped up remains lay on the floor.

A wide mouth, puffy lipped woman stood in the doorway between the kitchen and the living room. Her head cocked to the side, mirroring his own head's position. The woman's eyes were entirely white, as though they had rolled upwards into her head. Her nasty mouth was repulsive to him. Those puffy lips moved in continuous chanting.

The light overhead popped. Blew a shower of sparks.

The woman a name floated to his consciousness like the taste of rot inside cooked meat.

May

She moved towards him. Hips first, a sexual offering. His body, in thrall, responded, but his mind did not. Some other gagged on the electrical signals.

I have never had attraction to women!

Especially this one. She was horrid, rail thin and fish-faced. His thoughts stuttered and finally asserted control over his body. He pushed the woman aside and ran away. Her words floating at him from behind, infecting his thoughts, telling him in lurid detail what he had just done.

But he did not stop. He kept on walking until he was outside, undeterred by people who stared at him with utter horror. Recoiled in fear. Then his feet stopped. Seeming to understand he had reached the proper destination.

The Omni Royal Hotel.

He went inside, took an elevator to the top floor, climbed three additional flights of stairs to reach the roof. The night sky wheeled overhead, full of uncaring stars in leering patterns. Twirling clouds banked over a lit navy blue emptiness. He was there and here and they were separate and one. Just as he prepared to jump off the roof and end his life the thing inside him, in side *them* urged him to stop.

STOP.

His whole body trembled.   A fail-safe activated his cynetic devices, stopping-the mm cold. Literally cold. He was freezing.   The mm faded. MikeDev hovered on the ledge, fractions of a moment from jumping. Below a man was slowly falling backwards from the rooftop, unconscious toward the sky. MikeDev saw this form, the man's form in a ghostly outline collapse to the ground of the roof.

MikeDev's senses returned fully to the present. To the bright blue sky full of clouds overhead. The cold receded in a snap. Shining steel under his feet made up the present day roof of the OmCom energy tower.

Slowly, for a cyberian, sensory data faded. He was present again: a mass of incoming data processed by GAPIs. Hashed into reactions and actions. The past was gone. Ahead lay only the false color sky generated by the overhead dome, with its gentle blue color and artifically imposed warmth. Wafting clouds in nonsensical nature-driven shapes of no significance beyond the patterns of ice crystals floated along. The red-tinged sun hardly moved at all.

Cassie.....

MikeDev's head tilted to the side as he considered the face he saw behind his eyes.

Chapter 18 – The Most Selfish Spirit

Below him the space where the world had once been burned. It was not precisely below him. Nor above. Such directions hardly mattered in the vastness of space. Bereft as they were of the Earth's surface as a reference. No longer distant, the sun was a red giant, swollen and bloated. Like some diseased, dying thing.

Overhead - though again the term was more holdover than anything - less and less starlight reached the spot where the Earth had once circled its star. Yet still *he* floated. Chained to the spot, unable to leave.

He was not truly a *he* either. Both human sexes
had at times held him. Had give his form succor over the thousands of years he had lived among the humans. Before the humans fall and departure. Vainly, he had tried to leave with the humans, but instead he had ended up stuck in space. Drifting within the gravity well of a dying star and ashed Earth. Were he a human he might have possessed something like regret. As it was he could only layer what he knew of regret from his many possessions of humans. Layer it over his energy and simulate. It was by the same process he thought of himself as a he.

Though he possessed no form of body any

longer his spirit was no less potent than it had been
- save for being adrift and unable to leave. Some
things, by the forces of nature themselves are
precluded even from spirits such as himself. He
did not yet know them all. Though he had orbited
in space around this now dying star for billions of
cycles gnawing at the issue.

So he waited and hoped.

All it would take was one. One life form. One
ship full of meat-things. Of *people.* Of life-based
carbon artifacts, corporeal beings and he could
again live among them. Eating at them from the
inside, as he was meant to live. A grand hope and
one that sustained.

Over those years he had replayed his lives.
His meat-homes inside of people. Relived their
delicious tragedies. Delightfully, he examined
their beliefs, hopes, dreams and terrors - relishing
the vast amount of experience of them which he
retained. He had left none of it behind. It was not
his nature to give back what he took.

Because he was a spirit, a chip off the force
of nature itself he knew many things. But not all.
He had laughed using the mouth of humans who
wished so fermarvently to say a prayer. Had
scoffed at their religions. Blasphemed their holies.
But he knew some things for certain which they
could not. There was most definitely a higher
power. Compared to the humans themselves he
was such a power. He was not the apex.

The Earth itself had been *alive* in ways those humans had not realized until it was far too late. A goddess they had ignored until she was all but barren. Some of *that* was his doing. Pride was not beyond him.

He had often explained such truth to his meat-homes. The better to enjoy the sense of power it lent. Some of those meat-homes were his creatures from beginning to end. Others simply those who loved his meat-home. None of them had borne the hearing of truth with ease. Such discussions had led at times to places he had not expected. Including the discovery he was not alone among the spirits who were tied to the Earth. He had so often thought he was.

One of the costs of living within the meat-homes, of possessing their bodies, was living within the limits of their minds. They could only understand and process so much. He laughed in the bitter emptiness of space as this thought occurred to him yet again: how had the humans created a way to operate outside their own limits? He had never rivaled the trick.

He knew the answer. At least to the human solution. They had merged themselves with machines of their own creation. Opened vistas of thought far beyond what was possible on their own meatspace. He had devoured some of these pioneering creatures, did not really think of them as humans; they had been something else entirely.

He had not been as satisfied by the experience. Like all things in nature to achieve the greater understanding required
the loss of some lesser things. Emotions. Affections. Personalities. These things had eventually become superfluous to such hybrid beings. With their eschewment those beings had surpassed everything that was a human. Become thus mostly useless to beings such as him.   When all of the meat-homes had merged with machines the spirit had fled. And gotten stuck in space.

Though he possessed no physical form any longer, he could not coalesce without the Earth's presence and force.   A being of pure energy, part of him recoiled as a memory arced across his being. Had he had meat-form it would have shrunken and shriveled. Become less, like a child who after being spanked and beaten curls into a ball and tries to be unseen.   Unwilling but unable to resist he relived the memory, that terrible conversation.

...she was not a pretty a thing. Her skin had long since
begun to droop and fall in crevices, folds. Was covered in
spots. Her eyes were still good but most of the rest of herwas not. She had been fatter before. The years had flayed the weight off her. Her gnarled hands, bent with arthritis, no longer functioned as

anything resembling their intended purpose. She could neither walk nor crawl. Her only ability to move entirely dependent on the wheeled chair she spent most of her days in and the beefy woman behind her pushing it. There was no hair left on her head only more wrinkles and spots. Nor were there teeth in her mouth. Her daily food intake consisted entirely of ground up meat, vegetables, and milk. All unceremoniously poured down her gullet three times a day.

Once she had a name as well. Though she had not heard it spoken aloud in longer than she could remember. All her days simply ran together since her hearing had gone.

Her name had been Edith.

She was one hundred and one years old. Had outlived everyone she had known, her only living connection to her past was the banker who monthly sent monthly checks to the home for her care. Though he eventually stole most of the money and left her to die, for nearly ten years her money kept her alive while her body hung useless around her spirit.

Yet she was not diminished. She could still see and she saw deeply. Her memories were intact. They had sustained her like food and mobility and hope could no longer. Most who saw her recoiled in pity and disgust, but she saw past this to the reality behind it, the fear of their own mortality. Despair that no amount of life well-lived could give them more than what she had had. It simply was not possible then.

Edith was not alone though. Another lived within her. Inside of her. It was this other more than any factor which kept her alive. Full of hope after each loss, each victory, each cresting year. She never spoke of this other to anyone. Though she did speak to the other, when she was alone. Out loud sometimes, other times in direct speech inside her own mind.

The other had a name also, but it never told Edith what it was. Edith had taken to calling the other Mya after her first daughter. The one who had died as a little girl when war had come in the form of waves of British soldiers. None of them aware the war had already ended.

Though Edith could not recall when Mya had joined her, she did remember a time before the other had lived within her. Before Edith's body had begun to fail around her. At first Edith had thought Mya a demon. Then an angel. But after much discussion with Mya she had learned this was not so.

Those terms were human appellations for something which humans could not understand. Mya was beyond them: humans and their terms. Edith had then assumed Mya was God herself, but Mya had denied this so many times and so fervently Edith had eventually concluded it was not so. Mya was simply Mya. A force of nature which lived within Edith. A spirit who guided her and took sustenance from Edith's experiences, as spirits sometimes did.

Despite this Edith *could* recall the first time, and only, she had discovered another like herself. A fellow vehicle for
a spirit like Mya. She had known instantly, without Mya's telling her, something was different about the woman.

The woman's beefy hands had sent rolling spikes of energy through Edith when they first touched her. She lifted Edith out of the bed and into the wheeled chair to be brought outside for sunning. She had now been cared for by this possessed woman, this supposed nurse, for nearly twelve years. For much of that, until Edith lost her hearing, they had spoken a great deal of many things both human and spiritual.

"But, Mya dear, and Darl," Edith had said. Though the other spirit had not given her its name, especially not as Darl, it answered to the name when they were alone. Edith's first son-in-law had been named Darl. The bastard who had beaten and killed her second daughter shortly after the North invaded.

Edith had hated Darl more than anyone she had ever known. Had never thought to hate anything so much. She felt it appropriate to name what she saw behind the nurse's eyes, using *Mya*'s sight, after the man. Despite this they had not fought or been enemies, for Mya knew Darl was alike to him and was neither her better nor her lesser. Edith was protected from him, though her offspring were not and over the centuries Darl would torture many of them in retribution for memory of Edith's words. They had argued a great deal.

"Surely there must be SOMETHING after?"

Inside Edith's mind Mya laughed. A trilling sound like rain falling under a sunny sky on roses and grapes. Darl, although speaking through the nurse, heard the laughter. The nurse scowled, mirroring Darl's feelings. He did not allow her the latitude Mya allowed Edith. The nurse was *his* and he manipulated her accordingly: his toy and puppet.

"Why *must,* Edith?' Darl sneered, using the nurse's mouth. She leaned in close and whispered the comment into Edith's ears, knowing the smell of her tobacco-ladened breath made the woman uneasy.

"Because of you. And Mya. If you exist and are forces of something beyond the body, spirits in the *truest* sense, then surely that means there is some place natural to you and yours. Some place where those of my kind can go after we pass."

Mya remained silent to this. Edith could feel her other brooding and itching to explain something she was not sure she could translate to Edith's limited mind. They had discussed these limits before. Edith was well aware of her own limitations.

It was Darl's sneering laugh Edith noticed most.

"You think *YOU* humans will become like *US*? Surely you have read that rag you call a Bible? Or are you truly a godless woman?"

"Mya said the Bible was mostly folk-tales." Edith replied.

"Did she?" Dan said. "Mostly." Another laugh.

"But there IS a god or goddess, as far as you *HUMANS* are concerned. Far above you. And beyond. Spirits like myself, we are truly a part of the higher power! A *real* expression of it, an actual piece of its life-force." There was obvious pride in the nurse's tone, all Darl.

Mya spoke, entirely to Edith's mind. Though it was clear Darl somehow knew the words. "And to the goddess we must someday return." Edith was moved. It was the first time Mya had actually mentioned an afterlife directly. But Darl's reaction was far more visceral.

The nurse stiffened and gasped a cry, as if her body was in pain, as if her muscles had all cramped at once. Inside her head Edith felt Mya's mild satisfaction. She had known the comment would bother Darl and likely said it for that reason. Edith wondered at that, Mya had never done such a thing before.

When Darl was able to speak again his voice

was tight with anger. "Not all."

Mya laughed, richly. "Then you will spend the cycles of your existence in the coldness of space, bereft, alone and toothless. Waiting. Watching. But the Mother will have already passed beyond, she will not come back for you."

This was the first time Edith had heard of this Mother. She asked, in her own thoughts, which she was relatively sure that Darl would not hear.

The Mother?

Mya sighed with reluctance. "What many call god. *The* goddes. The highest power of this place. The Earth and the Sun. Together they form the spirit of life within us all, they are the Mother."

Edith nodded, her head drooping a bit as though weighted by the new information. But Mya was not done.

"That is all we are, we spirits, part of the will of the Mother. Shades of her power and glory. Most remain with her, part of her, but some of us chose to come amongst you. We are the source of your myths, your fears, your faiths and your dreams." Mya paused. "And your nightmares."

Darl puffed up. "I have always loved that word."

Mya brushed this aside. "It is part of the purpose of existence, that we are here. Though he does not like to believe that. He chooses to think of himself as separate. He refuses to acknowledge he came from the Mother or he should eventually return to her.'

"All things!" Darl said, spittle flying from the nurse's mouth. "It MUST be."

Edith did not understand this at all and Mya felt her confusion. Darl did not.

"You cannot see it, -----------" Mya said, uttering a name that was not a name. It was a sensation of things twisting in the dark, of implosion and stone grating on stone, of wearing and wearying and devouring. It was, Edith knew, Darl's true name. A screech like sound pierced her ears and even Mya flinched from it in the spirit. Mya trembled, almost detaching entirely from Edith. Flying out of Edith completely before she settled back down, giving off the feeling of a dinosaur with its feathers ruffled.

"I see!" Darl shouted in the mind and out of the mouth of the nurse. "What is redemption but weakness? Those other frail demons shall fall in upon themselves and return to the seamless whole, rejoin the Mother, but I shall NOT. I will be APART and TRIUMPHANT. I will be -------- !!"

Another bundle of sensation struck Edith.

...a mother refusing to give her milk to a starving baby, a child hoarding toys from others, a rich man getting richer, a being looming above all ordering the world according to whim deaf to prayer.

Edith recoiled from this utterance as did Mya. She might have died right then, her heart burst,

343

had Mya not sustained her.

And suddenly Edith's brain, with Mya's thoughts, understood something of Darl.

"The most selfish spirit." Edith murmured. "The one who refuses to ever give back of itself. That's what you are, the very opposite of the goddess!"

Darl shoved the wheelchair angrily, the wheels rolled and careened-until Mya suffused Edith's limbs with the strength to stop it. But the nurse was undeterred. She stomped forward and spit tobacco juice into Edith's face. "There *IS NO GODDESS*! There is *ONLY ME*."

"You *would* say that." Edith retorted, and expected Mya to agree with her words, but she felt the kind spirit's hesitance. Darl was laughing.

"You will suffer greatly in the end, EDITH." Darl said. "And *she* will abandon you. To rejoin the seamless whole."

Edith clucked deep in her throat. "Mya?" she asked, but Mya was silent. Edith had learned Mya could not be forced to talk. Something had upset the spirit greatly.

"You could cast her out, Edith..." Darl murmured into Edith's ear. "I can show you how. There is much I can show you."

Sensations burst into Edith's mind unchecked, like photographs bleeding together into motion, all herky-jerky as her mind's eye raced down paths into the future. She saw things she could hardly believe.

..bursts of energy and cries of pain. burning. rats scurrying through trenches, stick-thin impossibly wasted human bodies, rivers of poison criss-crossing the Earth. Men with metal bodies and eyes. A voodoo doll. Street lamps exploding. Bubbles. A little girl's body covered in bloody handprints.

Finally something pushed the sensations out. Edith felt Mya's presence reassert itself.

"*Enough.*" Mya said.

Darl sneered. "She is less than me, Edith and she knows it. I *can* destroy her. Consume her and become greater. You would not like it. She would not let it happen though, she would sacrifice you first. She would abandon you."

a meat cleaver raised and flashing with reflected yellow light. A Chinaman wearing stark black clothing and a rapacious grin.

Edith was torn inside. For the first time since she discovered Mya she felt dirtied by the presence of the spirit. When the nurse's hands stroked her head, a loving gesture that was all cruelty disguised, Edith did not flinch. She did not believe in THE God, in the *Christian* mythology she had been raised on. She did remember her prayers. Long forgotten from when she was a very small child. She did not say them.

"*I will not.*" Edith said. A previously unknown strength rose within her. Her back, long stooped from years in her wheeled chair straightened and her eyes cast upward to the bright sun. "*I* will not be your slave, nor *his*, nor *hers*." Edith murmured.

She felt Mya within her expand and grow warm, suffuse her body with strength. Love and hope. But not power. Then Mya was gone.

But Darl was not.

Darl strode over to face Edith in the wheeled chair and leaned down to whisper in her ear again. The beefy nurses breasts were as hard as old wood. With Mya gone Darl could no longer speak directly to her brain, Edith assumed.

"You will die old woman, but know this. I am - ------- and I have chosen you and yours. I will *abide* among your kin. Twisting them and those whom they touch! I will delight in their suffering, I will revel in the...."

But Edith did not hear the rest. She up and died...

Floating, though the word does not truly describe the motion of the most selfish spirit, the last, the final one - he recoiled from the memory of that conversation. He had been true to his word. He had tortured Edith's descendants for centuries. At times splitting himself so fine he could manifest in only the smallest, meanest ways amongst them. So dispersed he could feel the seamless whole beckoning him to return to it. Yet he never had.

He always jerked away. Became

concentrated again and continued to issue his spells of despair and terror amongst humans who bore Edith's blood or touch those who bore her blood. Most had no idea at all. Had never imagined themselves connected to a past containing Edith. Those who did never understood who he was or why he tormented them.

But for all that he achieved, until the last of Edith's innumerable brood choked in the fall of the Earth, he could not satisfy his urge. His need to see the only human who had ever heard his name suffer for it. Because she had fled to the one place he would not go.

The End.

www.ingramcontent.com/pod-product-compliance
Lightning Source LLC
Chambersburg PA
CBHW070639180626
46817CB00006B/2176